MOUNTAIN *of*

FULL MOONS

MOUNTAIN *of*
FULL MOONS

a novel

IRENE KESSLER

SHE WRITES PRESS

Published 2020
Printed in the United States of America
ISBN: 978-1-63152-860-6
ISBN: 978-1-63152-861-3
Library of Congress Control Number: 2019911277

For information, address:
She Writes Press
1569 Solano Ave #546
Berkeley, CA 94707

She Writes Press is a division of SparkPoint Studio, LLC.

Interior design by Tabitha Lahr

This book is dedicated to my family who supported me from beginning to end. Your love gave me the courage to keep going.

CHAPTER ONE

I dare not move. The hut is dark but I can still feel my mother's black eyes glaring at me. The sun is not yet up over the horizon in this Land of Canaan and my father, my Abba, is waiting and must be angry. The men need to make fresh mudbricks for the huts and I promised to bring a basket for them to collect the chaff. Instead, I am forced to sit here and listen to my Ima and her usual long list of complaints. I know them by heart. I sweep the floor, but it is not clean. I am never there to grind the flour and it is not done properly. Even animals will not eat the flatbreads I make, and I do not wear my shawl when I should. The truth is my parents want to keep me from playing my harp and singing. Did they give me grandmother's harp to stare at? A harp is made to be played and a voice must sing.

My mother is finishing her morning tirade. This daybreak is not much different from any other, but before the sun disappears, my life may never be the same.

· · · · · · · · · · · ·

It seems like forever before the sun is into its final descent. My last chore is the flour and it is done. If I do not hurry, my parents will send me to help gather the animals. I am disobeying, but the Council of Elder's meeting is about me. I must attend. The meetings are forbidden to women, but I must hear their decision. It is about my future.

Which hand will the council cut off? A picture of my arm, bloody at the wrist, makes me ill. That cannot be their choice. Can it? I am not a thief. The queasiness in my stomach makes my insides quiver. My legs do not want to hold me up. The ends of my curls go into my mouth. Ima is furious if I chew my hair. She says, "A goat in the field looks better than you."

I climb the rise and hurry to my shrubs. Then rid myself of the shawl. I hate wearing it. The bushes are mine because no other female dares to eavesdrop on the men's meetings. My favorite spot is not far from here. From there, I gaze down at the thirty-one beehive-shaped huts of my village and a long-ago memory returns. I was young and tried in vain to use all my fingers and toes to count their number. I could not. My parents always tell me how stupid I am.

· · · · · · · · · · · ·

The faraway noise of men's voices sends me back to my shrubs. With the shawl under my head, I nestle into the leaves. This gathering will begin soon. My family does not know the many times I listened to other meetings.

The period between light and dark began a while ago and the council fire is already lit. The whole village is aware the flames burn for me. Warm for the season in this northern part of Palestine, the air is overladen with the harsh odor of red-hot wood. The atmosphere is heavy, not with rain, but with judgment. The sun heads to its rest, and the stars will soon come out of hiding.

On my knees, I pull the branches aside. The greenery wobbles from my shaking hands. The chief invited the village men to express their concerns. They form the usual half-circle. Those men believe that if they touch me their teeth will fall out, that I consult with dark spirits, that I indulge in conjuring and trickery.

Will the punishment be about talking to the women? Why do men become fearful when we speak up? The first council meeting was at five seasons of growth. My family was shunned, but soon after the council relented. Change is coming.

"Sandalphon, my guide, why are you not here?"

"Do not worry, I am always here to help."

Banishment alone in the wilderness is terrifying.

· · · · · · · · · · · ·

The council members make a second half-circle behind the villagers. Abba might be late. Work must come first. The din of men's voices grows louder as the Chief of Council nears the circle. His frame is massive and his tunic is the single one draped over the left shoulder and decorated with red and blue threads. His long black hair is fixed in place with a matching cap.

The chief rings the bell. "May I have silence?"

His face is stern. A biting cold comes over me. The villagers relate tales of his compassion, but those piercing black eyes are frightening. The gold pendant around his neck sends out flashes of light in the declining sun. His cover is held together with a clasp made of gilt and precious stones. His right thumb lays on top of the clasp.

"Come to order." He rings again. The mantle he pushes to one side is held on his shoulders with a large red thorn. He sits near the ceremonial bell. "We gather to decide the fate of Galina Bat Shamgar, daughter of Shamgar, who named herself Elisha. We met many times about her. She is now almost thirteen—a woman—and unmarried."

How many times do I have to tell him I did not name myself?

He rings the bell and bows his head in welcome to my abba's arrival. The men laugh at my father and taunt him for his failure to control me. Abba's answer is to pull on his beard.

My father's hair used to be brown like mine, and we both have red streaks—Abba in his beard and mine in my curls. We also have the same brown eyes. I am happy to be like him and not like my ima. Abba stares at the men until they make room. He may not take part and only attends to hear the complaints against me.

The men argue, and the chief stands. "Silence. We have already considered banishing her." A new member of the community yells out, "Get rid of her. She is making trouble between my wife and me."

Not trouble. Truth.

The chief turns toward him. "Thank you, I am aware of that." His eyes are on the assembly. "We will come to an agreement or the decision will be mine. Does anyone from the community wish to offer an opinion?"

A harsh liquid comes into my mouth and makes my throat burn. For a moment air is hard to take in.

"Yes, chief." The black of Gerah's beard is streaked with white. It is the longest of all the village men and still does not cover his big belly. I am glad he is the first; he is the one villager who is kind to me.

"Chief, I cannot solve this dilemma. Galina's behaviors have not changed."

"Yes, yes," the men yell out. "We agree."

Gerah pulls his shoulders back and smiles at them. "I recognize that Galina should not speak to our women as she does. She also talks to the air as if someone is there. But the fact is, she did not one sinful thing." The men use both hands to bang their disagreement on the ground. "She did not one evil deed. That should be considered." The men bang again.

The chief nods. "I am in agreement."

Gerah scowls at the ground. "Her name is another problem. What man would marry a woman with a male's name?" The men bob their heads.

The chief stands and paces. "I had the same thought."

Our neighbor, Qayin, comes into view as he stands. The flames from the fire seem to lick at his face.

"Yes, Qayin."

My hands turn to fists. This man collects gossip and uses what he can gather to make others believe he is shrewd. Qayin's heart matches his pitiful stature. He gives my father an arrogant stare. Abba's shoulders straighten and he refuses to lower his head.

"You are mindful we are neighbors, and I observe this family's behavior." He walks around the half-circle keeping his chest held high, tapping on it with his right hand, and gazing into the eyes of each man. "Therefore, my information must be considered." The men snicker.

He also spies on everyone, including both his wives. His brother died and Qayin took his sister-in-law as a second wife. Ahlai is a fine and sensitive woman near to my age. We often chat and I grew to enjoy her company. Her face changes when Qayin approaches. She told me that after his first wife's death, he began beating her until she could not walk. I would run away before I let a man do that.

"Yes, yes, Qayin." The chief sits and leans his head on his hand. "What is your point?"

"Galina is strange, different." He holds up his right hand and points toward Gerah. "Talking to the air means she is crazy." He turns back to the chief. "Galina watches each move I make, and I fear she will set a spell on my family."

The chief stands. "In all this time, she did not do so."

Qayin's nose flares and his lips tighten. "Her Ima beats her because she terrorizes the children telling them her guide will make their legs fall off if they are mean to her."

The children love me. I play with them. My father's face turns red and his jaw moves like the time he chewed meat that was not cooked through.

The chief is irritated. "You stated this many times. She is not evil."

Qayin flies into a rage. "Is that true? She bewitches our wives. Galina told my wife to demand I do not beat her. She told my daughter that a man cannot tell her what to do. She claims women are as strong and as clever as we are. Her curls show red like fire and escape her shawl as if the devil wants them for its own. She brought unusual herbs to my wife and claimed they were for cooking. My first wife died of poison. I suspected Galina then."

I bury my fists into my cheeks to keep from screaming.

The chief stands, his black eyes examining the circle. "Qayin, we do not know why your wife died. You are right. Talking to the women is a noteworthy problem we will address." He turns to the council. "Remember, the former chief met with Galina when she was young and declared she was not dangerous. He found no evil intent. We judged a child's mind, and we forgave her. Were we too lenient?" He raises his hand to ward off replies, then shakes his head.

Qayin jumps up. "If she continues our huts will become places of opposition. The village will be overrun with hate and anger. If she is not banished, there will be no peace."

"You made your point. I will meet with the council to consider your contributions."

"Cut out her tongue and throw her out," Qayin demands.

"Please do not take my tongue." The words escape my mouth.

"Galina. Get yourself in front of me without delay." His voice is harsh. I scramble down. "Where is your shawl?"

"I am sorry, my lord, in my haste to obey I left it up the slope."

He signals with his head for someone to fetch it. "You eavesdropped and ignored the edict declaring women do not attend these meetings. This rashness will not bode well for the judgment."

I grab the shawl the council member hands me and place it over my head. My skin feels like insects crawl all over. "I ask for your understanding, but my lord, it is not fair for me to not know what is said."

The chief stands up to his full height and moves closer. "How dare you? Who do you think you are? Do you make the laws? Silence yourself." His gold pendant shakes so close to my face I tremble. "You caused those dearest to you to be shunned. Must I now banish them?"

That pains me and makes me angry. "How do you punish my family?" I point toward Abba. "That is justice?" Abba's mouth is agape at my insolence. I take a step back and turn away. What did I do? I am so foolish.

The chief rings the bell. "By the next half-moon, there will be a final answer."

All the men turn to stare at me. I straighten my back to stand as tall as this small frame allows. I want to disappear into the sky. My pleading eyes are fixed on Abba. *Please forgive me,* is the message they send. My father glares at me, his brow furrowed, as if to shout, *You are finished. You are lost to us.*

CHAPTER TWO

Without a glance back I run, not knowing where to go. There is only one place where I feel safe. I rush to the fields where my brother is tending the flock. The love Nathan gives to the animals, to nature, to everything, brings a smile and allows the fear and sadness to be forgotten for a moment. The older sheep have been trimmed, and his shearing tool is tucked in the rope around his middle. He is the one person who knows my heart.

"Nathan! Nathan!" A lamb scurries away in time for me to fly into his arms. The eyes that gaze into mine are brown softened with yellow flecks. I drop my head onto his chest. His strong hands hold me tight.

"They have banished you?" His tone is warm but does not veil his concern.

There is no control of my tears. "I would rather be banished than hurt but pray they will let me stay. Their decision will come by the half moon." He lets go of me and I turn away. "They want to cut out my tongue." I turn back. "Please assure me they will not. I listened to their meeting from up the rise. When they said that about my tongue, I begged them not to hurt me and revealed my hiding place."

Nathan reaches for my hand. "Will you ever learn to keep quiet?"

"Do not be disappointed," I plead. I tell him all that happened at the council meeting.

"Perhaps they will shun you. They did it before."

He lets go of my hand and stands waiting. "The tongue was Qayin's idea."

"No one else would say such a thing."

I move closer. "Pray they will relent and let me stay." I wait for reassurance. He remains silent. "Abba sat stone faced and never said a word."

"He does the best he can."

"You always protect him. He did not try." I turn aside to wipe the tears.

"He could not. He would be asked to leave the village. Can I help? What will you do until the decision?"

"Wait and live through the torment. What else is there to do?" I slip to the ground. "How will I make a life on my own?" With my arms fastened around my legs, I rock like a child.

"You are aware the Council takes their time. They do not wish to make mistakes."

I turn to face him. "If banishment is their decision, must I go?"

"You will have no other choice." He glances toward the animals. "You still cannot be sure of the outcome, but something else is disturbing you."

"I also told the chief that it was not fair I could not listen and defend myself. Then I ran from the Council."

"You have never changed, never tried to make our lives easier. After you stood in front of the Council many times, one might expect you to understand how they work. Our parents let you know what you must do, and you refuse to listen. You know that this had to come to an end."

"Now you sound like Abba." I get up. "What does the future hold?" I reach for a handful of hair.

Nathan shakes his head. "Stop. If Ima finds out you are chewing again she will be furious." Tears run down my face. "I am sorry if I yelled. Sorry I could not help. Our parents do not understand why you will not change." He grins. "Neither do I." He shrugs his shoulders. "They fear what else you might do. I do not. You changed your name to Elisha and I trusted your sureness. They did not. But our parents agree you mean no harm."

"You are the one person who has faith in me." I take his cheek in my hand. "You are right. They will never accept I am not wicked."

We walk a few steps toward the hut. "Dear sister, you are not like the rest of us."

"Am I so different? I laugh and cry like others. I want love as all do."

He stops. "What will you do until the decision?"

I take his hand. "The only thing I can do. Carry on." A single lamb stands in knee-length grass far away from the herd. Why did her clan abandon her? She voices a pitiful bleat.

Nathan hears the call and his attention is on her. "And afterward?"

My brother is a bit older than me and taller than Abba. As a boy, he saved me from pranks and ridicule and now he is a young man. "Pray I will live and come home. Hope I will be shown the right end."

"I also pray all will be well."

"The way cannot be eased. I may not survive."

Nathan takes me in his arms and holds me until the trembling stops. "I should get to the stray lamb." He returns to the animals, and I turn toward home.

Nathan said the outcome is not sure. My insides announce it is settled. I want to run away and not hear my parent's harsh words, but I must go to our hut. If I do not help with the evening meal, my mother will be irate and her coughing will start again.

The sun has almost finished its descent. The smell of herbs

reaches my nostrils. Our women are at their fires making the lentil stew. The same aromas were in the air when the tribal elders decided I was not like the other children and the demons inside made me do evil things.

. . . .

Walking back toward the hut, I try to soothe myself. A few moments with my harp would help even if Ima punishes me with the stick. I remember when Abba gave me the harp long ago. He explained about the body being hollow so it is light enough for females. He thinks we are not as strong as men. Plucking a string made from dried and twisted sheep intestines makes a musical tone. That never ceases to astonish me. I hope the animals are not killed for harps to sing.

Wrapped in flax and on the floor next to my sleep mat the instrument is safe. My parents were sure I would tire of music. They were wrong. I would never give up my favorite thing. What I do not understand was why they allow me to keep the harp if they do not let me play it. It does not make sense.

Ima may be close by, and I do not dare play. Instead, I whisper, "Sandalphon, please come now. Ima is outside at the cookpot and will soon call for me." He is my friend, my cloud, my teacher, the voice who helps me, the one who changed my name to Elisha. He said the name would give me courage, but never told me why courage was needed.

He always arrives the same way, as a cloud with rippling movements. The cloud drifts down with grace. A rainbow swirls around him. His colors are mostly those of the time of year, but I always look for the one that stands out. It delights me and I laugh. The cloud's music rings out, his harmonies are like the golden sun. They fill me with cleanliness and warmth. I am the only one who hears his song of joy. An orb larger than the moon and with a color I do not recognize is his companion.

As a child I jumped behind a tree and peered from side to side to find who made him talk. No one was there. He spoke again and I knew he was a friend and now I reveal all my secrets to him. Most of the time I call on him when the pinks, yellows, and oranges of the sunrise dance at the horizon. The sun is disappearing, making me sad.

My cloud sets down on the ground and the orb backs away. "Peace be with you," he says.

"Thank you for coming. Fear has me in its prison. Is there some magic to help me?"

"No magic. Humans are able to learn and grow and that can bring joy. What would you like me to do?"

"The Council of Elders will pass judgment." I hesitate. "You guide me. But why did you never tell me not to talk to the women? Now I am in trouble."

"The meeting was also about other things, your name and speaking to me."

"I was trying to help the women."

"You are angry. Do you wish me to leave?"

"No. I love you and need your help. What will the council decide?"

"We spoke of this. If I knew, I could not tell you."

"My friend and teacher, will you be by my side?"

"I am always at your side and always will be. But remember, you have free will, and I cannot interfere in your decisions." With those words, he joins the clouds in the sky. Knowing he is near makes me less afraid. I rush home and clean up the remains of the family's evening meal.

· · · · · · · · · · · ·

I wake before light. When I return from relieving myself, my mother is bent low over the broom. Even when the sun is high, the hut is dark inside—as dark as the sorrow which torments me. She is jabbing at the floor with the bundle of shredded branches and leaves the same way she stabs at me with her stick.

Ima straightens her back. "Why do you wander when you know it makes me angry? You were late to the evening meal and you disappear when you are supposed to work."

"You do not want me to sweep. You said what I do is sloppy and does not remove the dirt. Teach me how to do better."

"Do not show me your anger, or I will show you mine. I cannot take care of all the work myself."

"Yes, Ima." I wish I understood why Ima is so mean.

The darkness of the hut hides the wrinkles on her face. "Abba told me what happened at the meeting. You refuse to accept the edict stating women are not permitted. At almost thirteen seasons of growth, you still have a fantasy you are powerful enough to change things. You are not the leader of this village."

"Do you not understand the men say things about women but they cannot defend themselves?"

"Be careful of your mouth."

Her voice chafes on my skin. "Yes, Ima." I do not understand my mother. She wants me to improve and do better but when I ask a question, she does not answer. It is as if I am not there.

My mother's attention is on the hut's floor, my father's proudest achievement, except for the son he sired. Abba pounded the muddy sand for seven suns until it was smooth. I was born soon after.

"You disobeyed. Who knows what will happen now? Stand still."

"I need to walk; the air soothes me. Fear of cutting out my tongue or facing banishment alone in the wilderness is terrifying."

"Tame your curls before anyone sees you. Gossiping with the women brings problems. And then there is your specter. You talk to the air, scare the villagers, and dangerous temptations control you." I am her embarrassment. "You are impossible and do not listen. We explain how to fix your troubles. Stop the chattering.

You are stupid. God made us mere insects to be stepped on. You are no better than the rest of us. Go ahead. Leave. You always do. You are stubborn to the end." Scorn passes over her face. Her eyes are on fire. "You will finish all the wheat in the jug and portion out the flour for baking."

I am her regret and her failure. "But Ima, it will take until the sun disappears."

"It is your work. No more chatter. Go."

"All I want is to stay with my family and get married like other girls."

"And how will it happen? You give yourself a man's name. What man wants a woman who declares men do not treat them well? What do you expect? Take your shawl. Abba will be cross. You should know that by now."

Calling me Elisha was the one thing she and Abba ever agreed to. I fought them for a mountain of full moons until they were worn out. But she is always enraged. "The shawl is in my hands, Ima." She saw me pick it up but cannot help making threats. Walking has to wait. I must do the grinding.

. . . .

The wheat is spread on a large flat stone. A great many strokes of rubbing the grinding stone against the grain are necessary to become flour. That is why it makes my hands sore and hurt when I strum the harp. Ima refused to show me how to grind better but wants perfection. Abba will be angry if I do not finish all she asks.

The sun is returning to the horizon and the evening meal is ready. The three of us wait in awkward silence for Abba's return. This tiny place houses my parents, my brother, and me. This place where I grew up. This place the Council may well declare I leave.

Ima turns toward me. "Why were you not here to help make dinner?"

"You gave me more wheat than usual and I ground it all as you asked." Ima's face clouds over. "May I bring you something?"

She glares at me. "Were you at your music?"

"No, Ima, I worked." Her eyebrows are raised. She doubts me. "Go and look. The jugs are all filled."

"Are you going to eat?"

"I am not hungry." Despair comes too often and robs me of any appetite. I sneaked a few fig cakes and a bit of flatbread she will not miss.

Abba joins us, the sun's descent drawing shadows on his face. I run to him. "Abba, I brought some herbs, mint and aloe, to help your digestion."

"Thank you, Elisha. I will try, but they will not help."

We sit on the mats. There is no conversation. I watch my mother's face, but she shows no trace of upset. Ima's signal of distress is wrapping her fingers into her tunic. Then the threads she carefully tied into a fringe wiggle like worms climbing up and down her cover. Maybe the difficulty is between her and Abba. No, they are furious with me.

The meal is not quite done. Ima turns to me. "You did not eat so what do you wait for? A celebration? Clean up and put it all away." Nathan turns and the slight shake of his head tells me not to argue. I scour the remains and settle everything back in place. When I was a child I cried because my stick doll was nowhere to be found. My mother explained that putting things where they belong meant we could find them with ease.

Their bellies full, my family enjoys a respite after working hard. It includes a goblet of libation. With the water muddy and impure again, grape wine follows the meals. I stay on my mat, near, but not close. They ignore me and chew on gossip.

What if I am banished? I depend on my family. Yet why should I stay? People here just tolerate me. Except my brother. At sleep time, it will be peaceful, and then I can think. Daybreak will bring clarity.

I wait for the stars to appear, the proper moment to excuse myself. "Good night and sleep well."

Lying on my back, my arms are over my head. Is what Ima said about insects and God true? Some villagers have idols, others are like my parents and pray to the One God. The villagers are sure God punishes them if they are bad. If God is in charge, then he should consent to the good. I am not a good person and without doubt not an obedient one. How will any god accept me? I turn on my side and hope for sleep.

"Please, Eshmun, the idol who heals. Help me. Then I will have the energy to do the work Ima wants." I do not know about this God thing. I pray because it makes me feel better.

CHAPTER THREE

I must have fallen asleep some time during the blackness. The sky is still dark and the stars still shine as I wake with the same thoughts in my head. I leave the hut on tiptoes and make my way toward the fields. The dimness makes it safe to run to the olive trees with my harp in hand. Our olive grove offers a scent which lightens my heart. This is my private place, where I make up songs and meet Sandalphon. My mother calls him my specter. He may be a cloud, but he is real. She refuses to accept that.

The despair that comes over me is one which nothing but music can soothe. Melodies fill me and I need nothing else. They lift me to play in the clouds, to touch the sky, to fill with joy, and reach the stars.

Will I wake Qayin if I play? I am far enough away. I gaze at the harp. The first time I saw it, the shape struck me as strange. My fingers caressed the wood around its four sides. The top was small, the two sides, front and back long to house the strings. Without music, the deep sadness consumes all my energy. Holding the harp to my heart always brings the words I need.

New verses come to me and whispering them brings a comfortable rhythm. Soon a tune comes, and I hum under my breath so no one will catch me. Abba's ears are always listening, but I must be sure my new tune will not be forgotten.

The sun is at the horizon. The village is awake. I took too much time and rush back to store the harp before they find me gone. Ima is standing at the entrance to the hut. She holds her chest and coughs. "Get to the garden."

"But, Ima."

"Not one word or excuse." She scowls at me. I lay the harp on the ground and follow her.

The stick comes out and her fury is worse than ever. The men in the fields ignore my screams. When she stops I cannot stand straight, but my harp needs to be rescued. I pick it up and hobble inside. I save it from Ima's anger.

· · · · · · · · · · · · ·

Ima goes to work in her garden, leaving me to limp through my duties. I shove some food into my mouth while scrubbing the hut. They never understand that with little sleep getting up is difficult. And work even harder. All through the night fear of the future made me shiver and moan. I woke up many times. My father yells my name, interrupting my cleaning. It will take more than fingers and toes to count how many times he called me the past three full moons. I pull my shawl over my head and run to the community planting area.

"Elisha." His voice is usually harsh, but now it is kind. "What did I hear while it was still dark?"

"What do you mean, Abba?"

"No games please. Did you enjoy yourself?" His voice changes. "The humming?"

"I am sorry. I was excited to find words for a song and did not want to forget the tune. You do not like my composing, but I did not think you would mind. Do not be angry."

He pulls on his beard. "You are well aware I mind, and this must stop. We try to accept you are different but living with you is most trying. You do not consider how we suffer each time they shun us." He moves closer. "This is what happens. Silence. Do you have any idea what your actions cause?"

"I do understand. That is not fair. I try."

"The villagers used to have a word with us, now they do not. They do not help with animals or harvests. We are outcasts because of you. To my shame, they do not want our help. You must recognize that you are part of a family. You refuse to listen, and we suffer."

I am an outcast, but he does not accept that. "But Abba . . ." He moves away.

Will he take away my harp? I wanted to sing for a birth celebration because they were serving roasted meat, a delicacy I have never had. Abba said, "Music wastes time and keeps you from meaningful work. Be aware of grave consequences. I will take the harp if you sing, and I will know if you disobey." I never had to hear those words again.

Humming my tunes makes me happy. If Abba hears music, he sends me to help with the cooking. "Women work. That is what they do," he said. I cooked a lot.

Abba stares at me. "You are of marriageable age. You learned as all youth do that harmony in the huts means marrying young. Not one man, young or old, shows any interest. You bring disgrace and shame upon us."

"Those men decided I am evil." I face him. "You do not listen. How could I care for those who judge me wicked?" I turn away and my eyes squeeze tight to hold back tears. "Why would I change to please them? Is it not enough I am embarrassed in front of every last one? That is not fair. I care. More than you think."

"Now you may get us all banished, cast out of the tribe." He searches my face. "Not another word." His cheeks are red. How do I please him? "You avoid doing your share of work in the house and the fields. You will work, or else I will take your harp." Abba's jowls jiggle. He turns and walks toward the hut.

Is threatening to take my harp a way to make me work? Abba thinks composing is idleness. I work in the fields and the hut and do all they ask. He does not understand about tiredness from not sleeping.

But I did this to them. What kind of person am I, not understanding, not realizing their hurts? My heart is in music. I cannot give it up but perhaps I can find a path to fix the problem. If I try to work more, the council may relent and my parents will be happy.

My brother works hard watching the flocks. He has no time to find enjoyment. It is acceptable that he does not marry. Abba has no contract for a wife for Nathan. Yet customs dictate I should already be in my husband's house. Why is it that way for women?

CHAPTER FOUR

Abba is tramping about the hut and wakes me with a jolt. He never gets up before me. My sleep was interrupted with bad dreams of living in a forest and fighting with animals. This sunrise marks the passage of five suns since the council meeting and everything goes on as usual. The longer they deliberate, the more frightened I become. More suns will pass before they decide.

After we eat, Ima goes to the garden, Nathan vanishes into the fields, Abba disappears, and my task is to tend the cook fire, clean that area and the hut. When all is in order, I resolve to make a fresh beginning. Sandalphon will continue to be my guide, but I will no longer speak to the women about their problems. I can do it this time. I must.

Abba returns as I set out to prepare the middle of the day repast. I tell him of my new resolution. He stares at me. "I understand you believe what you say, but this is not the first time you promised to change. Finish your preparation. I will return shortly. Before I go, let me admit the herbs did help." My smile cannot be hidden, but he is right. Many promises were made, and I broke them all. Why am I not more like Nathan? He does no wrong.

The Council does not move with haste. In the past, I found it hard to endure. Now I am determined to be patient. Abba returns and the basin waits on his mat. He takes a few bites and calls me to his side.

"Elisha, I met with the Council, and they will attempt to take your promise into consideration."

"Thank you, Abba, thank you." My father gave me hope—if just for the moment.

The sun shows its full light. Ima comes inside for a respite and a goblet of libation. I am finishing sweeping the front of the hut. "You are needed in the garden. Go. Now." She turns and goes back to the vegetable plot.

I put the broom where it belongs. "I am on my way, Ima." My steps are quick. She is digging up the sandy dirt. "May I get something for you?"

"You moved so fast. Are you sick?" I am puzzled by her answer. "In the past you never stirred the first time I called. We need to plant the seeds Abba bartered before the wet season arrives."

Nothing pleases her, not even obeying. "Ima? If I dig up the soil, will you set in the plants? If I do it they are crooked."

"Yes, Elisha." She is annoyed and her expression is severe. "Something else you want?"

"Can I ask some questions?"

"Our attention should be on the seeds."

"What do you suppose the council will do?"

"In my experience the person gets what they deserve."

I will not let her make me cry. "Why am I always afraid?"

"You are so foolish. You are not fearful."

"I feared my childhood friends." I continue to dig. "After they saw me talk to Sandalphon they frightened me and called me names. They teased and refused to play with me. Then they trapped me in a circle. I could not find a way out. I cannot remember what they did to me."

Ima turns away. "You are different. But teasing? That is your fear? Such a delicate flower. If you stopped doing things that frighten people, you would not be afraid of them turning on you."

"Why do you make it about my difficulties? Is it not enough the whole village is aware? I ask you about being afraid and lonely and find no answer. My troubles have nothing to do with this."

"I am certain they do."

"May I be excused?" I start back to the hut.

"Get yourself back here or you will be the sorriest young woman in the Land of Canaan. Do you want the stick again?"

That stops me. "I am sorry. Please, Ima, not the stick." The bruises from the last time she thrust the stick into my sides have not healed, but there is no more pain. No matter what I do, she gets angry. The punishments began as a child. Was I so horrible even then?

"The truth is that you do not work and run to your music."

"My head is filled with worries about the future, but I do not forget work." The planting comes to an end and there is no more conversation.

"Ima, may I go to the olive grove? I will return soon." I still ask though she always agrees. "My head is full of many uncertainties to sort out."

She brushes me off with her hand, like a piece of dirt on her garment. "Be back in time to help with the meal, or else," she calls after me. *Or else*, means the stick. "And no harp."

The scent of olives draws me. When the tribe settled here, the trees were saplings. They are now full grown and hold our tribe's history. As a youngster, Abba fixed me on his shoulders and gave me a small staff. I hit the branches like the men and made the ripe fruit drop to the ground. That made me proud for many suns after.

I thought of one way to make everyone happy. Become what they wish me to be, force myself to denounce my detestable behavior. Work and give up music. I repeat that in my head. The words that cannot pass my lips burn my tongue and bind me like a lamb ready for slaughter. I lie on the ground sobbing and wanting to die. I might as well. Without music, my life is over. My chest is so weighty it makes the whole of me hurt. My legs turn to slush as if I climbed mountains or walked until another full moon passed. It seems that my arms are pulled in opposite directions, and in the end, nothing will be left of me.

A new song is the one thing that can make me feel better. The ballads remain in my head. They are my secret. My tears have calmed and I wonder if my father will be successful with the judging.

A deer passes in the distance. She is sad, her head and shoulders hanging near the ground. The animal is powerful and fast. The tribe is convinced that deer are alert and cautious. That they depend on intuition to solve their challenges. Can I be mighty like the deer?

. . . .

Three suns later with all my tasks finished, I hurry to Nathan in the fields. When we were young, the villagers spoke about me in his presence. First they eyed me. Then they said, 'she is a follower of the Tempters, is evil, and will do harm to the poor and those desperate to survive.' I had no scar to mark me, but I was a curiosity for the villagers to stare and poke at, for the children to tease. I could not escape the whispers, the laughter, the fingers pointing. It made me hurt inside. Even Nathan could not help.

"Be well, my brother. It comforts me to see you with the animals."

"I do enjoy the care of them." The goat offers milk, and Nathan is on his knees with the jug. His eyes are on me while his hands continue their labor. "How are you?"

"Nothing is easy, and it is all confusing."

"The wait must be difficult but the council will make their decision."

I kick at the grass. "I know that." Nathan puts the jugs aside and takes the shears from his belt. He makes sure to leave a thin layer of wool to ensure the animal escapes being burned by the hot sun, yet still stays cool. We are blessed with a flock that produces the most wanted of all—pure, white fleece. Abba has been working from dawn to dark gathering what he can for a merchant. Even if he was here he could not help.

"Elisha, you must not go away. How will you manage?" Nathan sets the shears into his belt. He slaps the goat's backside and sends her on the way.

"Nothing can be done about it."

"You do not want to leave. We can take care of you."

"You said that before. Do not tease. Not now."

Nathan's jaw tightens. "If you can live by yourself, I will set up a tent outside the village and bring you food. You will not mix with the villagers."

"Please, Nathan, stop. I will be all alone and a bandit might find me, or villagers might come upon you going back and forth and wonder why. Someone could chance upon the shelter. I love you for the offer, but it will cause more complications."

"You act like a child, and this decision is not acceptable."

"Nathan, think. No matter how faultless I am, no one will forget my cloud or talking to women. There is no other way." I grab some leaves to wipe my nose.

"But you can be safe here." His voice catches in his throat and belies his words.

"Nathan, please listen. It is not because of my waking too late or too early, my harp, or my songs. You understand how they are and they will not change. I must find a way to create and sing my songs or I will die inside. If I am banished, death may come anyway."

"If you are determined to obey, please take this blade."

Nathan set the blade into a precious bone handle, and I run my hand along its smoothness. My loving brother made it for me. He turns around in a circle and lowers his voice. "The council men spoke of an area down river with different people. But you should understand that these men, wise as they are, were not aware of whether those others are like us, or how they might be unique. They had no idea of where they live."

"You are not supposed to share this with a woman. Thank you." I take a few steps toward the field. "The truth is, no one can help."

"Maybe there is a chance they are like you and you will be welcomed."

"Thank you for trying to make it better, but I have no idea how to find them." I stare into nothingness.

"Be aware. You are loved." He turns and sets off toward the hut to sharpen his tools.

I turn to leave, and Abba calls. "Elisha? Elisha? Where are you?" The urgency in his voice makes a cold sweat drench me head to foot. Nathan's face turns white.

"I am scared for you, my sister."

His face makes clear how much trouble I am in. "You are not more afraid than I am." My father's call fills the air and echoes in my head. I hurry toward the sound. My body is burning and threatens to burst into fire. My legs are stiff and I force myself to lift them up and put them down. My chest pounds. Why did he choose an unfamiliar area away from the community, one the tribe ignores? It is bare of greenery and flowers.

The dash to get to Abba leaves me breathless. I stand before him. Abba tugs at his beard while I quiet my gasps.

"My daughter, I chose to speak with you away from others' ears."

It is the council. The decision. "Yes, Abba." My mouth is dry. I swallow many times, but the dryness refuses to go away.

"I am not well acquainted with songs, so perhaps I have been unfair. Sing one of them for me." He sits on a nearby rock.

"You never listen to my songs and do not want me to waste time composing."

"You always question. I want to hear one. Now. Sing."

I clear my throat and choose one of the first I wrote about the sun and the stars. My tune finished, I watch his face for an opinion.

"Your song is nice, the words somewhat appealing. What you can do with all that is another question. You are not married. Perhaps you are talented and can find a way to make a life with music."

"Thank you, but what do you mean make a life?"

"We have no way around the council's declaration." The words are pronounced without a gleam of expression. "Let us return to the hut. Your mother is waiting."

I nod. I will not cry. If I argue, the family will be exiled. My fate is settled.

I trudge through the high grass toward the hut. Like an elbow in my side, a feeling bothers me. It counsels that it could be better to leave. Nathan insists I stay. If I could marry and have a family, but that will never happen. Hope and fear compete for my heart.

CHAPTER FIVE

I am banished. My fate is settled. The decision was up to the council and what I want does not matter. All I can do is hope. During the next two sun cycles Ima weaves soft cloth for my new tunics. One of sheep's wool and one of goat hair. Two are necessary in case my blood flows and stains what I am wearing. She also makes a rough cloth for a new sack to carry food and clothes. Her back hurts from bending over the loom on the ground. She works hard, and little sleep makes the persistent cough start again.

"Ima?"

"Yes, child. Do you not notice I am busy?"

"But I brought something to help you. Aviyah, the root gatherer, gave me mustard seeds. She said to soften them in water, then put them in a cloth and place the mixture on your chest. She promised the cough will go away."

"You choose to indulge in many fantasies."

"But, Ima, why will you not try? The herbs helped Abba."

"Foolish nonsense. Fine for cooking, not for health." I try to make it better but even that does not please her. "Your father is saving extra goat milk to barter a small skin to hold water."

"Thank you." I go back to my work. Will she be happy or sorry when I leave?

While my mother is away helping Abba, I bake fig and date cakes and flatbreads for my journey. I am afraid she will be angry I used her flour. Perhaps she will not miss the wheat I grind. Not that it matters. I will be long gone. I feel bad. It will not be long before Ima must do all the work. The baking finished, I roll the cakes and breads into old flax cloths and bury them near the olive trees. The olives are not ready for picking. We had no rain to water them.

I go back to the hut, and Ima is not there. Perhaps she is helping a sick friend. Carrying my harp, I head for the olive grove. Do they not want me to be hopeful and happy? Only music does that. The harp is on my chest. My arms are around the case. I try to imagine my life. Will anyone help me, love me, want me? I hum all my songs in a soft voice, so no one hears them. They do not help.

I return to the hut and Ima is standing in front of the door. I stand still, harp in hand and wait.

"I am so tired of you not listening. I hope you will obey wherever you go and not shame us."

. . . .

The sky is dark. The half-moon arrived. Too soon. Before anyone was awake, I dug up my provisions, shook off as much dirt as possible, and stored them in the olive tree praying the birds would not find them. I stand near my mother in my sleep space. Her tired eyes avoid mine. My stomach is churning. I hum one of my songs to feel better.

"Must you hum? Wake up. No one will listen to your songs. They are not pleasant enough for anyone to hear."

"Yes, Ima." The cruelty of her words surprises me. Long ago she listened to one song and said nice things.

While my mother prepares the jug of water for the men, I sneak my food and Nathan's blade into the sack. They are secure on the bottom. I try to be careful with my new tunics and under shifts, but my hands shake and I drop them. Why are her words so mean?

"Ima, do you not understand how worried I am? You hardly speak, and your words are harsh." I pace back and forth rubbing my arms. "This is hard." Both arms fly out with fingers splayed clasping my fears and wave in the air. "Do you think I want to go?"

"It is possible you do. Pure stubbornness makes you disobedient."

"That is not true." Her tone holds as much resentment as mine.

She pulls my failure out of the sack, makes a face, refolds, and takes care situating them. The shawl on top is a reminder for me to wear it. It is sheer great fortune that the food and blade escaped her fingers. She bends toward me with distress in her eyes. "The sun is at the horizon. There is danger, for soon the light will be gone."

"They are cruel to make me leave my family."

Her face softens. "We may never be together again. Many families lose their daughters if they marry outside the village. This is different. There is much in the wilderness to trouble you. At least you ate a decent meal. I have many concerns for your journey. Especially not having enough food or water."

"I have the same worry."

"You are not strong like your brother."

"There is no choice."

Her nostrils flare. The small packages of bread and cheese she prepared go on top of my other things. This woman of few words appears harsh and indifferent. Yet I am sure she loves me. I must have faith in that.

"I am sorry to cause such heartache. I did not intend to."

My mother twines her fingers into her tunic and twists the cloth. She turns away. "Not your intention? We told you how to stop. This is as it should be."

"Will the others not come to say goodbye?"

"Things need tending to before dark. Much is left to be done." Her eyes are everywhere but on me.

Perspiration drips down my neck. Why did Abba not come? What is not on Ima's lips is that I will not be here to help, and they will have more to do. She thinks I am not aware of that.

"Elisha. You stand here, eyes down, shoulders slumped. Your hair is unwashed, uncombed, and your eyes wide, your face filled with fear." I fix my lips against my teeth. "You are a fighter. I birthed you and my tube, the one that sustains life in the womb, wrapped itself around your neck. You screamed when the women had a difficult time prying the tube away. They cut and tied it. We could have lost you." She turns away, her back toward me. "The women blessed and accepted you into our tribe. They bathed the blood from your tiny form, anointed you with oils, and wrapped you with swaddling cloth to let you know you were safe. You were in my arms and as I held you close you screamed. I could not stop your shrieks and that made me ashamed. I thought I was a bad mother." She turns back. "Young and unmarried, you go to a new life, which will change you."

"What are you trying to tell me?"

"This is a difficult burden, my daughter, and I wish you well. You fought to be here. That is who you are."

She picks up the water jug she prepared and goes to set it down at the door. It is for the men to wash before the meal. I sneak my harp into the sack and recall that as a child I imagined the harp called me to create my songs. Ima returns. I put my arm over the sack to hide its contents.

"Do not forget to have a long drink of water before you leave," are her final words.

I could have died when I was born. Did she mean what she said, that I am a fighter? She never told me that before. Determination is in her stance as she heads for the fields to call the men for the evening meal. I do not take my eyes from her every step. Please, my mother, please turn back and look at me. I cannot control the quivering of my lips.

· · · · · · · · · · · ·

The miniature statue of the idol, Eshmun, goes on top of my shawl. It is not mine but they will not miss him. The villagers claim that deities oversee the sun and moon going up and down. They are afraid of them.

The sack is on my shoulder. I hoist the small water skin over it. The precious liquid will last but one and a half sun cycles. The cook fire is the first thing to walk past. Many hours were spent here, learning to prepare the food and make the cakes. My clumsy hands could not put the bread dough into the tabun without tearing them apart. My loaves were so stiff they could not be bent to make a ladle, so gravies and juices were left in the basin. But it was easy for me to fill the tabun with dung and heat it well.

Nathan did not come to see me off. I am sure he could not leave his work, or it was because men do not cry. I search the fields from one side to the other. Abba is not in sight.

I freeze when arms suddenly will not let me move. "I could not let you leave without a farewell," he whispers. His hold is so tight it hurts.

"Nathan, why did you not come sooner?"

"I had to help Abba with the fleece the merchant ordered."

I nod. "I had to do all my chores so I am leaving when it will soon be dark. I wrote a song for you, but I should go before I make more trouble. The words are my thanks for your kindness, your understanding, and your love."

"Go, Elisha, and make music many people will hear. You will sing for me another time."

"I wish for that to happen, but no one can predict the future. It does not appear happy."

Nathan lingers. "I should go." One more long, strong hug and I watch him head for the fields. I turn down the path that leads the other way. Both sides are filled with villagers. One side yells, "How dare you take your time." "Get out of here." "You had better move fast." "Never come back." "You are not wanted." "We do not want a Tempter." The chief is standing at the end of the line, and I take a step back. My family knew the villagers were here, but shame made them stay away.

I ignore the throng and hold my head high. I continue down the path and on the other side are the friends I played with. They scream at me and turn away once I pass. The women shriek words I cannot make out. Qayin stands with victory on his face. His wife steps back so he cannot see and throws me a kiss. I smile. Let him think it is for him. The men yell, "Do not come back." "You are evil, a monster." "You should die." "No one here wants you." "Good riddance." Gerah has tears in his eyes.

I reach the chief and my legs wobble, but I refuse to hurry. I steady my steps as I pass him.

"Galina." I turn. "Goodbye," the chief calls, "I hope your journey will be easy, and know that I do wish you well."

I run down the remainder of the path. His remark, so sincere, reached my heart. I grit my teeth and hold back tears.

The crowd's rants continue while I walk to the olive trees. I stop for a moment to thank them for their divine smell and the happy hours spent with them. "Farewell my safe place, I may never sit under your branches again." Weeping makes it difficult to see the way. A long time ago, the chief appointed Abba to find new fields to plant. He took me with him, and we went this way. I remember him saying the Jordan River was straight ahead.

. . . .

All I have ever known and loved is gone. I continue in the direction Abba showed me. He said our village was not far from the Jordan, a walk of a few sun cycles. Whenever my father and I walked about,

I tried to make my strides lengthy like his. I yearned to be like him. At eight seasons of growth, I understood what being a man meant. He made the decisions. The ground I walk on moves under my feet. It slips back to the past and disappears.

Women of my village are not supposed to travel alone. Yet here I am. Darkness will soon take hold. The area is full of rocks. With each step, I pray to be kept from harm. I am sure of just one thing. The food and drink need to be divided into the smallest amounts necessary. That is not hard. Not eating is one of the things that made my mother angry. As if I did not like her cooking. She refused to understand it was the sorrow that did not let me eat. That began as a child.

This is not the time to worry about where I will find safe places to sleep or pure water. That is for the morrow. Strangers or animals may discover me. I lingered too long because I hoped someone would come and assure me it was a mistake. I push the thoughts away. The threat of darkness is upon me. A pain shoots through my foot. "Ouch." I stubbed my toe on a rough-hewn log. Did anyone hear? I wait.

I lean on the log to rub away the hurt and it sways. I inspect it and the center is hollowed out and perfect for sleep. I climb in and lie down with my head on the sack and the water pouch hugged to my chest. Please, let me rest and forget. But sleep does not come. Pictures of my family, followed by each villager yelling and screaming parade through my awareness. It seems like half the night disappears before I feel myself drifting off. The morning waits and I must face it. My last thought is, *I am a pitiful excuse of a proper young woman.*

CHAPTER SIX

I roll out of the log to stretch against the soft grass. It could have made a wonderful sleep mat but would also expose me. Worry, sadness, or both woke me well before dawn. I hoped that being away from home, I would sleep better. The shawl goes into my sack. I am on my own and can do as I please. Abba said this part of the country has wild animals and unsavory men on the hunt for innocents to rape, rob, or kill.

My head is filled with all that happened and makes my heart gloomy. The sight of the sunrise helps me push thoughts to the side. "Ouch." I wait. There is no one to hear me. My toe grew large during the night and I sit to rub it. A line of ants parade in front of me. They are searching for food to bring to their families. "Good luck, little friends."

Sandalphon's orb is in the air, glowing with a pretty red hue. An unusual blue is in one part of the heavens and a sandy blue in another. My cloud twirls around like I do when I am happy and floats down to the ground. As always, the orb guides its arrival, then stays to the side and waits.

"Peace be with you."

The voice sounds different. Alarm takes hold and I dash to the far side of a bush. "Who are you?"

"You know who I am. I am your cloud and visited many times in your village."

"Sandalphon? You sound different, like the men in my tribe."

"Perhaps it is you who have changed and hear me in a new way. You are a composer and singer and your tribe banished you." I step closer. "I am here to help along your journey. Some happenings may be difficult to deal with." The cloud moves nearer. "I can assist after a quarrel or if you do not understand."

"If you can do that, why did you not help before they banished me?"

"Waiting for the council's answer was painful, and I could not offer any soothing. Everything happened as it was supposed to."

I come out into the open. "Supposed to? Now you make me angry."

"This is not easy to understand. Humans go through things in their life to aid in their growth. Not every experience is easy."

"Growth? Am I not tall enough?"

"This is about learning, and I will assist you with finding teachers."

"Women cannot study so how can you help?"

"I have guided many souls. Do not fear. My strong point is helping those who make music."

"Music? You did not tell me that before."

The cloud comes closer. "You did not need to know. But you are embarking upon a long journey. In this new life of yours, you will need to make many decisions."

"My parents say I am stupid."

"Not knowing is an opening to new learning, not stupidity. It might also be better if you will examine your heart for answers. Enjoy your walk."

I do not understand but give a polite nod. "Thank you for offering to help. The orb's color is pleasing."

"The color is called turquoise and like the sea, is blue and green blended into one."

"I never saw a sea." And he joins the clouds in the sky.

. . . .

What can my heart tell me? How will I study? Were my parents wrong and I am not stupid? Each stride takes me farther from all that I know. Did Abba see me leave? It seems to be time for the sun to reach its peak but that globe has not moved much at all. "Which way do I go?" Sandalphon, you assured me of your aid." My words fly into empty air.

In front of me are grass, trees, and shrubs, but no flowers. Nathan said somewhere down river people are different. If I survive, happiness might be possible with others who are unusual. I need to be brave and hold that with my whole heart.

The villagers said that everything I did was wrong or evil. Sandalphon said, "You will have a new life." The cloud assured me he guided many souls. I am in a tangle.

. . . .

A rustling sound comes from the shrubs. A bandit? A bird? Maybe an animal. A fast moving snake? I run to the nearest tree. My toe is not healed and I hope to not have to scramble up. "Sandalphon," I whisper in my head, "I do not see one place to hide." My palms are wet and I wipe them on my tunic. Trees stir. Perhaps it is only the wind. Each moment seems to be forever.

Sounds low to the ground assure me something is nearby and it is moving. I clutch the lowest branch, the rough bark pressing into me. I cannot make out where the creature roams, but the sounds are coming closer. Watching out for my toe, I climb as high as I can. The creature moves, but still does not show itself. My back is against the trunk of the tree, the branch is thin and I fear it may break. The longer I am caught here like a trapped animal, the more the fear grows.

Hissing makes me flinch. I try not to breathe, the smell is horrible. The animal appears and I hold back laughter for fear someone might be near. Abba called these animals 'the unclean ones who creep,' and warned us to take care, for their bite is vicious. This ferret is in no hurry. There is loud crunching and I shudder. He must have found some bones. His meal over, he moves like a snail. Is he looking for more to eat? At last he passes by and is out of sight.

The animal is gone and I am secure in the tree. "Sandalphon, please, which way? Why are you not here?" The cool grass would be comfortable but could be dangerous. The tree is not at all pleasing but I decide to rest. I am safe.

· · · · · · · · · · · ·

When my eyes open the sun is past its peak. I climb down. A short while passes and there are areas of fallow land followed by others that are lush though not a hand has marked them.

I take a large step, trying to convince myself that I am on the way to a happier place. In front of me is a fertile spot. More bushes, shrubs, and trees abound. The sun flickers through the branches and fashions a glint on the greenery. The air holds a crispness, reminding me of clarity after a storm. Its coolness bring freshness and joy to my heart. A bite of bread and a date cake enlivens my mouth. That is surprising because hunger never bothers me. My food and water are nowhere near enough. If I die, it will not matter.

A short walk and an open area is not too many steps ahead. There is a mixture of many colors in the greenery and the abundance of grass. This meadow is unlike where my tribe lets the animals feed. The grass here is a deep green. Flowers of all hues fill the space, some resembling the pastels of the clouds' haze. Others are cheerful reds, purples, and blues. Their scents make me giddy. This place exists not one moon cycle from home and is so different. It is too soon to come upon another city-state, but a hut is in sight. Could there be another village nearby?

"If I bruise you, beautiful flowers, I am sorry. I love sitting next to you." Lying back with my eyes closed, the sun warms me.

"Peace be with you. And welcome."

Jumping at the sound of a man's voice, my response, respectful as my parents taught, is still cautious, "Peace be with you." I leap up and back away. The glare of the sun makes it difficult to see the man standing in front of me. I shade my eyes with my hand. He is bent over at the shoulders and his face reveals stories of many years of hard labor. His gray hair is matted with perspiration and his dark eyes flash.

"Do not be frightened. I mean you no harm. You walked a long way. Your hair is full of leaves." I reach to touch them. "Twigs poke out of your garment." I bend my head to see. He laughs. "Are you here to visit?"

He seems no different than my people. "No. I live in a small village north of Shechem and go south."

"To the south?" he hesitates. "Do you not know you are headed east, toward the rising sun?"

"I will track the Jordan."

"Once you reach the Jordan you can follow it, but you wasted time. What is your destination?"

I peer in one direction. Was my father wrong? I turn to another direction. Now I must walk farther with not enough food or water. Can I trust this man?

"You seem confused and I am concerned. A young woman might come to harm. Why are you alone?" His hand tries to repair the disarray of matted hair.

"To find people like me."

His hands sweep over his torso. "We are the same as you. Two arms, two legs, and a body," he laughs.

"No, I do not mean that way."

"My name is Pinchas. Would you care to come with me? My woman would enjoy female company. Not many people happen this way." He points toward the other side of the field. A woman outside is sweeping and waves a welcome. A grin beams across her face. If he has a woman in his hut there should be no danger.

"I am about to go to her and our meal. You are welcome to join us."

His demeanor is kind, his appearance tidy. He is not dressed in the way of the law-breaker who was punished in our village. That man's clothes were ripped and tattered, and his beard and mustache were unkempt. He spoke words children should not hear. Ima covered my ears and dragged me away before I saw what happened.

The meaning of this man's name is mouth of brass and that concerns me. The promise of a meal and a family, maybe a new life, all help me ignore an uneasiness that might be foolish. "I would be pleased to join you. I am called Elisha."

"After the meal you can relate the story of your man's name and the concern about people like you." His mouth laughs, his eyes do not.

Discomfort takes hold.

· · · · · · · · · · · ·

His woman, Carnia, welcomes me as if I am family. She is respectable and proper, older than my mother and her face is marred with spots of brown. The deep wrinkles on Carnia's face remind me of our tunics after we ring the water out of them. The females of my village are sturdy, but a powerful wind might fell this speck of a woman. She shows me into a one room mud-brick hut that resembles mine—what used to be mine.

They help me feel comfortable, almost like kinfolk. Not what I expected. The room is large like ours but the area for sleep is in plain view. At home, we each have a private space with a curtain.

"Put the young woman at ease. She needs care."

Carnia backs away, turns, and leads me outside. The sound of water comes from a narrow stream. Trees surround the nearby cook area. Carnia fills the basin with heated water. "Take as much time as you need." She returns to the food preparation.

"Thank you," I call after her. With all the foliage removed, the tan tunic Ima made is ready for a thorough scrub. I hang the wrap on a tree branch to dry. My tribe taught respect for your body and keeping yourself clean.

The moment of discomfort with Pinchas makes me think that as kind as these people are, they might watch. I leave the under-shift on making it impossible to wash all over. My curls will take time to dry. The sun will hasten the process. The brown tunic on, I join them at the front of the hut.

The aroma of olive oil, rosemary, and cinnamon fill my nose. I can stuff myself and save my food. Carnia brings the two-handled cook pot to where we sit. Curds, barley, and chickpeas fill the vessel.

Walking must make me hungry because I almost fall onto the mat and eat quickly. The last of the food has soaked into the flat bread. I pop it in my mouth and the basin is clean. I look up. Carnia and Pinchas are staring at me. My bodice is wet from dripping hair. Is that what they gape at?

"Do not worry. My master and I have been as hungry as you are." Carnia's smile reminds me of my mother. "Ima provided what little she had to give."

"I understand." Carnia rises to clear the used vessels. "Where is your village?"

I brush the food off my wrap and with the few worn wooden basins in hand I join her. We get to the washstand and she invites me to clean my hands. "I am from a small village not far from Shechem. Where can I put the clean basins to dry?"

She points to a small space nearby filled with rocks. "You are alone?"

My heart tightens, but I answer with my head held high, "I am not married."

"And your parents." She turns toward me.

"They are in my village."

Her chin dips down and up. "Where do you go?"

"I must go south." She asks a lot of questions.

"Maybe you can stay. We are far away from people."

"Perhaps."

"Let us join Pinchas or he will soon be impatient alone."

Pinchas begins to speak as we sit to join him. "I want to know more about the people you seek. You said they are like you." His tone commands. The way of most men.

"My lord," I hang my head in apology. "My family would not appreciate our discussing that. I hope you understand."

"We are kind and will not judge you." Pinchas's smile is false.

"You are tired. Stay." Carnia wraps her voice in fleece. "You can sleep with comfort, eat a little food, and then continue your walk." She sounds like a mother.

"I agree. You can be safe with us, not out in the wild," Pinchas adds.

I wish to stay, but is he being polite? "That is true, and my journey is long." I adjust myself on the mat.

"Carnia." The sound bellows so loud she jumps up and moves back two paces.

"Yes, my lord. What is your pleasure?"

"Where is my libation?" His tone is brusque.

"In a moment, my lord."

She cowered as she answered her husband. Ima calls my father lord and master at times as a sign of respect. Carnia's name means bird. This bird has a broken wing.

"May I help?" I follow Carnia into the hut. She lets me pour the libation while she stores the utensils. "May I ask a question?"

"Please do."

"You live in the wilderness. No one is near. Is there no danger?"

Carnia smiles. "Pinchas was brought up here and I came to live with him and his parents, as is the custom. We had no reason to leave." I nod. She takes the libation to Pinchas. I stay behind to inspect a tiny crystal on a little wood stand. The color is turquoise like Sandalphon's orb. I could tell by her discomfort, Carnia did not tell the whole truth.

Making my way toward the mat, Pinchas speaks before I am seated. "About your man's name?" The request is plain spoken, the insistence is in his tone.

"Excuse me, my lord, my tribe would be upset if I spoke of that." Please, my cloud, my voice, my friend, pardon me for the lies.

"That is a shame. I missed out on two stories. Your water skin is small. Fill it and go on your way. We do not have a lot of food to share." Carnia looks up.

"Thank you so much. I do not wish to bother you."

"It is my pleasure. That is unless you are moved to stay."

But he just said . . . "May I take some time alone to make a decision?"

"Do not take too long."

"Excuse me." A polite nod and I take my sack and walk to an area behind the hut for privacy. I take out my harp and drop the sack on the ground. Holding the harp helps my head to clear. The way Pinchas addresses Carnia troubles me. He reminds me of Qayin and makes me uneasy. Perhaps it is merely his way of speech.

"Sandalphon, where are you?" He sets down close by. "Please guide me."

"You know I cannot help with decisions. You must choose your next step, and I will be here as you need me." The cloud and his band of colors disappear.

First, I decide to stay, then five steps later choose no. I do not know these people or trust Pinchas. Sandalphon said to examine my heart. I was taught that I should draw in air. Deeper breathing helps my body to relax and after a short time brings a message. *You do not want to be alone.* I let out another breath and feeling even more at ease, I return to the couple.

Pinchas raises his eyebrows and twists his mouth to one side. "Did you decide?"

Carnia motions toward the mat. "Please sit. I hope you will stay. I poured the libation. Drink. Drink." She encourages me with a wave of her hand.

The quality of her tone is sweet and her eyes plead for me to stay. My decision was to leave. For Carnia's sake I will wait. "I will stay for the night. Thank you for your kindness and hospitality." One night might lead to more.

"Now," Pinchas hands me a full goblet, "about yourself." The grin filling Carnia's face disappears.

"Where shall I start?"

"Can you explain what took you so long to decide? It seemed you were hiding from us while cleaning yourself. Do you think we are the kind of people who would hurt you?" Pinchas prods. Then he scowls at his wife daring her to say a word.

A sip of wine delays my answer. My words, chosen with care, are truthful. "The women of my tribe taught us that if we have a difficult decision to face, to go outside, take in air, and wait until our heart whispers instructions." The couple glance at each other. Concern is on Carnia's face. "The answer becomes clear, making it possible to move ahead."

Pinchas sneers, rolls his eyes, and stops me with the palm of his upraised hand. "Consulting your body is ridiculous. Decisions are made by the consideration of affairs. Men are aware of that."

I draw back. Anger fills the deepest parts of me. I want to be close and shake my fist in his face. Instead, I stand there.

"The women of your tribe told you. Your ima." His voice drips with scorn.

"My ima is a grand woman. She works hard and is amazing and bright."

"Your ima told you how to make decisions. No wonder."

I stare at him. "I said it was the women of my tribe." I grit my teeth. He is trying to make a fool of me.

"Women. Of course, no man would make such a declaration."

Disgust covers his face. His words make me squirm. The villagers showed me that sort of face enough times to recognize its meaning. His wife turns away.

"My thoughts have changed, and I will leave you in peace."

"Did your heart tell you so?"

His laugh is wicked. I pick up my things and go to the tree to collect my tunic. The crunch of footsteps makes me turn. It is Pinchas. I step back.

"A bit of advice. If you wish to get along in this life, do not talk about what women say. Your tribal women may mean well, but you must listen to the men. They distinguish between truth and fancy."

He is like the men of my tribe who turned me out. "Many women are strong and clever. They are as courageous as men."

"How dare you speak to a man in this tone of voice? Go. Now." Pinchas shakes his head and stomps off a moment before Carnia comes out of the hut.

"Men do not always understand the way of women. I am sorry if my master made you feel unsafe."

The one person I ever saw so alone and desolate as Carnia was Ima after a fight with Abba. Does Pinchas beat Carnia? My father never beat Ima, but they fought and yelled so loud the whole village heard them. He called her disgusting and hurtful names. I cried the tears she should have.

What did I do? Will his anger make trouble for Carnia? She returns to the hut, her feet heavy into the ground, her back bent as if her entire being is in pain. There is nothing I can do. I want to speak but cannot.

The still damp tan dress goes in the sack. Wagging my head helps my curls dry. I scurry down the trail to get away from the humiliation choking me. I made things worse. I spoke up and had another failure with a different family.

CHAPTER SEVEN

I reach the meadow and take time to walk through the flowers. They are as beautiful as when I first saw them. The sun has begun its journey downward, and I hurry to the trail. The turquoise orb appears but does not bend to present the cloud. The colors surrounding Sandalphon are brighter than usual.

"You are doing well."

"I am glad you are here. You do not understand how much I needed you."

"Why would I not? You had to embark upon this trip on your own, to depend on your instincts. Your time with Pinchas was not happy but it was good learning."

I turn away. "It was more than difficult."

"You have a 'poor me' part of you. Do you need sympathy?"

"You are being mean. I failed again and feel like an orphan."

The orb moves away. "Your parents are alive and Pinchas a passing encounter. You began to prove you can survive."

I look at him. "That is true. I guess."

"Something made you want to stay."

"The longing came back. There is a part of me that is miserable and wants a family. What did I prove? My instincts were wrong. I want to go home."

The cloud swirls. "Is it your family you need? You were not happy at home, so why would you want to go back?"

"They take care of all my needs."

"Do you not think that is self-serving? Would you expect a new family to do the same?"

My face is hot from the tears I hold back. "I could have been more helpful."

"Is that the whole truth?"

"I avoided helping as much as I could."

"Why?"

I walk away. "I was angry. They refused to give me permission to make new tunes or talk to the women."

"You made them angry."

He surprises me. "Perhaps what you say is true."

The cloud is at my side. "The decision to leave Pinchas shows your instincts were right."

"I did not want to be around a man like him."

"You made a valuable conclusion. You recognized a clash for humans, a strong divide between two parts of you having wants and needs and creating a battle."

"What do I do if they fight?"

"You will learn."

"How will I learn?"

"I cannot say. You will arrive in Urusalim and meet with Abram. He will tutor you. He is the first Hebrew, an immigrant, and a wise man. You have a long journey ahead and it is not to be hurried. You will learn much."

I shake my head. "Why a Hebrew?"

"His family worshiped many idols, like your parents. And like your parents, he now prays to the One God who cannot be seen."

"What does that mean?"

"God is invisible, so no one can create a picture or form."

Does he know I took Eshmun? "Oh, I knew that. But, why Urusalim?"

"Abram is now consulting with Melchizedek."

"Why would I want to meet him?"

"You might choose to admire someone like Abram or his wife Sarai, or you may choose your own path."

"And who is Melchi . . . whatever his name is."

"He is known as the Righteous One. All your questions will be answered. The timing must be proper. Be aware you follow in the footsteps of a great man."

"I do not understand, but I will obey." Sandalphon's tinkling fades away. Abram is a great man. Could it be I have a future ahead of me?

Because of Pinchas, I forgot to fill my skin. It is light on my shoulder, and I pray a stream is not too far. Both Ima and Carnia discount their own needs. Who put men in charge, so women have no chance to speak? We have opinions. Carnia is like my ima. They are twigs in the wind, always bending in the same direction as their man.

· · · · · · · · · · · ·

The Council knew of my promise, and I prayed they would let me stay. They did not. How do I trust anyone or anything? I have no idea of my next step.

Flashes of light between the branches catch my eye. It is too soon for the sun to vanish. A stillness enters the top of my head and fills me down to my toes. "Thank you, my dearest friend."

I lie down on the soft ground. The blue of the sky is above me and my arms reach to the sides and take in the fresh sensations of peace. It gives me new words to consider. "Be still inside," it says. "And remember, all is well." What does that mean? I sit up. I must keep moving. Loneliness creeps up and grows heavier. How can all be well alone in the middle of the forest? Fear is weightier than loneliness.

· · · · · · · · · · · ·

I wake from the night's sleep in a tree and stretch out my back. The log was more comfortable. My first consideration is the recent happenings. Ima and Carnia convinced themselves that all was agreeable. I choose to face the truth.

My arms, confined all night by the branches, stretch out into the cool of the morning air. Being surrounded by the fresh aroma of foliage brings a measure of calm. Down from my roost, my walk is slow. I make a game of trying not to rustle even one leaf by raising my arms and sliding sideways between the bushes.

My cloud spoke of a new life. My destination is ahead, and the journey could be successful. I crave the lightness of a new happiness. Cheerful thoughts do not help the sorrow go away. My belly will not tolerate much food. I sit to enjoy a bite of Ima's bread and cheese and complete the meal with one bite of a fig cake. The swish of grass, the crack of a broken twig, and movement of leaves startle me. Two dark eyes shine from behind the panthera's dripping snout and sleek coat of yellow with black spots.

The cake falls from my hand. If he smells the provisions, will he kill me or steal my sack and leave me with no food? The animal's whooshing sounds are low to the ground. The blade Nathan gave me is in the sack. I cannot reach it without drawing the panthera's attention.

Long ago, Nathan told me that one of the men spoke of dangerous animals. "Do not stare into their eyes, for that will infuriate them. He also said not to move any part of yourself." I will stay like a stone. I lie down and attempt to play dead.

The panthera sweeps by, his fur tickling my right arm. The fur is warm and soft, reminding me of playing with the sheep as a child. His low grunts make me shiver. Where did he go? The whooshing is back. His sniffing moves with painful deliberateness up and down my left side. The warmth from his nostrils makes me quiver.

With my eyes squeezed tight, I call for Sandalphon but do not move a muscle. The animal nuzzles my feet, but I do not even twitch my nose. The danger is real. My thoughts are stupid. I will be fine. I will survive. He licks the last of the dried blood. Or will I? Please, let him not want more. Sandalphon, someone, anyone, help.

The panthera is over me. His four legs grip both sides of my body. His hot breaths are on my face. He sniffs me up and down. Stops at my neck. His snout roams about my hair. His warm spittle drips on to my lips. I tighten them. The thought of his spittle in my mouth makes me nauseous. Think about something else. Will he tear me to pieces? No, not that.

My arms. He is at my arms. Licks each finger. I must not stiffen. That is also stupid. If I take in less air will he think I am dead? Or will he finish me? I tighten my toes, my thighs brace, ready to run. That is ridiculous, he moves faster. Pictures of the family flash by and I wish I could spend time with them once more. I stay still and pray the panthera does not notice my shivering.

Time passes and I wait for what is next. He comes back and sniffs the whole of me again. Do not make him angry. It will be over soon. One way or another. There is sudden quiet. The stillness which should bring serenity, frightens me. Much more time goes by. What is his plan? I hear the swishes again. Which way does he go? Breathe. Breathe.

But I must hold my breath to hear the leaves move as he passes. There is no sound and I decide to look. He is nowhere to be found. I bury my head in the grass, my body free to shake and sob tears of release. I study the area. It is hard to imagine this peaceful place also holds so much terror. A long drink and the sack and skin go over my shoulder. I move forward. I was spared.

The sight of Sandalphon's orb makes me glad for the company. ""Well done," Sandalphon declares.

"It turned out well, but I still shake from the fright. You said you would help. Did you not understand I was terrified and alone? My life was in danger. Why did you not come?" I kick the fallen leaves.

"The helpless part is back. Do not lose heart. I am always with you. You wish for me to be here, but there are times when you need to work toward your desire." I sit on the grass turned away from him. "Your mood is that of a child. You are a woman and must think for yourself. Trust I will be here but not always at your command. Now, what did you learn from the encounter with the leopard or panthera as you call him?"

"I was never so terrified in my life."

"Ask yourself my question before you close your eyes. When you wake, it is possible you will know. We will finish then."

· · · · · · · · · · · ·

When I wake up, the sun is crawling over the horizon. Down from the branches of my latest sleep space, the date cakes are even more delicious. There are only enough to last for a short while. Sandalphon is not yet here and I am glad to be alone.

"Here I am, Elisha."

"I am sorry for being glad you were not here."

"Do not be sorry. The thoughts are yours and precious, and you are entitled to a respite. What else happened with the leopard?"

"The dread brought fear and excitement and somehow, I am different."

"In what way?"

"Just a moment, I am not sure." I take my time. "Though I am small, something makes me seem taller. You would say I lived through it."

"You did well. Remember, fear can warn that something is amiss. Its power can also have the ability to stop you from doing anything."

"I did not show fear of insects like the girls. I chose to be daring like the boys."

"Yes, Elisha. You must be bold and that takes courage."

"That worries me, and I cannot be sure of peace in Urusalim. If I return to my village, it will be no different from before and the chance to study with Abram will be lost."

"That is true. Know that I protected you from the animal."

"You did that? What did I do? I was there, too, you know."

The cloud twirls. "Fear did not overcome you and that changed the result."

"What does that mean?"

"It was meant to be." He lifts toward the sky.

"I did it myself," I yell after him. "If it was truly protection, why did you allow it to happen at all? I do trust you, but . . ." Too late. He is gone.

· · · · · · · · · · · · ·

I need to move on but decide to rest for a moment. An idea 'connect with joy,' comes to me like a command. It arrives with a brilliant light and a rush of energy. But it is too bold, and I am not worthy.

I gather leaves wet with dew and sit to clean my toe. More leaves remove the sweat on my brow. Not four strides later a voice brings me to a standstill. "Try again, one more time." Not sure where it came from or if it was my own rashness, I wait.

"Yes, Elisha. It is Sandalphon. Do not give up because something does not work the first time."

My jaw is tense and my lips are pressed together. I stand my ground on the forest floor. I take in one breath to relax and send it toward my heart. After a few more breaths my heart seems to grow full and opens like a flower. It's petals unlock one at a time. The heaviness lifts to the top of my head and floats away. It reminds me of the time when the stillness came and assured me all is well.

I lie down and there is an awareness of floating in the air and still being connected to the ground. The weight of this experience touches me. There is a knowing in my bones that to be ready to explore what I must, I need to stand solid on this soil. That all I do, each of my thoughts, are precious and connected to a larger inspiration. The delight I feel readies me to walk until my legs can go no farther.

I down two fig cakes, gather my things, and am about to continue on when the sound of rowdy men reaches my ears. Sandalphon, please come back. I move to the next tree. The men yell at each other and laugh the same as the men at home who drink too much. That sends a chill through me.

CHAPTER EIGHT

*A*re these men the bandits Abba talked about? I force myself into action. I can climb the trees, but the leaves are too sparse to conceal me. The decision that must be made frightens me more than the panthera. Those men could be sneaking around, and if I run they can catch me. Their sounds grow louder. Then there is silence. My chest relaxes. They come closer and my chest clamps down.

More silence. Maybe they changed direction. Or are they sneaking closer? Another tree is near, and though not the highest, offers the most leaves. A booming sound breaks the stillness. "Here. This is perfect."

I scramble up as high as I can. The branches scratch at me through the tunic. A perfect roost sits in the middle, the branch bigger than two men's hands. It is easy to settle into the narrow slant it makes with the trunk. I hang the sack and skin on a different branch, then curl myself into a ball, pull more leaves in front of me, lie there, and wait.

They are quiet and I steal a glimpse between the leaves. "Hey, let's stop here," one of them yells. I pull back. The men stopped at the tree next to mine.

"Where is the food and wine? We are hungry and thirsty."

"Just a little while more," another answers. They sit to enjoy the meal. My mouth waters from the smell. They must have had a sizable amount of libation, they stagger all over. With elbows pressed into my sides, I try to make myself smaller. The men's laughter is boisterous and harsh. It could cover any sound I make but I cannot chance it. My throat is dry, and my water skin is out of reach. The voices move under my perch.

A branch snaps back and a twig makes a cut on my ear. I jump but do not risk making a sound. My spittle soothes the hurt. This spot is not as comfortable as I hoped. Where the branch becomes two, it pokes into my back.

One of them yells, "I can shoot my arrows farther than you." They play with the bows and arrows shooting them into the trees. The knife is at the bottom of my sack and there is no way to defend myself.

"Perfect shot," one yells. "Now over there," another one says. They scream with laughter at each arrow leaving a bow. I grab my legs and pull them closer. No supplies are available to cleanse a wound or staunch the blood if an arrow hits me. Their cruel laughter is scary.

"See what I found. Someone left a woman's tunic. Would anyone like to guess what happened?"

I peek out and see my tunic fell out of the sack. The one Ima stayed up the entire night to weave. The men below say nasty words.

"Here, get this," one yells. They make a circle and with the points of their arrows throw my cover around. Over and over they catch and send Ima's hard work. With each successful snare they share more drunken laughter. I am glad Ima is not here to see her efforts gone in a few moments. If they catch me, will that be my finish? I swallow hard. The end could be horrifying. What if they find me? I am not strong enough to stop one of them.

My eyes close and I curl over. Is this my fault? My back curves nearer to the branch, its jagged edges sticking into my skin. Please do not bleed. I pray my weight will not break the bough. These men are hunters.

"Hey," one of them yells, "the sky changed." They glance up. "There is an unfamiliar wind. We are going to get wet."

My nose itches and I need to sneeze. They say it is a divine sign but now it is dangerous. My fingers creep up and knead my nostrils. Without warning the wind whips at my hair. The branches bash into my face. I fight them off. The rain soaks everything and I shiver. Did the end of the thirsting season need to begin now?

"Let us move on to a drier place." A few of the men gather the strewn arrows on the ground while others wander farther away to find more. The man who noticed the sky walks toward my tree. Does he know I am here? I grab the closest arrows and hold them in my hand, high and ready. I slowly move the branch in front of me to cover what it can.

The man stands underneath where my cover drips from the rain. He reaches up. His hand is near mine. Almost close enough to touch. He examines the tree. His eyes widen. They land on his prize.

"Here they are," he yells, and pulls arrows out of the bark. He turns and walks away. It takes time for my chest to calm and I still do not move. When the courage to peek out is strong enough, the men went on their way.

My body aches from hugging it tight for so long. I wait a few moments. Climbing down from my perch, I search in every direction to make sure the men do not return. My cover is waiting. It is full of holes and as forlorn as my heart. I hold it to my breast, then drop the mess into the sack. Should I give up, go back home. They will not accept me. I must go on. Will this be my life?

A bush is nearby, and I crawl under its leaves. This journey of being led is one of wandering as if caught in a web, not knowing what to expect next. I am the one who must survive. This is too hard. If the men killed me it might be better. Or I could starve myself, no longer eat or drink. End the questions, the dreams, and the desires.

· · · · · · · · · · · ·

Darkness is falling and it is time to check my stores. The breads are moldy and I throw them to the birds. Ima's cheese melted and I scrape what is left into my mouth. I eat a date cake, and it is time to move on. What I realize now is that I need guidance and accepting Sandalphon's help means an agreement to listen to his suggestions. If I want him to continue coming to me, my whole heart and willingness to do the work must be present.

This is the season of my birth. If I were with my people, we would celebrate. We had many trials. Still, my heart aches. The family is no longer mine.

The cloud whispers in my ear. "Excellent. You recognized a feeling. However, you did not name it. It is called sadness."

"At home I knew what to expect and who would say what." The memory pleases me. "I was safe."

"Are you sure?"

His question feels like Ima hit me with the stick. "You are right. It seemed so." I stare at the cloud. "How can I do anything when I do not know what will happen from here to the next step?"

"Does it remind you of home?"

He surprises me. "I suppose so."

"Life is like that, and you managed to survive. Go and sleep well." His colors fade and the sound of gurgling reaches my ears. That was the strangest talk we ever had. I hear the splashing water. Could it be the Jordan? That would raise my spirits. It would be my first destination and a chance to fill my skin.

The sun is partly below the horizon. I hum a song from my childhood as I walk. The one I sang for my father before he told me the council's decision. I try to quicken the pace but my legs will not let me move faster. The blueness of the water appears before me and the sun is almost gone. The stream is small, not the Jordan, and I get some sleep.

· · · · · · · · · · · ·

The air is already warm when I awake before dawn. The soft waves and blue of the stream lift my spirits. After filling the skin, I gather my things and start out.

My legs are still stiff. "Why do you not heal?" Perhaps moving will loosen them. Progress must be gradual. There is no pain, but their heaviness weighs me down.

What torments me? My family's faces full of disappointment flash by. My heart hurts with dark regret. I did not want it to be this way.

"Stop for a moment and tell me what you learned from the last task."

"That is a difficult question, Sandalphon. I do not know. But I did learn that if I pay attention to what you teach, there is a greater chance of success. And I need to choose what benefits me."

"As each insect chooses to feed on certain greeneries or other specific parts of the tree, the choice of prospects for your new life belong to you."

"Leaves? What are they supposed to teach me?"

"When you are in Urusalim and have choices you will understand. Working with Abram will open up many new ideas."

"What will he tell me?"

"It is Abram's teaching, not mine." All that about leaves has no meaning. Sometimes he rambles on. "Do you understand my description?" I nod. "You did well. I leave you to continue."

"Was I right about the last challenge?" He is gone.

I did well? Then why would he not say more about Abram? Is what I am to learn a secret? The sun rises and each tree, each branch, each leaf delights me. The yellowish-green of the moss is unlike any in my village. I put the sack and skin on the ground, freeing my hands so I can touch the smooth surfaces. They make me laugh and

I roam through the foliage. The sweet perfumes call me to inhale their scents. The pungent ones make me heady, and I back away from the sharp ones.

The warmth of the sun helps me come alive. A light rain falls while the sun is still shining. As a child I went into the sprinkles and my mother called me to come in. "Please, Ima, I want to play in the rain. It bounces off my skin and makes me laugh." Raindrops swirled around me. Ima made me come into the hut. "If you get sick, I must care for you and cannot do my work," she said.

I want to twirl with my arms thrown out like I did then. Would life be different if Ima talked to me about a boy I liked, or before the onset of my blood flow when I did not know what to do? I was sure death was near.

The rain stops and the sun shines a bit. The trees fascinate me and I ignore everything else. Their scents settle my fears but do not take away the hurts or bad feelings for the villagers not wanting me or defending me, for making me believe I was unworthy and useless, for the certainty I was evil. Most of all, for not being loved, except for Nathan, who never scolded.

Not too many steps later the sight of water brings a rush of playfulness. Is this the Jordan? The expanse though bigger than the last one, is also too small. I run toward it, drop my skin and plunge in. I am enjoying the respite when my belly interrupts. It needs food. I search but the sack is nowhere to be found. The skin is in its proper place near where the sack was. I inspect the surroundings again. How stupid of me. It has to be back where I met with Sandalphon.

"My friend, my voice, please help." Where do I go?

"Put to the test the position of the sun."

"Thank you." That is not much help, since the sun has not moved enough to give a sign. I attempt to retrace my steps with the skin clutched to my chest. Every area is the same as the one before. The next clearing shows nothing. Did I go the correct way? The next two regions also yield no sack. My curls are in my mouth and I chew. Ima would be angry.

Sandalphon tells me not to give up. The sun's movement now shows that I turned off course. I move to the right. The direction is still not true and I plod ahead on a new track.

I find the sack on the bank of the stream. I pick it up and my knees give way. I hug the skin and sack to my chest. "Please my family, I am so ashamed. I did not mean to lose your gifts. I will be more careful and responsible." I want to rock like a child but Sandalphon said I am now grown up.

When I was young the tribe said, "You became enamored of your environs and did not take care of your possessions." I lost one of Ima's basins. "You suffer from a lack of responsibility. Life is not to enjoy. Much needs to be done." To complete the punishment they gave me, I had to stand where they made the community fire from the rise to the last of the sun. I was five seasons of birth.

The tribe said I was defective. Sandalphon said I would be helpful. Who is right?

Now to deal with the trek back. The sun's descent is causing a change in the air. A welcomed dryness strokes my face. My cloud told me this last part of the trek might be finished with a reasonable pace.

I walk through an unending expanse of trees and shrubs. More than both hands many times over. I am hungry. The last of the water is finished quickly.

I survived Pinchas, the panthera, and men with arrows, but the scariest part of the trip is ahead. I should go home.

"Hope is a most valuable resource."

"Sandalphon?"

He is laughing. "Do you have other voices in your head?"

"I did not see your cloud, so you frightened me."

"The view you have about your journey is correct."

"You read what is in my head."

"I am able to. Consider each encounter. Each was done well."

I turn. "You call that success?" I wait and wait but he will not speak. "I managed to survive but lost my sack and wasted time." And my thoughts are not always nice.

"You are here, alive."

He makes me ponder, or is it become aware? "What are you saying?"

"Hope serves you and is not to be discarded. And you may have the chance for a bit of good fortune." And he disappears. He comes and goes at the oddest times. I needed him to say if the herbs in the desert are good to eat.

The region before me grows more arid. The tribe spoke many times of this location. Though the messengers who came from the south described the area to the villagers, this is not a vision you can imagine. The few trees I walk past are small, weak from thirst and unable to accommodate a child's form. White sand lays between the last of the trees and the desert's jagged rim, then bareness stretches as far as can be seen.

Nothing offers freedom from threats, nowhere to sleep and be safe. There are few trees and bushes. The sacks are on my shoulder and, to make progress, I alternate between running and walking. The sun moves toward the horizon. Overcome by a weakness which should not be, I kneel to rest. When I attempt to stand again, faintness overtakes me. I reach for the skin and my legs give out from under me.

My head is as tangled as sheep's wool. What should I do and where do I go? My throat is dry. I am such a fool to think this trek can be done by a woman . . . onward, upward, be near you, here, there. My head is a muddle, and I cannot get up.

My words do not make sense. My thinking is somewhere in the clouds. Nonsense roams . . . not agree, fight, do what, taste. What can I taste? The food is gone, nothing to eat and . . . someone shakes my shoulder to and fro.

"Go away, Ima. Go away. I cannot wake up."

"Are you sick?" The voice reaches through the jumble in my

head. The voice is not Ima's. Not Abba's, but a man. I can smell him. I try to sit up. Will he hurt me? My eyes will not open.

"Your skin is empty. My flagon is at your lips. Take a sip." The water drips down my chin and runs down, cooling my chest. "Now, another mouthful and try to open your eyes."

I sit up and raise my forehead as high as possible to pull the lids apart, but they are fixed.

"Good, but we must make more of an effort. Try." A tiny slit of green and yellow appears, but my eyes refuse to see more. "Here. Another drink." My head hurts, and I lie down.

With his arm under my back he pulls me up. The container is at my mouth and I drink. "Open your eyes."

There is a haze in front of me. Did someone spill goat's milk from the sky? I blink a few times and the man comes into view. "Thank you, my lord. Thank you. The rest of my water must have spilled when I fell."

"You seem better; your cheeks have color. You are well for now, at least for a while. Where are you going?"

"To Urusalim." I try to gaze into his dark eyes but mine hurt.

"You still have a long way to go." He hands me the flask. I long to drink to the bottom but will not profit from the kindness of this man.

"What is wrong with me?"

"There is a caravan over there." He points to the right.

"My eyes hurt, they cannot make it out."

"Our journey is in the correct direction, and we would be happy to have you join us. Try to stand."

He has been kind. "Are you a bandit?"

He puts his hand around my waist and pulls me up. "I will gather your belongings. Do you want the skin?" I shake my head, it is of no use. "The women will welcome your company."

Still a bit dizzy, I move ahead but trip and stumble. We make slow progress. When we are close to the caravan nervousness overtakes me. "Men are here, but I do not see women."

"We have a large cart and it is not far. See the yellow covering?" I nod. "The women are protected inside."

We reach the cart, he opens the covering and places my sack inside. He lifts me on to the edge, jumps in, grabs my waist and yanks me to the floor. He kneels over me. "Please, my lord, do not hurt me."

My hands are over my head. He ties them together. "Please, my lord, no."

"Do not worry, this is for your safety."

"My safety?"

"The cart is not steady, and you could get hurt." He ties my feet and turns to leave.

Hands on his hips he looks at me and laughs. My sack is in his hand. He shuts the covering.

CHAPTER NINE

I pray the cart is moving in the same direction as when I walked. He promised me it was. Twisting and turning my hands do not loosen the ropes. The caravan stops and I hold my breath. The man returns. Can he tell I tried to free myself? He ignores me and goes to the back of the cart. The small pieces of wood he takes to the men are soon burning and the aroma of food scratches at my stomach. The man pulls the covering open again and fear makes my back dig into the floor. Welcome light comes into the cart.

"Here. Food."

My back relaxes. "I cannot eat with my hands tied."

My hands free, he goes back to the men. No matter how hard I try, the ties on my feet will not loosen. The flap from the cover was left open and what they say terrifies me.

"She is young, there is no ring on her finger so she is unwed and pretty. We can sell her. Imagine what we can barter for a virgin."

The men laugh. One of them yells, "We should have fun with her first."

"No. If we want to barter, we need her untouched."

Those words could save me. Nathan's gift is in the sack, so is the slate and stylus and my precious harp. Working at the ties again fails.

He comes back to collect the basin and ties my hands when I finish eating.

"I must relieve myself."

"It cannot wait?" I shake my head. "Why did you not say so before I tied you up?"

He releases my feet and helps me down. It is the dark time of night. He slowly walks me to a clump of bushes and loosens my hands. He turns his back. "Go ahead."

I might be able to run. "I cannot with you standing so near."

"You will, or you will go back now."

He can run faster than me. After surveying the area, there is no safe place to hide out. If I can get back here again, maybe I can find a way.

The man yells, "We have lost too much time waiting for you." He grabs me at the waist and drags me back to the cart. "In. Now." As soon as I am tied up, he yells to the men, and they move again. Sleep never comes and I make no headway with the ropes.

. . . .

A different man brings food the next morning. He is not as careful. The bindings are not as tight. "Here. Finish at once, we are ready to leave." He comes back to pick up the basin and I ask, "Are you going to Urusalim?" He ties me up and laughs as he leaves. The caravan is moving. The cart rocks from side to side as if it could turn over. Maybe the first man told the truth. He saved my life. Would he hurt me now? But they talked about selling me like an animal. What if they are not going to Urusalim?

Daylight must have come and gone, and I see no one until the dimness shows. Another man finally comes to give me food. This man does not speak and is also careless. He does not come back. It takes until dark for me to free my hands. With feet still tied, I crawl to the covering and open a corner. The only thing I hear are loud snores. I peek out farther. The desert offers nothing to hide me. A feeling inside says it should be the morrow. I creep back and shut my eyes but am too afraid to sleep. I watch the covering all night. No one looks in.

My insides have been jumping up and down. The careless man comes with food. When it is finished, he ties my hands. They are not as loose as before. Darkness falls and it is quiet except for the snoring. It takes more time, but I finally work my hands from the bands. Forgive me my family, your gifts were precious but the bandits stole them. I untie my feet and climb down but cannot move. I shift my hand to my back. It takes a few moments to find the problem. The tunic is caught on a wood splinter. I rip it away, making a hole, but I free myself.

I take the path on the darker side of the cart. I move one small step at a time, as if I crawl standing up. I stop short. Did I step on a dead animal? My eyes had enough time to adjust to the darkness and the lump seems to be a sack. I bend to feel the fabric, pick it up, and Ima's scent is still on it. I hug it to my heart and feel a hard object inside. The sack must wait. I cannot waste time. I throw it over my shoulder.

I am free of the wagon. From the light of the stars I make out shadows of buildings in the far distance. Buildings mean people.

"Sandalphon, can you see? A city is not far. Is it Urusalim?"

Afraid to kick up any dirt or trip on a stone, I pick my legs up slowly and put them down with great care until well out of sight. When I try to find the city again, it disappeared. Was it my imagination or am I sick? The quaking of my legs is so bad they give out and I drop to the soil. The sack is near my hand. I grab it and thrust my arm in. Eshmun is there, and my stick doll and my garment. Though they cannot take the place of my harp or Nathan's blade, even my slate and stylus, at least I have these to cherish. Sleep did not come when I was tied up in the cart. I must accept that my body needs rest until it is ready to move on.

"Elisha." His voice is soft.

"Sandalphon."

"I did not want to frighten you. As you proceed, consider what you have conquered."

"Falling with words coming out of my mouth that make no sense, being frightened and not able to see, is conquered? I no longer trust myself. No one told me the lack of water did that. And then, I had to escape those men."

"Think for a moment. If you had an oxcart would you not check the cart and wheels before you took it out to work? You chose to trust the man who snatched you. Where were your instincts? You need to take care of yourself if you wish to survive. You were warned about bandits. Remember awareness."

My face stings with heat and prickliness as if thorns jab at it. "I knew it was wrong, but l could only think about having no provisions and they could get me to Urusalim faster."

"You were right but put yourself in danger. I am aware you could not have stopped this man from carrying you off. It was quite an accomplishment to escape. Congratulations."

"The cost was not my life, just things."

"Find some aloe for your skin. Remember, experiences teach lessons. And consider hope."

"I promise, this was my example." Sandalphon disappears into the night. I bury my face in my hands. What else can happen?

· · · · · · · · · · · ·

I wake to see the sun on the horizon. I wanted to ask Sandalphon if the buildings I saw are in Urusalim. "My friend, please advise me if I am wrong." The cart gave me safety and now I am exposed. I will never strum the harp again. The tears that come to my eyes do not want to stop but I must move on.

This could be the last of my travel. If I make it that far. All of my provisions are gone. I am being stupid and that does not help.

I need strength to get to Urusalim. I will do it. That helps me feel lighter and gives me energy, but my throat is as parched as my lost sheep skin. If I were to die no one knows where to search for me. That kind of thinking does not move me forward.

The shawl goes over my head and the sack on top of it for added protection from the sun.

"Please, Sandalphon, and anyone who hears, keep me safe throughout the journey."

"Have the courage to hope." His voice is comforting. "Be still inside and listen to forewarnings. If you can grasp how it works, you will experience exceptional wisdom."

That is the second time he said those words and it is nonsense. Animals and bad people are around.

The heat sears through the thinness of my sandals. It is severe against the bottom of my feet. I am too weak to tear pieces from my torn tunic to wrap around them. Ima always told me I am foolish and need to learn sound judgment. She never told me how.

A young gazelle scampers through the sand. It leaps with a grace I will never enjoy. Its forelegs thrust out, its back provides power and balance. The beauty of its elegance enriches the barren landscape. My body will never be as majestic as that animal.

I walk as fast as I can. What lurks nearby? Will Sandalphon come if I call? Shivers go through me. The possibilities make me uneasy.

The sun is not yet high and a bush with groups of fronds facing downward call me to it. I lick the moisture from its undersides to little help. Where is there safety? I must keep going.

The sun moves past the high point and I am still alive. I sit to rest and my fingers tickle. An insect uses my hand as its private crossing. It maneuvers the hills and valleys of my skin then makes its way to my smallest finger and returns to the desert soil. Eyes shut, I call on hope to help me put my fears aside and keep moving. It might be safer than lying here.

The sandals were not tight when I set out, but my feet are now swollen and bloody from rubbing against its sides. The sand is too hot to take them off. The walk brings me to a bush with dark green leaves. The branches are as long as my father's arm. The points are sharp, but no flowers bloom. How does it grow? There is no sound of water.

The area ahead is almost empty of greenery but will have to do. I drop my sack on the sand and sit. When I stand my legs are weak. I am afraid to move. There is nowhere to find a drink, but ahead is the expanse of the city. It shines straight in front of me. "Sandalphon, where are you? See? Over the crest. You said it could be reached before dark." The farther I go, the less progress I make.

"Yes, Elisha. You have a question."

"How far is it to the city?"

"Where is your determination, your boldness, your courage? Or did you agree to have fear stop you?"

His voice is warm but that is not the question I asked. "How far?" He is not answering. "Will I find others like me if any others exist?" My hand reaches for my curls and I pull on them.

"Why did you leave?"

"You say that as if I wanted to. Nobody liked me, wanted me or talked to me." I stop to think and inspect his colors for any change. "I do not know. You give me hope, make me want to continue, but will it be like home with no one caring about me?"

He begins to back away. "Do not consider the villagers. Consider your reason for leaving."

"They banished me. I would not have left otherwise. You know that."

"Is that the truth?" I nod. "How do you feel now?"

"Better."

"You spoke your truth. Now you must seek more of your truths. Ponder on the difference between wants and needs. Remember, you are a brave young woman. Until the next time."

I want determination, boldness, and courage, but how do I find them? Sandalphon gave me no information, but he hinted that I will feel defeated if I give up. I am brave. I will keep telling myself that.

My head fills with a picture of the city. True or not, it sets me off with a bit of ease in my heart. The sun already began its descent. I drag my sack and crawl. It is slow going but at least I am moving. I am brave. My knees hurt from digging into the grit. I make more of an effort. The sun's voyage is approaching the horizon.

The city is in the distance. The real city. My knees no longer burn, I am no longer hot, and my throat is no longer parched. I keep on going. The sun is at the horizon before I get close enough to see a low stone wall on either side of a breach. Tears stream down my face. I am brave. I struggle onward.

The last of my strength is gone. I can do it. I am brave. I will make it. My limbs do not want to move. I will get to the breach. Crawl. Keep moving. There is no way to tally how long it will take to edge closer to the finish, but I must rest. I lie there knowing I can almost touch it but cannot move. I must move. I am brave. I crawl a thumb breadth at a time until an open space between the walls is in front of me.

I roll around on the desert floor and stretch my arms as far as they can go. Lying on my back I study the stars. "Abba, Ima, Nathan, I did it. I am in Urusalim. It was a difficult journey, but I am in one piece and I am safe."

In the nearing black of night, my first impression of the break is that walls meant to surround the city were not finished, and the gate needed to close the center was never added.

I am here despite the trials, and I am brave. But what is next? I have no home to go to, I am alone with no one to love or care about me, and there is no sign of where to find a safe place to rest. The end of the wall is the farthest from the entrance to the city. No one can see me from there. I crawl to it, curl up on the hard surface, hold my doll in my arms, and at last sleep comes.

· · · · · · · · · · · ·

The hiding place is perfect. I can peek out and not be seen. My mouth is so dry my tongue clings to the top. The aroma of fresh baked wares makes my stomach growl.

Before me is a tremendous expanse filled with traders bartering their merchandise. It was the sound of people yelling that woke me. Goats and sheep wander the far areas while sleep coverings, mantles, olives, and other rations are a few of the enticements spread on cloths. Women are trying on necklaces, and one is bartering a small jug of milk for beads. In the distance, a couple stands next to each other. The priest in his dark robe and colorful hat holds a goblet. He hands it to the man first and then the woman. They each drink. The mountain looming behind them completes the picture. I wonder if I will find my love.

With an indifferent air, I move toward the blanket displaying the baked goods. I walk around as if to examine the delicacies, greedy for the instant I can grab one and run. The number of fig cakes, plain breads, and others with olives and spices is so great the cloth is concealed. The owner turns to speak to a younger man and I reach out my arm.

A hand from behind restrains and pulls me to the ground. A man with a hoarse voice whispers, "You do not want to do that." The smell of alcohol all over his clothes and breath makes me turn away. He holds me tighter. "I enjoy a decent quality stoning as well as the next man but would hate to watch a fine young woman like yourself have her hands chopped off, or worse, be hanged."

"Thank you, my lord. I am new to the city and walked for many suns to get here. My hunger wiped away my good sense." He removes my hand from the bread.

"It is obvious you do not belong here. I do not know where you come from or what you were taught but consider this a strong warning. If I see you stealing again, you will be punished. Next time it will not be painless."

"Yes, my lord. I will obey. Is this Urusalim?"

"Where else could it be?" He walks on.

My cheeks are on fire yet a biting cold runs through me. Another man startles me.

"I could not help overhearing your conversation." It is the man I tried to steal from, an older person with weathered wrinkles. He looks at me as if I am peculiar. "Your skin is burned, and your bones stick out." He picks up a flagon. "Here. Drink." Long swallows of the liquid relieve my throat. "Do not move." His command warns me I had better obey.

He walks a few steps and calls, "Nikkal. Come. Now." I turn to escape, and a tunic flared out on the bottom blocks my way. The girl is younger than I am, with black hair and the same dark eyes as the vendor. He whispers in her ear then turns back to me.

"Do not be frightened. My daughter will help you to our house. It is not far. My woman will feed you and make sure you sleep well." I nod. That is what I need, but are they good people? My instincts are too tired to answer me.

"My name is Nikkal. My mother is a devoted and kind woman and a fine cook."

My mouth has trouble forming a smile. "I . . . am . . . Elisha."

"Elisha! That is an odd name for a girl. We can talk about that after you fill your belly." She wraps her arm around my waist, then drapes my right arm around her shoulder. I hang on to her as we step past the missing gate at the breach and enter the city.

Before me stand row after row of large homes on each side of a walking path that winds in every direction. The houses are odd and more crooked than our funny looking huts. If I had the strength, I would laugh. They are of various sizes, some spread on the ground like ours, but others with a second layer on top. Like our huts they are built from mudbricks with mortar holding them together. City people must be rich.

A set of steps goes up the rise. At each one, Nikkal hoists me onto her hip and then sets me down on the next one. Who are these people that help a stranger? They are nice, but what is their intention? The house is not far. The wayward path makes it seem so. I stop many times to breathe and repeat, "I am sorry for the effort you must make." Nikkal's face lights with kindness each time.

"Are you here to find someone in the city or for a visit?" she asks.

"Someone told me to come."

"Why?"

"I am to study here."

Nikkal hoists me up the last step. "What will you learn?"

"I was not told."

"I understand."

How does she understand? I do not. We walk to the back of the house and there is an open courtyard with a garden of vegetables, a washbasin, and a cook fire, like at home, except it is larger and a house. "This is my ima, Kotharat."

I manage a half nod. Kotharat tosses back her long black hair and stares at me. Nikkal whispers to her mother. They only word I hear is study. She waves goodbye. "I need to help my father at the market." I nod.

There is shade over the eating area fashioned from branches and flax cloths. No one in our village has that. Kotharat sets out a mat for my meal and the sight of food makes me weaker. I drop to the mat, ignore its hardness rubbing at my sore knees, and stuff big chunks of bread and cheese into my mouth with both hands. The fragrance of the food fills my nostrils as it melts inside. The goblet is near my hand. Each bite is followed by gulps of wine, so more food can be shoved in.

Kotharat appears at my side, her dark eyes inspecting me, "No, my child. Slow, slow or it will come back up." I turn back to the food and force myself to chew a little at a time.

The meal finished, Kotharat leads me inside to a small area behind a curtain. A covering in which to wrap myself lays on the mat. "Here. Aloe for your burned skin. Sleep as much as you need." Her tone is not harsh, but her voice is.

"Thank you for your care to a stranger." Eshmun comes out of the sack and I hold him tight to my chest. How long I slept I do not know but arguing in the center room wakes me. I recognize Kotharat's unforgiving sound.

"Nikkal said Elisha is here to study. Did I not put up with enough learners who passed through this house? Because of Melchizedek? Do I not have enough work to do? I do not want another lazy student."

Next is a young male voice. I make out some words. Journey and Melchizedek.

House, help, water, and grind come from the next one. The deeper voice sounds like the man I tried to steal from.

Kotharat's tone rises. "How do we know she is here to study. Consult with the Righteous One," Kotharat commands.

"Enough. Get his opinion." The baker is last and loudest.

"Sandalphon," I whisper, "this is the right house. I am afraid for them to find out about me. It could ruin my chances. I will be reliable, do what they ask, and speak little. Then there will be no trouble."

"Do you have questions for me?"

"I am so glad you are here. Will life be better now?"

"Why do you ask?"

I hesitate. "May I question something?"

The cloud bends toward me. "I will be as helpful as I can."

"I was different from those at home. Tell me why."

"Why do you think?"

The glow of colors wraps around him as if to assure me we are protected. "If I knew I would not ask."

"My answer may not be what you wish. Are you sure?" I nod. "You do know. You are distressed and afraid to find the answer yourself."

My fingers make tracks in the sandy dirt. "Did anyone there speak to you about me?"

"No, they did not."

I turn away from the cloud. "I did not belong, though I wanted to be the same as other girls."

"Is that all you wanted?

"You know I wanted to make up songs and sing."

"It is possible you will be able to do that now."

"I hope so and do not want to destroy my prospects." With that, the voice is gone. I shut my eyes not sure if I belong anywhere.

· · · · · · · · · · · ·

The sun is well above the horizon, and I crawl out of my mat and go through the center room to the courtyard. Kotharat points to the washstand. She busies herself with the basins from the first meal while I wash up. She hands me a cap.

"In Urusalim, women wear a cap."

"Here is my shawl." I hold it up so she can see.

"You will wear the cap when you are out in public," she hands me a long cloth, "you will wrap your hair in this. Your shawl will go over the cap. You will wear this rope at your waist, around your cover."

Each tribe has different rules. "Please excuse me for sleeping late and disturbing you with serving again. May I help myself?"

"Not this morning. Sit." The not quite veiled command makes me feel like a child. "Here is some barley gruel. We will talk." Kotharat sits close to me, too close and I move away.

She moves nearer. "Eat."

"Yes, my lady. Thank you." I almost drop the basin.

"Do you intend to stay in the city?"

"That is my plan."

"Did you work with your ima?" She stares at me.

"Yes, my lady."

"What did you do?" Her eyes narrow.

"I did what Ima asked, my lady."

"Did you grind the flour, wash up after meals, and go to the stream?"

"Of course, my lady. Girls must learn before they have their own families. My mother taught me how to cook, but I do not bake well."

She nods approval. "If the family agrees to allow you to stay, I expect you to carry out the duties you mentioned and others I require." I nod. "Have you heard of Melchizedek?"

Her tone grew softer with the question. "Someone spoke to me and said by finding him I would find Abram."

"Are you aware of what he teaches?"

"That information was not offered."

"Really?" Her manner is one of disdain. "Who informed you of this?"

That look is one of authority. A second mouthful of the now cold barley gruel is my excuse to delay. If I tell the truth, she will know I am peculiar. The promise I made to Sandalphon was not to lie, yet they come with ease. "Someone on my journey." My attention turns back to the food.

"That is all for now."

"Thank you, my lady." She goes into the house.

Kotharat is a strange and scary person, but she did not throw me out. This is the start of my new life and with a family. Abram is here and will help me find ways to be acceptable and return to my people.

It is hard to contain my joy. When I think about last night's conversation, I realize they were deciding what services might be performed for my keep. I can be perfect and do what she asks, just the way she wants. Then there will be no trouble and I will have a new family.

CHAPTER TEN

How odd it feels as a stranger to wake to an empty house and walk around as if I live here. Their center room is more spacious than my family's entire hut. Three more skins hide sleep areas. On my way to the washstand, I note an unusual sunrise. The colors are vibrant, the air cool, the plantings happy and their scent sweet. The soil is damp. There was some rain during the night. I must do everything these people ask, so they will keep me.

Fruit and bread lay on the mat near the cook fire. How thoughtful. Kotharat left it for me. I wash up and go to the food. A young man still dressed in his night wrap comes into the courtyard and walks toward the washbasin. It is hard to turn away from his striking face. I try not to lose my footing and sit with haste but not with grace.

"Peace be with you." His deep voice resounds in my body. "My name is Resheph," He washes the dirt from his hands, turns, and raises dark eyebrows. His glimpse is one of approval. No man ever did that before. I want to run yet want to stay in this moment forever. He grins, turns around, and disappears.

The resemblance to his sister and Abba confirms he is a member of the family. No one mentioned a son, but a second male spoke during the argument last night. Besides, walking around anywhere else half-dressed would not be tolerated.

Resheph reappears a few moments later and indicates his night wrap. He bends forward and motions with his arm to apologize for his state of undress. The short wrap starts to part. I force my eyes away. Girls at home said men wear nothing under their night clothes.

"So, you are Elisha. I assumed you were still asleep." He sits close by. "Welcome to our home. I am sorry for not being here to greet you."

"Do not be concerned." His man's smell is strong and makes me uneasy. He is comfortable and will not move. Polite or not, I shift away. He moves closer. I grab the basin of food, stare at it, and put it back on the mat. Politeness demands I speak. "Pleased to meet you."

The curls on his chest wind around like my hair. I want to touch them and find out if they will bounce back up after I press them down. The muscles moving underneath his chest have a strange appeal.

I fasten my attention on the bread and fruit. "I am sorry. The food was here when I came out. Is this for you?"

"No," he laughs, "my mother left it for you. We ate long ago."

My mouth is dry, but if I get up, he will see my clumsiness. He moves his head and waves of dark hair fall onto his temples and drip with water or perspiration. I want to run my hands through and put the strands back where they belong. Instead, I eat.

"Ima suggested we go for a short walk so you will know where things are in the city. Are you strong enough?"

The 'yes' I want to yell is trapped in my throat. I clear it and make my voice sweet, "Yes, my lord, I can walk quite far."

"My chores will be completed in a short while and we will leave."

I manage a nod before he turns to go. One sight of his rippling back and any discomfort vanishes. This house is now a far more inviting place, and my imagination soars like a bird. He is the reason I am here. I found my mate.

As I shove the food into my mouth the picture of us living here with our five beautiful children forms in my head. I clean the used basins and run to my sleep space. His mother gave me salve for my burnt skin. I spread it over my body and hurry back to the main room.

He returns with combed hair and a shining face. He wears the same kind of tunic as Nikkal, almost reaching the ground and wider on the bottom. His is made of a finer flax and the neck is embroidered with many colors. There is one I do not recognize. It brightens his eyes.

"What is the name of this hue?"

"It is called purple and made from sea snails. The two threads were a gift from my parents for my excellent studying. They are quite dear."

They are rich, and he is smart. "Where shall we go?" My cheeks are burning. I lower my head. He will never want me, my parents are poor.

"Do you not wish to visit the city?"

"Why my lord, of course I do. Are there many places to see?" Except for purple, the same colors as in the neck of his garment curve through the rope at his waist. I sneak another peek at his pleasing face and run my hands through my mess of hair to make myself presentable.

"We take pride in a few things."

"That would be nice." Do I seem too anxious?

He grabs my hand. "You had better get your cap and shawl."

"Oh, I forgot."

When I return, he takes my arm. "May I be your guide?"

I pull away and step around him. He rolls his eyes and joins me, his smile self-assured. He is aware of how handsome he is. Resheph ushers me out of the courtyard and onto the lane.

"We will go first to the center of town," he points to the right. "Please keep up with me." I hurry to be by his side. "The most important place to see is where you will collect the water each morning." He gestures to the right again.

"Me? No one asked." That is what the walk is about.

With eyebrows raised, his sideways gaze expresses his annoyance. "I have many other responsibilities. If you do not want to be of assistance, you can find another place to live. Are you not willing to serve?" He crosses his arms and waits.

They want me to stay. That makes me feel different. I now have responsibilities and duties and can help this family. "Oh, of course. I did not mean . . . your family has been more than kind and generous. I will fulfill any obligations expected of me."

"My ima will be pleased. You are a fine young woman."

My heart soars. As I hoped, this family will become mine. But he said serve, not help. I will not think about that.

We walk along and what I notice first is that the houses are on both sides of the lane. They are all the same but larger than the ones near the entrance to the city. Their color is somewhere between yellow and white and are not as lopsided as those near that breach. Between every two houses there are alley ways but they are narrow. Where do the children run and play? I am confused by the oversized jugs on each side of the route. "What are those?" I point to the containers.

"They are called cisterns and preserve the rainwater."

I hesitate to question him. "I am bewildered. The containers are along the lane." Resheph nods. "Then why do we make for the center of town?"

"That water is collected for emergencies during the season of dry and thirsting."

Now he is sure I am dull. "The people at home could make use of those." My voice sounds too cheerful.

We move on, and I realize we passed just a few people on the lane. The men must be at work, and I wonder what they do with no fields to care for. Resheph mentions the family names for many of the homes we pass. "Are you acquainted with those people?"

"Yes, we are familiar."

"Does the closeness of the households in a city make people friendlier?"

"In a way. There are always those who choose to argue. Is it not the same in your village?"

"We have those who are agreeable, some who argue, and those who accuse. Before my birth, the tribe were wanderers. They decided to band together and live on the land with the animals." What else can I say? "With few provisions my journey required me to walk as fast as I could. The few stops I made were when I feared starvation or becoming a tasty morsel." Words escape. I say too much but give no answer to his question.

"That is quite a story but let me continue the outing. To a large extent, we are merchants." He turns toward me. "There is no room to tend animals." The tone is one of teaching a child. "People come from the surrounding areas to our market and bring their wares and beasts. We barter with each other for what is needed."

"You are describing the marketplace I saw upon my arrival."

"Correct. Here we are. This is the spring I told you about. Its name is Gihon, which means 'gushing forth.'"

"Gushing forth?"

"It does not flow but spurts and is the one source of water except for streams which may not be healthy." The teacher is back.

An oval basin is carved into the limestone and the liquid flows in from a hole on one side. "This is very different from at home. This basin is large and fine in appearance."

"Again you do not recognize that the liquid is provided for a whole city."

I did not consider the number of people and made a fool of myself. The liquid and its vessel gleam in the sunlight. Filled more than half-way it is inviting. A goblet is laying on the side. I pick it up, dip it in, tilt my head back and pour it into my mouth. "It is delicious, but not cold like at home."

"The collecting pool spurts bit by bit and is exposed to the hot sun." He acts like he is my father. "Women come here to fill their jugs, take a swallow, and gather for a talk."

"But there are so few people now."

"They come before sunrise and again before sunset."

The breadth of the vicinity is larger than our entire place for gathering. "Where I come from there is a tiny campfire ground where meetings are held with the Council of Elders." My eyes water.

"What is wrong?"

"Nothing." It would be wonderful if he put comforting arms around me, but different from Nathan.

"You are sad."

"It was a memory."

"Do you miss your family?" He brushes against my arm.

"Of course." Tears burn my eyes.

"Being away from home must be difficult. Yes?"

Is he trying to make me cry? My heart hurts and my insides insist I move on, move away. "Where shall we go now?" I sound dull, not how I want.

"I will show you where Melchizedek lives. He is a king, high priest, and chief. Do you know of him?"

His ima asked me the same question. This is his reason for bringing me here. "Someone told me of his wisdom and kindness."

"He is honored with a visit from Abram, who is on the way south from Harran. They have been chattering for the last three full moons."

I want to throw my arms out and turn in circles. "Did you meet him? Abram?" It is happening the way Sandalphon told me. "Is he handsome? What color are his eyes?"

"Perhaps you will be lucky and have a chance to find out."

"That is mean. Can you not tell me?" Resheph remains silent. "Is he nice?"

"You speak like a child."

He will not ruin my joy. "Are you an old man?" My words escape again. "Sorry. I am excited. Abram came to Shechem and my family went to visit the altar he built near an oak tree. I was too young to join them but they told me stories." Stop talking. Resheph is silent. What can I ask? "Uh. How did the two men meet?"

"Abram assembled many men for a night raid and they rescued his nephew, Lot, from our forces. Melchizedek went to the battleground to assure Abram he was not angry for the slaying of his relative. After that, he invited Abram to meet at his house."

And I walked from my home to be with him. "This story is new to me." My insides turn cold. I am so dense. He said our forces. Resheph's family is Canaanite and I did not suspect.

"He ordered a great banquet and blessed Abram and the God who delivered the enemy into his hands."

I was not listening. "That is lovely." Canaanite. My parents would be outraged if they found out how much I like him. I need to chew on my hair but not in front of him.

Resheph stops walking. "This is the house where he lives and teaches."

The dwelling I stand in front of appears the same as every other house we passed. "As king and high priest, should he not be living in grander quarters?"

"He chooses not to. He wants to be near the people."

My eyes do not move from the building. A troublesome idea makes me shiver. "Why did you bring me here?" Kotharat told him of our talk.

"To show you the important places." His demeanor says, *how could you think otherwise?* "Let me introduce you." He grasps my hand and does not take his eyes from me. "Your hair gleams so in the light."

A tingling sensation sends a stirring through my body and for a moment takes away any sureness I might enjoy. "Oh, no." I wrench my fingers away. "Not now."

"Why not? If not now, then when?" A peculiar smile plays around his mouth.

Up to this moment the single male who touched me was Abba. I hugged Nathan, but he is my brother. "It is too soon and I am not ready."

"What will change? The morrow will be no different."

His all-knowing posture is back. "I cannot."

Those big eyebrows raise again. He shrugs and makes a face as if I am a nuisance. "You are sure of what you want." He turns and starts for the path.

His rudeness makes me ill at ease. Did I spoil his efforts? That must be why he walked away. "Wait. Perhaps. Give me time to think."

He walks back and stares at me. Does he have no understanding of my nervousness at meeting such an important person? He outranks our chief of council. And this meeting can change my life. I wait until I am sure some quiet found its way to me. "I am ready."

I stand next to him, unable to say another word, more frightened and excited than any other time in my life. He knocks on the door-post, and my throat dries. A young gentleman dressed in a tan tunic greets Resheph. They move away. I am not able to listen. What is Resheph saying about me? The young man comes back.

"Welcome, Elisha, I am Yadid." He opens the gate. The two men stand aside allowing me to enter first. "Thank you." I stand there as if frozen. In the dimness the one thing that can be made out is a sleeping space at the rear. The skin to hide it is pulled to one side. A huge person stands near the drape.

CHAPTER ELEVEN

Melchizedek turns toward me and opens his arms wide before I can bow in respect. "Come here, my child." A quick glance says no one else came in. "Yes, you. Come so I may greet you."

My walk is unsteady. What makes me uncomfortable is his examining me. My legs wobble as I stand in front of him. He must be the tallest man in Palestine, and his presence overpowers the almost bare room. His importance alone would tower over our chief. His authority frightens me yet the dusky black of his eyes are lit with kindness.

"There is no reason for unease. I am a man like any other." He puts his hands on my shoulders and I fluster at the power of his touch. A second male touched me and I dare not object. "Welcome. When Resheph came to class, he mentioned you suffered a demanding trip and showed much courage."

How dare he? "I had no idea he spoke to you. I am not courageous." Now I understand, this was Resheph's task.

Melchizedek appears older than Abba and his chin is stronger. The wrinkles on his face remain soft. Only the crinkles near his temples show the years of study needed to become wise.

"You tremble, but there is no cause to fear me. How did you come here?" He sits on his bench. The gray of his hair is mixed with white and sticks out. It is as messy as mine. The tall hat with green and yellow stripes tries to control it.

"Thank you for your kindness, my lord." I relate the trials of the trip and leave out nothing.

"You are not one to boast. I enjoy that. What made you leave your village?"

Do I speak another untruth? I will make less of this. "I was forced to."

He watches me. "Yes?"

"I made the chief angry."

"Why do you hesitate? Do you have a problem?"

A problem. His face is relaxed. I must answer. "I was less than truthful. Sandalphon said it was because no one in the village wanted me, and not one man chose me for a wife." Sorry for the lie, Sandalphon. I bite my lip and study the king's face. Will he discharge me?

He nods. "An unusual group of students meets here. More than a few were made to leave their homes. You did say Sandalphon sent you."

"You are familiar with him?"

"Not myself," he beams, "but through some of my old students. Like you, he guided them here. But that was a long while ago. His reason for bringing you to me is promising. Do you not agree?"

"That could be, I guess. But I do not understand. I am not gifted or witty, and I don't consider myself worthy of this honor."

"That is my task. Permit me to be the judge." I glower at the floor. "Do not be self-conscious. If you are correct, the evidence will soon show. Sandalphon has never been wrong."

"Never? Is that so?"

"I do not lie."

My hand hides my lips. "I did not . . . I am so embarrassed."

"I understand. You are still tired. Come back with Resheph after you give yourself enough rest and we can begin the teaching."

I fill with joy and pray to all the Gods to help me learn but dare not look at him. "I will do as you say."

"Yes, you will," are his parting words.

The family needed the king's approval. We walk no more than three steps from the house. "My lord, may I ask what he meant by the last remark?"

"It is his way of saying there is much work to be done, and you are expected to do it without questioning the objective. The reasons are not always apparent. In time, you will learn to trust him."

"Thank you." He will teach, not Abram. Can he help with my trouble? I want to go home.

"You made a perilous journey for a woman alone." I do not know what to say. "You are brave and agreeable in appearance."

He said words I want to hear. "Thank you, Resheph," I stammer. This is the second time he spoke well of me. Does he care for me? So soon?

After a delicious evening meal, I clean up and store everything where it belongs. The family watches me. I must look tired. They urge me to go to my mat. The outing did leave me more worn out than I expected.

The sun, the walk, the meeting with Melchizedek, and the odd yet delightful feelings about Resheph mingle together and keep me from sleeping. I turn from side to side on my mat until the sleep cover twists around me. Resheph is like Nathan, someone I can depend on. At last I am settled in and ready to sleep when the family's discussion creeps into my ears.

"What information did Melchizedek share with you?" Kotharat's high tone makes her sound anxious.

Resheph describes the events at the king's house and adds, "Elisha is willing to work as much as she can and Melchizedek approved. He is ready to teach her."

While Resheph speaks with softness, Kotharat does not. "Of course she is willing. We will provide a roof over her head. What other answer would she give?"

"Oh, Ima." That is Nikkal. "Do not be that way. That girl is nice."

"She may be agreeable but she is not Canaanite. Elisha is Hebrew."

"But Ima, why does that matter?" Nikkal lets out a brusque sigh.

"I need her to help me. She is appealing to the eye and from the way your brother gapes at her, I do not need a talisman to foretell what might happen."

"Your mother is right." The tone that chides Resheph is harsh and grating, not concerned and helpful as it was with me when I arrived. "A match of that kind will never be. Are you listening, my son? I also noticed the way your eyes keep track of her every move." Baal's voice is rising. "You are too absorbed with her."

"I tried to make her comfortable."

"Your father was across the alley and heard you say she was agreeable in appearance. He watched you try to take her hand." Kotharat's voice shakes with frustration. "You listen to me. This will go no further. My son will not wed a Hebrew."

"Ima. You may wake her."

"I do not care. I am trying to save us from heartache. We will never tolerate this happening, Resheph. Are your ears wide open?"

After much mumbling and grumbling the house grows still. Their words chase each other around my head. Though I made this family my own they made clear he would not be mine. My heart does not agree.

"He is yours," it yells at me.

"It will not be."

"Your heart keeps telling you so."

"It can never happen."

But in my heart of hearts I am certain I will find a way.

· · · · · · · · · · · ·

The first meal is over and I hurry to take care of my duties. Being in a new place makes me uneasy and the longing to be with my family is strong. Resheph finishes his tasks.

"Are you going?" He posed the same question every morning for the past three suns, each time his tone scraping closer to my bones.

"Yes, my lord. I am ready. Nervous, but well enough thanks to your ima's care."

"We need to leave. Get yourself organized."

We hurry down the footpath. Resheph ignores me. His conversation was spirited before. I want to run back to the house and pull the cover over my head.

He stops and turns to me. "Elisha." For a moment, he seems like a little boy afraid to ask me a question.

"Yes?"

"Do not be bothered by me. I am fine."

"Please, you can ask."

"You make me uncomfortable. We live in the same house, please do not call me my lord."

"I am sorry. I did not mean to do that. Of course, I will abide by your wishes."

"Your appearance is quite fine."

We are near the house and my throat is completely dry. My fingers move though I did not command them to, almost as if I am playing my harp. We are at Melchizedek's house.

Resheph throws open the gate to my future and ushers me in. Unlike my earlier visit, the house is bright, lit with many oil lamps. What is not clear is why the king of Salem, who is rich, lives in a house sparer than my host.

The cheerful pillows on the floor give a hint of wealth. Their colors shine, so they are made from an expensive fabric. The cushions are placed in a half circle around a woven floor covering. Resheph comes to me. "That picture is of the Great Vulture."

"I was told it is the Nesher."

"I believe you are wrong. Melchizedek would know."

I am glad I did not say I heard it at a men's meeting I eavesdropped on. The picture shows the bird's commanding wings in gold, a bald head, large curved beak, and powerful talons I would never want to be near. Close to the vulture are gentle doves, painted with silver wings and feathers of white touched with blue.

Three young men who seem close to Resheph's age are deep in conversation. Another female is here, a woman of great beauty, older than me. Her eyes are decorated with black on top and bottom, her hair is perfect, her face is glowing. She is too attractive to befriend me. I choose a golden yellow pillow and hope the students will be kinder than my friends at home.

Melchizedek comes in. The sight of his elegant strides tells me I am awkward. He is not the problem. The trouble lives in me. Can I do the work? A woman and slow will I understand this important man's words?

He sits and waits for us to settle. After a short greeting he stands. "I will not be teaching."

One of the men yells out, "Are we dismissed?"

"If you wish to miss Abram's lessons, go." The whole group yells over each other, but quiets as he raises his hand. "I must leave for a while and Abram has consented to teach this gathering until he and Sarai leave to continue south."

The deepest most rooted center of my being stirs like a pot of thick stew. What Sandalphon promised is about to happen.

Melchizedek claps his hands for attention. "Abram pursues truth and dedicates himself to finding a worthy way for people to live. I pray to El-elyon and Abram calls him the Holy Spirit. God sent him from his father's house to wander through Palestine."

If I lived with Abram, I would be afraid to say one word. He is wise and I thoughtless. Melchizedek's softer tone interrupts my reflecting.

"We grow up with loved ones and where they are will always be home. The connection is one of the deepest we will experience. Yet, God said to Abram, 'remove yourself from what is dear.' How many of you did something similar?" I will not cry. Only Resheph and the young woman with the fine-looking wavy black hair do not raise their hands.

A man comes into the room and peers around. The sight of him makes me gulp. He is younger than I expected.

"Abram. You arrive before time." Melchizedek rises to greet him. The others do the same, but I cannot move. The glow surrounding him overpowers me though the features I study do not stand out against other men. Trying to stand and join the group, I stumble.

Abram smiles at me. His eyes shine brightly next to Melchizedek's dark ones. I never saw blue eyes before. "No, my child. Raise yourself and do not stoop before me. I am not the Holy Spirit, but his messenger, no more and no less than you. Rise and let me see you."

I struggle to stand and seem like a fool again. This would not happen to Lady Beautiful. Resheph runs over to help me.

Abram's skin is darker than mine, the color of sandy soil. His dark hair is wavy. The thick and unkempt beard reaches below his chest and is so inviting I want to climb into the fur of his chin to escape his gaze. The curly hair of his mustache battles its way along the sides of his mouth to join the whiskers.

Abram takes his time observing each of us as if that will tell him our deepest secrets.

That makes me squirm. His eyes fall on Resheph.

"And your name is?"

"It is Resheph, my lord."

"Ah, yes. Melchizedek spoke of you doing well in your studies. He said you wish to be a teacher like he is."

"Yes, my lord." Resheph tidies his hair. We sit to listen. It seems Abram assumes Resheph is the best student in the class.

"Beware young man," Abram goes on, "while you do well in that area, there are dark places like a pestilence in your soul. You have little regard for the safety or feelings of others. Know that your acts, harsh as they may be, will be returned to you tenfold. Punishment for misdeeds will be administered."

With his head held high, Resheph walks away without answering. I lower my eyes as he goes by. His cheeks are red. He was haughty, and with a wise man. If Abram talks to me like that, I will die right here. Abram may not be as wise as people make him out. Resheph has been kind and generous. Abram sits and points to Yadid who approaches with slow steps and wide eyes.

"Do not be afraid. Your name?"

"I am Yadid, my lord." He is the one who opened the gate on my first visit.

"You are a beloved friend and an able student." Yadid smiles. "Others take advantage of your kindness and you accept it. The result of gentleness spread too far can be resentment of the time and effort you put forth when others do not return the same. Fill your spirit with love, young man. When you do, you can give without reserve."

Am I gentle? Will Abram speak to me?

"Who is next?"

"My name is Yardin." He walks with a sure step and stands gazing at Abram.

"You are brave in your stance and sureness of who you are, yet you doubt your abilities. The underbelly of bravery is thinking you can do it all which may produce a conceited and self-centered man. Your name carries the essence of descent. Take care and lift yourself. You are meant to overcome your name."

For me, doubt is always present. I might as well give up if I do not try. I do succeed at times if I am not stopped by fear. If Abram tells me I am a fool, I will walk back to my family and accept any punishment.

The beautiful one does not wait to be called. She walks with her hips swinging. How can I fix myself to walk like that? Ima said, "Your nose is too big, and your mouth turns down." I do not chew on my hair if Resheph is near. What can Abram say to her? She is perfect.

"Peace be with you. Your name?"

"I am Adi, my lord."

"If you wish, you can become the jewel you are named. Your parents spoiled you, so you expect each and every person to bow to your needs and wishes. You are forward in your dealings and arrogant with the men who come into your life. If you continue, there may be grave consequences." He waves her away.

She skulks back to her seat with her head lowered. With my jealousy of her I could not imagine beauty caused challenges. Abram understands people without ever meeting them. Am I too forward? I like Resheph so much but he does not speak of how he feels. Abram may be wise but he is wrong about Resheph.

The youngest of the men approaches as if he must put his hand into a fire. "Peace be with you, Abram. I am Calev."

"Peace be with you. Why are you so frightened of what I might say? Not a word has been uttered."

"I fear the worst."

"Are you so unsure of yourself?"

Calev bows his head. "I guess I am."

"Has no one told you how wonderful you are?"

"No, never." His laugh mocks himself.

"What a pity. Your name means 'like a heart' and says you are compassionate. Each of us is unique and born with a special gift, which helps us to deal with problems in a different way. Your way of serving allows you to help someone I cannot. Hold your head high and claim your gift."

Am I compassionate? I have no special gift except maybe my songs. Calev moves away and Abram stares straight at me. "You had a respite and now please." He motions for me to come forward. "Your name?"

"It is Elisha, my lord." Fingers, arms, toes, every part of me needs to fidget.

"Your eyes speak of a simple life. Wounds affected your youthful years. Those experiences taught you to open your heart, though you do not yet consult this greatest friend. My hope is for you to use these gifts well."

What does he want of me? My voice catches in my throat and comes out choked up. "Thank you, my lord. I do not understand what I am supposed to do."

"Be open to what is taught and trust you will find the information you seek. Most important, you will not learn to find joy and a way to express your feelings unless you are open and honest. Then you can speak without restrictions. Think of a way for your words to sing or become poems. Do not hide what you think is undesirable about yourself. When you do, that which holds you back for fear of being wrong will disappear. You will find your strengths and be free to choose what you want. Your passage requires small steps like a child. It is a long and sometimes demanding journey." Abram dismisses me.

He sounds like Sandalphon with his leaves. I return to my pillow. My wandering attention removes me from the surroundings. What are my better parts? My heart is open. The bad? I do not speak with freedom. Is that dishonest? I do not make choices and hide the desirable. He did mention songs and words.

"Thank you." Abram's voice startles me. "I will be here for a short time and am honored to teach what I can. Our studies commence."

He continues teaching about what you do and knowing who you are. I do not listen and try to write a new song Abram will approve of. My head is too crowded to appreciate what he is saying.

Lessons are over. This is my first time here, and already I struggle to keep up. The determination to focus was not successful. My body is awake but my head is stuffed with confusing thoughts. I try to ponder Abram's statement. My insides shake and I want to go home. Resheph is busy gossiping so I leave for home. He runs to my side. "Thank you for helping me stand." I smile then lower my eyes.

"You are welcome. Next time, you will stand up yourself. Did you see Abram's tunic? It is of the same tan linen as yours and it is just as plain."

"Yes, but mine is not as fine."

"I will say this. You look lovely, but your garment is horrid. Holes go through in many places. Yet you still wear the cover." He laughs.

I grit my teeth and tears come to my eyes. "On my journey men put their arrows through this tunic and the other one got caught on a piece of wood. My family is poor and my garments but two. Your ima refused to allow me to weave a new one."

"I am sorry. I had no way to know."

"One more question. Every Canaanite prays to the One God because Melchizedek does. Why does your family keep idols?"

"My parents think they are nice to look at. No one cares as long as we pray well."

"That is like my home. We also have both."

He is not willing to say more. I think Abram's seething comments demand his attention, but I am not done. "May I ask you another question?"

"You are full of them."

"It is confusing. They both pray to the One God, yet Abram and your king have different names for him."

"Melchizedek says the prayer is important not the name one uses. He and Abram think alike."

"Do you believe God gets angry?"

"My teacher said he does. Everybody gets angry, so why would he not?"

"Does he bring the floods?" Resheph does not answer. "Do any of the others in class come from Hebrew parents?"

"That was never discussed."

I nod. "Was Abram right in his opinions of us?"

"I think perhaps in some instances."

I turn my head away. "Do I speak untruths?"

"I heard none."

"He said words about pestilence for you."

Resheph moves ahead. "I do not understand why he said it and do not agree." I catch up to him and there is silence the remainder of the way home.

· · · · · · · · · · · ·

The evening meal cleaned up, I run to my mat. Away from the family, I consider Abram's meaning. Why did he mention my wounds? He said what we do needs to come from the heart. Does he mean to invent songs from there? Do we open the heart and let it pour out? The impure pieces would taint the clean. What my heart can say to me is a big question.

These ideas urge me to try again to create a new tune. My songs belong to me. I shared them with few others, but not because I did not want to. What will happen if Abram's teachings are in my songs and many people hear them? That could be my answer. Is composing a challenge to courage?

I search for the phrases to use. The first words Abram spoke before my head was too filled to listen were, "Always do what is right and be sure to use the right turn of phrase so no misunderstanding can occur." I want words to give people new ideas to think about. Like Abram's messages from his God.

My cloud appears. "Why do you make up songs?"

"You scared me. I am happy to see you, Sandalphon," I whisper, "but can you not creep up? And be careful or someone will find out you are here."

"Do you not remember they are not ready?"

"You forget I yelled, and they can hear that."

"What do you like about singing?"

"It makes me feel agreeable. It is the one thing I know I can do well."

"Is that all?"

I turn away. "What do you mean?"

"Think about why you use certain words when others will do."

"To make the songs appealing?"

"Many people use them to better understand themselves and the realm they live in."

"Do I do that?" I study my feet.

"I hope so."

I look up and he is gone. He left me with no answers. I need time alone and must not wake anyone. I tiptoe out of the house. The moon lights my way to a place I found on the lane away from the dwellings. Sandalphon said being peaceful and out in nature before composing aids the words and melody to appear.

I sit in contemplation. What will help people appreciate Abram's wisdom? An idea forms in my head but it is not right. The words are not skillful enough. Fear raises its head like a snake. I will not let the voices in my head tell me how bad my composition is. I send them to sleep on a cloud. "I will listen to your concerns when my work is done," I chide and return to my thinking.

The song comes together and I speak the words twice more. They do not say what I want and not enough exist to make a real song. I am disappointed.

· · · · · · · · · · · ·

My time is filled with the chores Kotharat gives me, gardening, grinding, cleaning, and I am sad that I do not have enough moments to appreciate the trees, or music.

. . . .

Filled with sluggishness at the next morning's rise, I force myself to get up from the mat. I woke before the others. Is gloom about to take possession of me again? I am irritated. Doubt and fear gnaw at me. I rail at myself for not being able to make a good song. Something else grumbles at me. My stomach. I cannot fix my ballad, but I can have something to eat.

I grab a date cake and run back to the quiet place on the lane. No one is here. Dare I sing? I push the desire away. I had better not or there may be trouble. I return to the house and eat more though I am not hungry. I clean my basin and put it away. Later I will clean up the family's food.

I must go to the spring. I prefer to stay and think but we need fresh water. And I need Kotharat to be pleased with me. About to leave for the limestone basin, Sandalphon arrives, his greeting is gentle. "I hope you are well."

He stays by my side as we walk. "As well as can be. I have so much to think about it is hard to sort it out."

"Could it be that you are fearful? Also, you are not quite recovered from the journey and . . ."

"I am well but tired. Can you help me?"

"Much of what you say is to complain and find fault. You convince yourself how terrible you are and that prevents you from being content. If you continue, you will never trust you can do well."

I stop walking. "I do not do that." Sandalphon does not answer. "Do I? Can it be changed?"

"I do not need the answer. You do. Take time to think about what I said. We have one more point to speak about."

"Must you say it now?" I sit and close my eyes.

"As a human, incidents arise when you are small, which make you assume you are lacking. Others can do what you cannot." I open my eyes. "Children do not understand the reason is that the adults are older and they learned more. We can always find reminders of inadequacy if we choose."

"And when you are grown?"

"Each time humans are chided for a wrongdoing the same lack overtakes them. You can understand how the effect may be long lasting." He moves away. "You gave no consideration to wants and needs." I did not do as he asked. Again. "You should. It is important, and you might want to change some behaviors."

"You are right. I told myself I cannot do the work and will not have what I want and need and we just started."

"You are beginning to understand, and I wish you well." My heart swells.

· · · · · · · · · · · ·

I get home and store the jugs. Another decision faces me. The sadness is back, and though it is exciting to enjoy new understandings I do not have the energy to go to class. I need to be alone, away from chatter and discussion with the freedom to think. But if I do not go, Abram will have a disappointed face. Nothing should go wrong. If it does I will cry and embarrass myself.

I wait with patience to discover the reason. Distrust and worry came because of the beautiful one. I overheard her talking to Yardin. Adi said, "Elisha is having trouble, she is slow. She will never understand the teachings." Resheph is the only one who is aware I worry. Did he tell her? Then the beauty whispered to Yardin, noticed me, and laughed. I did not hear Yardin's answer.

Resheph returns from his duties. The basin of bread and fruit I prepared is waiting. I would like to throw it in his face. Could he be so mean to tell my secret? What does this mean for our future? He ignores my mood, eats, and we leave for class.

Melchizedek's house is in sight when Resheph says, "I am concerned. What is wrong with you this morning?" His tone is gentle and caring, unlike other times.

"Nothing."

"Elisha, you cannot fool me."

"I am out of sorts and do not understand why. This is new to me, so there is much to think about. The confusing part is that I wrote a new tune and that always makes me happy."

"A song? You make them? That is splendid."

"Do not congratulate me. You may not like my music."

He cocks his head to one side. "That might be true. I will let you know."

We arrive a bit late and the rest of the students are waiting on their pillows. We hurry to the last two seats. The beautiful one is at the other end, and I am happy to be far away from her. Abram sinks on to his bench. "Settle in. I need no noise so I can teach."

Resheph raises his hand. "Abram, I hope my speaking does not interfere with your plans. Elisha told me she wrote a song."

I stare at him. I did not give him permission to talk about my music, about anything having to do with me.

Abram turns to me. "Elisha, is this true?"

"Yes Abram, it is." I am on fire.

"Congratulations. May I ask you to sing it for us?"

"It is not complete and I am not ready."

"You are shy but people here care about you. Please."

These people are not my family. How can they care? If I say no I will be more embarrassed. "Yes, Abram."

"Come to the front and stand near me." He beckons.

Unsettled and struggling for breath, I walk to the spot he indicates. I take time to calm my anger and breathe. "My song is called 'Always Plenty.'" The song ends and no one moves. Abram slowly claps his hands and the others join him. I stand rooted to the ground. There is no praise in the applause. They smile and pretend to be nice because Abram would be angry if they were mean.

"Let us get back to our seats. Thank you, Elisha, for attempting to use my teachings. The song is nice, and my hope is that you will continue to create music." He turns to the class. "Elisha is an example of finding your passion. If you are sure of your desires and work hard, you can accomplish what you wish."

I pass Resheph on the way to my seat. The smirk on his face says, *Do not try. You will never succeed.*

Composing is my passion, but did Abram like the song? The way he spoke, careful with his words, gave the impression he wanted to dismiss me. I want to run, be anywhere else. It is not possible to give him my attention. Like me, my songs will never be good enough.

CHAPTER TWELVE

The teaching ends later than usual. "Resheph, I must go." He does not finish his conversation, and I move down the path.

He catches up. "What is wrong?"

"Your ima decided I will make the evening meal from now on and requires me to observe how she prepares the food. You know very well how she likes when comings and goings are proper."

"We will hurry." He moves faster than me then peers over his shoulder. He wants to race, and we do. All the way home.

"What fun that was. I am winded. You won only because your legs are longer than mine." He laughs, and I get into the house first.

Kotharat's cooking lesson entails her being on top of me and over my shoulder, informing me of the particular tool to use, and not agreeing with the way my mother taught me to measure. I am surprised she never follows me to the well to make sure I collect water properly.

Cleaning up over, my attention wanders back to class. They applauded and said nice things and were polite. Abram's words fit the melody. They applauded but only because Abram did. My song was not acceptable.

. . . .

The morning brings no sun and dismal darkness. The rainy season is coming. My sorrow is worse. Is it worry consuming me? First I was not wanted by the villagers, now my music is not good enough. I need my brother.

Resheph and I sit across from each other and I can barely make out his face. In this darkness you cannot see past your nose. At least we are contained by the walls and will not get sand in our eyes. The rest of the family is gone. The silence between us feels cold.

I decide to break the quiet. "It is late for a windstorm."

"How would you know, you do not live here."

"Where is your mother?" He does not say a word. "Why is she out in this weather?"

"She is tending to a friend who is sick. My father went with her, so she is safe."

"Will your abba go to the bake stall?"

"Will you stop asking questions? He went to the flour storage."

They are gone, and I am trapped alone with him. With each bite of food my body strains to speak of what hides inside me. His interference made me sing. He made me find out my music will never be good enough and he does not care.

"Did you sleep well?" Resheph does not bother to lift his head.

My sleep was broken with dreams of running away and falling. "Yes, I did." Resheph peeks at me and turns his head away. I find myself doing the same thing.

"My ima is not an unkind woman, yet at times she appears so."

Why did he mention his ima? She is like a sentry watching my every move. "My ima, as well. Working so hard makes them impatient."

"They spend too much time with work and no time for enjoyment."

I nod. For the first time, we are not comfortable with each other.

I am relieved when Kotharat's voice invades the house before she does. "The wind has let up and extra water is needed. My friend is too ill to go to the spring. Take the jugs and go at once."

I grab my cap and shawl. Still not light, at least the gusts have quieted down. We reach the path. Each person is rushing somewhere and we are obliged to walk close to each other. We push against the wind and if someone passes close by Resheph brushes against me and presses his elbow into my side. He would not say so, but I am sure he does it on purpose.

I try walking to one side of him and then the other. "Your quick pace is trying on my shorter legs," I lie. He slows down.

We fill the containers and turn to go back. The wind is almost gone and after the first few steps he brings up a subject I hoped to avoid.

"I heard about your journey when you told Melchizedek. Before we reach my father's house, one detail needs explanation."

"What shall I explain?"

"Your name." He stands still.

Why does it bother him? Was this Kotharat's idea? "What about my name?" I want some distance and walk ahead of him.

"Where are you going?"

"I am heading over to the rock so I can rest. My story is not exciting." I put the vessels down and sit.

Resheph laughs as he puts his down. "I am sure you have an explanation. No woman has a man's name. I do not understand and I am waiting." He is standing behind me.

"But wait, we need to hurry. Did you forget your mother's sick friend needs the water?" I try to get up and his hands are on my shoulders holding me down.

"You are avoiding my question making me more curious. I will not let you move until you answer." He sits next to me and crosses his arms over his chest. The rock is not big. I move as far away as I can. "It is hard." He moves closer, his man smell is intense. I turn away, so he will not notice my cheeks growing hot.

"You said your story is not interesting."

"That is true but does not make it any easier." I squirm in my seat waiting for a remark, a question, someone to interrupt, so I do not need to continue. "Lying under a sapling near my home I . . ." If I tell, he will be sure there is something wrong with me. "I was a small child . . ."

"Go on. I am listening."

The sweetness in his tone makes me melt and assures me I am safe. The words flow. "A strong kindliness inside me demanded my attention. The feeling was tender and loving."

"Out with the remainder."

I nod. He smiles and his face is peaceful. "This knowing sensation told me to use the name Elisha from then on to gain courage and that advice stayed with me until . . . Can we walk? I am afraid your ima will be angry."

"Yes, but you must finish."

We pick up the jugs and move on. "The notion grew to be mine and became strong within me. The children called me boy-girl and made me feel horrible. Sandalphon assured me that this was a proper name and would give me courage. He comes to me still." I turn toward Resheph. "Do you know anything more about Sandalphon?"

"I remember someone who was here long ago spoke to him."

Melchizedek said the same. "My entire village thought I was sick in the head and said I spoke to the air. Your knowing Sandalphon tells me another person talked to him and what Sandalphon said is true." Resheph roars with laughter and I want to run and hide.

"You are slower than I supposed. I thought you understood there are people who believe many things but many possibilities are not taught. They think things cannot be when they are quite common."

"You mean there are people like me?"

"Your eyes are as wide as the desert. Yes, others see, listen to, and are aware of things most of us are not."

There are more as strange as I am, and they study with a great man. It is possible I will be accepted. I want to rise above the ground and walk on clouds or twirl around and around with joy. If I do, Resheph will not view me as grown up. But a giggle escapes. "Do you do that?"

"I am not blessed."

"My tribe believed I had devils in me."

"That is not unusual. Others suffered the same, but their walk was not as difficult as yours."

"Why not?"

"They did not travel alone, nor did they encounter the dangers you met."

. . . .

After the teaching, Sandalphon joins me on the way home.

"How are you?"

"Well, thank you. Resheph went to help his father."

"I am aware. Did you enjoy your chat?"

"Oh, yes. I found others like me."

"I know."

"Of course you do." The orange in his colors is brighter than usual. "Now that you are learning, there are some important issues to be considered about females."

"About females?"

"It is a complicated problem. According to your society, even prior to her birth a girl is blemished."

My hands are on my hips. "Sandalphon. What are you saying? Blemished? Is this true? If it happens before you are born how can you do anything?"

"First, you need to ponder the reason for this difficult lesson."

"What are you telling me?"

"Think about Eve's story and its connection to the scars that were left. This is important. We will consult soon."

The sound of his words concerns me. Am I damaged? Sandalphon wants me to ponder on it, but I will not think about the dreadful meaning. What does Eve have to do with me? I will think about her another time.

I run home while the sun is hanging in the sky almost ready to go down. My head roams through my discussion with Sandalphon. "Girls are marred before they are born," he said. I push the thoughts from my head. Kotharat told me she would tend her ailing friend. This is the first time I must cook dinner.

With the jugs on my shoulders, I run to the spring. No one is on the path and my thoughts return to pondering the meaning of blemished. It can be soiled, broken, disfigured, or damaged. Am I all those because I am a woman? Who decreed it? Women could not have.

The well is a happy place. The coming sunset fills the area with shadows. I must be late because no one is here to gossip. It makes the stillness peculiar. With the vessels filled, I hurry back to prepare the evening meal.

The bread comes first in case Baal Hadad barters all his at the bake stall. The keep is full of vegetables that need to be used before they rot. With great care, I cut them into like-sized pieces that fit into our mouths as Kotharat instructed. Lentils, garlic, a pinch of cumin, and the cinnamon I like to use are added. Water goes into the heavy pot and I drag it to the fire and hang it on the hook.

· · · · · · · · · · · ·

The family is seated on their mats and the flatbread I baked is piled high. Its fragrance calls to our bellies. I set the cook pot in the middle of the eating space. The heaviness of the pot is comforting. I made enough for the family to eat well and plenty for the morrow.

Baal Hadad readies a piece of bread. Drops of perspiration drip down my back. He is about to dip the bread into the pot. My nails bite into my palms. He brings the bread to his lips. The family waits for his reaction. "This is delicious, Elisha. But I would like to teach you more about baking." His eyes smile.

"Thank you, my lord. My ima never taught me how." I am sure no one tasted the tiny bit of anise I picked.

Resheph's arms are crossed over his chest. "I do not like this. Ima's stew is much better. The vegetables fell apart." Sometimes he is like a child, making everything a contest.

"If you do not like it, do not eat. That will not make your ima happy."

Kotharat glares at Resheph. "Thank you so much for your opinion." Then she turns to me. "Where did you find the vegetables?"

There is only one place. "I chose the ones in the keep that lost their freshness and had to be used before they were thrown away."

"Did you use them up? There is no market on the morrow."

"Most of them are gone but I made enough for another meal."

"That should have been my decision, not yours. You did not ask what plans I had for the food."

How could I ask? She was not here. "I am sorry, Kotharat. I will do better next time." She is never satisfied.

"This is a delicious meal thanks to Elisha." Nikkal always rescues me. "No matter. We have enough and we always have plenty of baked goods."

I send her a sideways glance of thanks from under half-closed eyelids. She shows me a slight parting of her lips.

The cleaning is done, and I go to my sleep space to call on Sandalphon. While waiting for the cloud to arrive I come to a decision. I will not waste time pondering on Resheph. He enjoys being unkind. What needs attention is my reaction that men's opinions are more important. That Baal's thoughts were more precious than anyone else's. Why, as a woman, am I not concerned with females who also want to be pleased?

I cannot help pondering on Eve. If she was made from Adam's rib, then she was the same as he. Why did men decide after she ate the fruit that she was wicked? Sandalphon arrives with the turquoise ball and his vivid colors.

"Well done, Elisha, but what is disturbing you?"

"Kotharat. I do not want to be mean like she is."

"Do you remember the time at home when you had so much kindheartedness for a lame boy? What did you say afterward?"

"That I am dull and do not belong anywhere, and will not be able to understand, and will never do anything well. And I am a waste of time."

"You were fault-finding again. Picture saying kind words to yourself and how it makes you feel." He waits. "Now place the compassion for that boy inside of you.

I close my eyes. "I am content, as if someone wiped me clean. Showing kindness to yourself was not practiced in my tribe but I am willing to consider it."

"You are not with your tribe. As to your other question, you are a member of a society where women are not considered intelligent. You needed approval. It is no wonder you wanted Baal to confirm your work. Know when you do well and consider approving yourself." A delightful green color trails after him as he lifts up to join the other clouds.

My tribe was sure of working without end. While it is necessary, it also made them appear cold and distant. There was no tempering with softness, especially for oneself. Learning to give myself a positive reply may be difficult but Sandalphon said it is my way forward. It would be wonderful if it means more beautiful words will flow for my songs.

CHAPTER THIRTEEN

All my early chores are done, and I am ready to leave. Kotharat stops me. "You are not finished. From now on you will clean the vegetable keep."

She is well aware this keeps me from going to class. Is this a punishment for using up the food? I work harder and am still unable to please her. When she releases me I run as fast as I can to escape the clouds overhead and be on time for class. Abram will be annoyed if I am late. Something makes me start. A tree cracked and crashed to the ground. Rain may be coming. I move faster in case I am right. I hope it will pass by. I do not want to get soaked.

The problem Abram put to us last time darts into my head. "We must reflect on and question who we are. That is the most important knowledge we can gain. Knowledge of ourselves brings wisdom. Then we can study other things."

The whole class was confused. "What does he mean?" "If one is what one is, what else do we need to know?" they asked each other. Their questions caused more confusion and Abram would not say more and dismissed us.

My voice arrives, colors twinkling like the stars. "Ah, we have a matter to discuss."

"Yes, but I am going to be late for class."

"There will be enough time."

"What do you think about Abram's question?" Sandalphon does not answer. "Abram talked about knowing yourself and posed questions like why do I do what I do, want what I want, where am I going and what will I do with this knowledge? I have no idea how to answer, and my head is about to burst." I decide to sit and listen to Sandalphon.

"Yes, Elisha?"

"What am I to do with this? Me, a young woman from the country who came here with no education and only you to help."

"First, stop making excuses. You are countless cubits ahead of yourself. What is the first question?"

"Who am I?"

The cloud comes closer. "What is your answer? Listen to your body and think."

"I am a daughter, a young woman, I try to be a friend, and now a seeker of knowledge. But is that all I am?"

"Think and I will wait."

"A lover of nature and beauty and maybe Resheph, and singing, and composing, and a man who speaks to the Holy Spirit is teaching me." Sandalphon knows what is in my head and is aware of my thoughts about Resheph. If I spoke from the boasting place in me, he would not approve.

"I am glad you were honest about your friend. And you did not boast." His colors twinkle faster, as if he is laughing at his little joke.

My spirits lift a bit. "I would like to be wise like Abram, but how much wisdom can I have at my age and coming from a poor village?"

"You are here to absorb a different way of seeing life and people. And how you wish to be as a person. Do not expect this knowledge to become part of you in a moment. When you have the knowing remember, the gentle spokeswoman is the one whose words are heard."

"Why gentle? Because I am a woman?"

"Because the listener must be more attentive."

I smile. "I like that. Let me say how pleased I am to be here and learn. I am sorry for not saying it right away."

"There will be more ideas in the future, so I will leave you with a question. What makes your soul vibrant as if it shimmers and is strong?"

My brow wrinkles. "My soul? I never thought about that. I do have some ideas I grasp and did not expect to. Is that wisdom?"

The cloud rocks from side to side. "It is possible. Ponder not on wisdom but on your soul and what makes your spirit happy and consider composing more songs."

He is gone. An idea lights me like an oil lamp. He is saying my songs and my soul are connected. Maybe they will be my way for the whole world to hear Abram's words. Are we supposed to do what we love? That would be astounding and everyone would be happy. Abram said music is my passion. It would be wonderful if it is true.

Sandalphon did not help me clear my head about the work and except for being late, the morning goes well. I did what Abram asked. But when the sun is high, I find myself running out of Melchizedek's house. I need to escape from the embarrassment burning hot on my cheeks. The whole group made fun of my question, "If all comes from God, is pain also from Him?"

Resheph rolled with glee, the loudest of all, and so did Adi, the beautiful one. She always copies what the men do. The fault lies with my task masters, Sandalphon and Abram. They put me in this position. They know how I struggle and now I convinced every one of my stupidity.

Inside me are rippling currents that will not let me sit. I am grateful no one is here. Do I go home or back to Melchizedek? If I knew how to read and write, the learning might come faster.

I go down the lane and sit on a rock to calm myself. The question I asked about pain was not stupid, no matter what they think.

"Elisha?" The voice surprises me. Resheph is here and I turn away. "What is wrong with you? Must Abram send me to find you?"

"I will not talk to you." How I long to be a cloud or unseen like Abram's Holy Spirit.

"Abram said to tell you he will discuss pain for the last class."

I want to make a fist and hit him. "Why did you laugh at me?"

"I did not laugh."

"Yes, you did. There was nothing else to laugh at."

"It was funny at the time. The class laughed and I chuckled."

The way he shifts his feet says he lied. "You were the only one to point your finger at me and roar louder as I ran out."

"That was someone else. Why did you run?"

He tries to confuse me. "You know. You were there." He no longer fools me. But we live in the same home. And I need to stay. "I made a fool of myself and you made everything worse. That is what happened."

"Are you upset because I am here?"

The worry on his face brings me misery. "No." I do not sound reassuring. "I am annoyed with myself for my dullness." Can it be? Someone else pointed their finger?

"You are too hard on yourself, and you are not dull. I would not like you so much if you were." His eyes are on mine and he lifts my chin to peer into them. "You are a talented young woman. You make wondrous songs and sing them with heart. Your singing sends shivers through me as if it heals me with its touch. Do you not realize that?"

What I realize is that what he said is not true. He heard only one song, but the expression on his face makes heat rise and course through me. "You are saying silly things because you like me." I watch his face.

"Now you are being stupid. Liking your song has nothing to do with whether I like you. The work we are doing with Abram is difficult even for a scholar."

I am surprised. "Do you mean that?"

"Yes, I do. I understand your frustration, but I do not understand why. Something is wrong with you. Study. Like I do."

"Somehow that is difficult for me. Can you help?" He is the best student so he should know.

Resheph's eyes are angry. "You are here for a purpose. To learn. Learning does not need to be perfect."

"I want to understand it all right away."

"Maybe you will."

I steal a glance at him. "Can you teach me to read and write?"

"I waited for you to be ready. Abram taught us. He learned when he lived in Sumer. We can begin after sundown."

"Why was I not invited to the class?"

"He taught us in between his ramblings with Melchizedek before you arrived. Abram wished for you to recover from your trip and have time to settle into this new life. That is why I waited for you to ask. Do not worry, you will learn well."

My heart is full. My arms wish to hug him, my lips to relish my first kiss. "You and your family give me much. How can I repay the kindness?"

"No payment is necessary. We opened our house to a guest, and we are the ones receiving the gifts."

"You are too generous."

"Let us go back to class."

We go inside and my heart fills with sadness. A moment before, I was happy. Both my throat and chest tighten. Resheph cannot help with my problem about learning. Am I mistaking his behavior? He wavers back and forth, seems to want to reveal his intent, but then words disappear and he is willing to consider one thing. Class work. His messages never agree.

· · · · · · · · · · · ·

A walk after class might help me to understand Abram's lesson. The funny lopsided path where the houses were built first and the lane tracks their direction is the long way home. That gives my body time to inform me of what bothers me. My chest is weighty as if I will soon be ill.

"Sandalphon, I need you. Please come."

"You are troubled."

"Is it Resheph or studies that bother me? He almost spoke of his love for me and what he knows I am feeling, but then . . ."

"Is that so?"

"I am not imagining he cares for me."

"You might be wrong."

I shake my head. "No. It cannot be. It pours out of him and wraps me in a glow. I would not make that up. But what keeps him from speaking? Does he not like what I do yet does not say so?"

"What if he has his own reasons?"

I ponder the message. "It is possible."

"Is there a truth you are not facing?"

"What truth?"

"The reality of what was spoken."

"What was . . . Oh. I am Hebrew?"

"Correct."

I move about unable to settle down. "My great love for Resheph will change his way of thinking."

"You have a leaf to eat. Now we must clarify intuition. It does not come from the head, though you may receive the message there. Insight comes from what you allow yourself to become aware of and is one of the feminine strengths."

"I was wrong."

"Remember Eve."

He is gone. What is all this about Eve? I do not want to be near Resheph if he does not feel the same. That would be torture and too much to ask.

I go from happiness to devastation when he ignores me. Abram would say, "You must have patience and focus on your own growth. Consent to having the angels send your heart's desires." He would also say Holy spirit, but I do not.

I no longer yearn to go back to my family. I am like a branch growing out of the soil but bending toward the ground instead of the sky. This branch is separate, not part of the tree, alone and spent, with no energy to lift itself. Yet its flowers are blooming in the cycle of life and hope.

Sandalphon would say we do not know Resheph's intentions. That may be true, but I behave in response to what he says and does. I grab a fistful of hair and shove the ends in my mouth.

CHAPTER FOURTEEN

The last meal of the sun cycle is filled with stories of the goings-on and gossip of the city. It is a placid evening. I try to sleep but my talk with Sandalphon keeps me awake. Why did he say it was my leaf to eat in that way? I did not understand his advice. Love can conquer the fact I am Hebrew. I was born that way.

The swaying of my curtain and the ripples from someone passing or fingers moving it sets me on alert. Resheph is going by. He is the only one who would do that, and his step is heavier than his Abba's. He clears his throat. It is on purpose.

I want to rip away the curtain that keeps me from him. I run to it and wait. A great joy runs through me and flutters like a sunbird drinking its fill. He walks by, without hesitation, and says nothing. He makes no other sound. He will never say the words I long to hear. What is left of the night is spent sleepless and fighting with the cover.

. . . .

There is no obvious reason for the house to be peaceful during the next three suns. I hear no demands, no arguments, no bellowing or screeching. On the last evening, I arrive home late from class. Kotharat is angry. She finished making the evening meal.

"Where were you? Why were you not here to cook?"

"I am sorry, Abram delayed me. Resheph will also be late. Abram had a new lesson for me, and it took him a while to explain it."

"I have much to do and that does not include your responsibilities." She goes out to the garden.

She did not fight with me. I did not tell her I took some time for studying. If my reason concerns Abram, she accepts it.

I collect the jugs and run down the side of the route toward the spring. I cannot get Resheph out of my head. The lady of the house across the lane waves and I return the gesture with a nod. Why does he tease? To what end? Does he wish to bed and not marry me? His behavior is confusing. I join the long line of women waiting at the well.

Weary of Resheph, reflections on Eve's story returns. She was blamed for what went wrong because she ate the fruit from the Tree of Knowledge. Who would not seek knowledge? Most females receive no learning. Is that not why I am here? Why is cleverness wicked?

The line is longer than usual. As I wait my turn, a girl up ahead stares in my direction. "Does everyone know about Resheph?" Her voice is loud enough to scare away the animals. "His father and mine are discussing my bridal gift. And there is another Resheph's father is bartering with but not the abba of the guest at his house."

The women turn, laugh, and wait for me to retort. I wish there was a hole I could disappear into. My skin burns as if I am in the middle of a cook fire. I command my limbs to do their duty and hold me up. My ears ring with their laughter. I hold myself straight and tall without a flicker of emotion crossing my face. When the jugs are filled, I race back to the house.

The jugs are in place, and I am ready to go to my mat. My mother could be strict and sometimes unforgiving, but she would never be as cruel as that girl.

CHAPTER FIFTEEN

Kotharat left before dawn to go to her friend. That leaves me to prepare the meal. It will not be difficult for she will not be at my side watching. Mix the barley in boiling water, stir until the mixture is thick enough. Then add the right amount of fat.

They ask for more and the request warms my heart. I smile and do not share my secret. A bit of salt made its way into the pot. The tiniest speck because of the lack and high cost. If Kotharat was here she would complain, "The morning meal should be the usual and plentiful bread and fruit." This family is lucky. There is always something to eat.

Baal and Resheph go to the bake stall to gather goods to set up at the marketplace. There is enough for Kotharat to eat before she meets them there.

The fact that I impressed them makes me proud. Is that bad? Should I ponder on it? Abram went to be with his beloved Sarai, so we are free. He will return on the morrow. Will that be the right time to ask about my problem?

My wish is to make up another song. Instead, Nikkal and I busy ourselves with cleaning and manage to put the whole place in order. We make the house shine like the stars. That way Kotharat will have nothing to complain about.

Our work done, we decide to go to the garden and enjoy the weather before picking out what vegetables to use for the late meal. We run out of conversation. The silence embarrasses me. I need to ask her something but do not want to start with that.

"I never answered your question about my name." My account is not as detailed as what I told Resheph.

When I finish, Nikkal is smiling. "That was an unusual journey. Do many people ask you about it?"

"Not many, but a few." I wait. "May I ask you another question?"

"Of course."

"Why is Resheph not betrothed? He is of age."

"Why do you ask?"

"A young woman at the spring said your Abba is bartering with the fathers of two women for a betrothal ceremony."

Nikkal laughs. "Women always say that."

"She spoke with sureness."

"I would advise you to stay away from that issue."

"Why?"

"My brother is a fine-looking man. There are many women who are attracted to him. Abram will soon continue his journey, and Resheph will study with Melchizedek until his learnings are complete. He wants to be the next Melchizedek and is not ready for a family. You should not get caught up with him."

"Does my interest show?"

"To those who are alert."

"I understand if he is not ready, but why do you warn me away? It would be fun to be your sister." Nikkal looks at the floor.

"My brother has his own ideas about women and how they should be treated. I would not wish to be a part of that."

Her words are confusing. "You make him sound evil. Can you explain?"

"I can but will not."

I do not believe her.

· · · · · · · · · · · ·

Nikkal leaves for the market, she wants to barter for a new shawl. I ask for Sandalphon and bring up the difficulties with Resheph.

"We must undertake another matter first."

"But he confuses me and Nikkal spoke as if he is evil."

"I am afraid I must insist. Trust me."

He was never so firm before. "That is not easy right now."

"Did you think about what makes your soul vibrant?"

"You asked but cleaning and studying needed to be done." I turn away, then grin at him over my shoulder.

The cloud moves from side to side. "All right. I will allow you some leniency. What are your thoughts?"

"I do not have any." I wait. "How can I be sure it is my soul?"

"A joy will fill you as never felt before."

"What I know is that I am supposed to have one and so does everybody."

"Why?"

He remains silent for so long I must answer. "The soul is in us when we are born."

"Why?"

Now he is making me angry, so I take my time. "I have no answer."

"Ponder on how your soul helps you." His voice fades with no mention of Resheph.

· · · · · · · · · · · ·

The morning's weather is perfect so it is hard to sit inside. To make it worse, Abram's first statement makes me feel bad.

"The way for you to grow is to study and learn. The most important learning is to first understand yourselves."

Sandalphon said the same and though I promised, I ignored his suggestion. Abram also hinted at this in different ways. I do not know how to do what he wants. The other students are nodding in agreement.

Abram paces the width of the room. "Can you identify why you think in a certain way or what you are certain of beyond doubt? But let us consider light and dark. Is one better than the other?" We nod.

Resheph decides to show off again. "Light offers us the ability to see what we are doing and helps plantings to grow."

"That is almost correct. They each offer a different point. But you did not consider dark. What about dark?" No one answers. "Dark brings bad feelings, bleak, sad, shadowy, dismal." Abram stares at each of us as if willing us to fasten our eyes on him. "What about good and evil? Is one better?"

"Yes." "Of course." "Trivial question." "Senseless." Remarks come from all over.

"Are you sure?"

Yadid, who opened the door on my first visit, has disbelief on his face. "How can it not be?"

"If you say it is so, Abram, then it is." The others laugh and Resheph grins.

Abram pays no attention.

"Can one exist without the other? If we do not recognize good, can we know evil? If we only experience dark can we identify light?" We glance around the room. No one comments. "These are called dualities or contrasts."

Abram's last word captivates me. The others sit back and seem puzzled by the new notions. Do Abram's words mean putting these ideas into our lives? Yet it seems more than that. He continues. "Our world is filled with contrasts and contradictions. Why? So we can make choices." Sandalphon's example about eating leaves. "We choose how we live by the selections we make. Do we do good or evil? Help one in need or walk away, give or withhold? Our behavior informs God and people who we are."

Abram sits on his bench. "Do we walk with love in our hearts or hate? Who do you choose to be?"

I take in a mouthful of air. The room is without a sound. The birds are chirping, and a conversation is going on outside.

"This is a most important task. It takes you to the core of your nature. I am dispensing with questions for now and dismissing the class. You are to go and consider. I ask for complete silence. Each of you go to a place where you can do the necessary work. Return when you are finished."

Resheph takes no notice of me as he walks off without a glance. What was in his head? He made a fool of himself. I watch him for a moment then turn toward where he told me the planting terraces are. There is so much to think about, so much to learn. There is never a right time to ask about my trouble.

I quicken my pace and as I come near, there is a smell I am accustomed to. The familiarity of it warms me. The hint of fields being set ablaze is still in the air. Those fields will now lay fallow until ready for new plantings. My tribe decided that this was the way plantings can be done in almost any season and there would always be fertile areas. The largest area is filled with emmer wheat. The next one, a bit smaller, is planted with barley.

The lentil vines need to be picked, they are more than two cubits long. Chickpeas were planted three full suns ago. It will take more time before they are ready. I continue toward the orchards to find an olive tree to sit under. Sandalphon arrives without the orb.

"How are you?"

His greeting stops me. "Abram's teachings are not easy to make one's own." I turn toward the cloud. "They make all I see or think about life appear different. I am shaken and at odds. His are new notions, which turn me upside down."

"I am sure you will right yourself again. You need time alone. I will leave you to your reasonings. Call if you need me."

I nod and continue to the orchard. I sit under one of the larger trees. As I close my eyes and take in the scents of the plants growing around me, words for a song flood into my head. I name it, "We Cannot Know the Other."

I finish the song and an understanding comes. There is more behind Abram's words than I grasped. Did he mean we need both because both are good? Evil is not good. I shake my head. Abram said to return after we are complete.

When I get back, the one missing student is the beauty who cannot think for herself. She arrives as Abram enters the room. "I am glad we are all here. Who would like to speak first?"

I move around on my seat but cannot find comfort. I am so nervous my hand shakes as I raise it.

"I do, Abram," comes out in a whisper.

"You have not spoken before but do not be afraid. Your hand was halfway up making me wonder if you needed to scratch your head or had a question." The class laughs and he stares at them. "It takes courage to speak in front of a group. Please, Elisha."

"There is still confusion in my thinking. Is there more behind your words? Are you saying we need the, um, contrasts because they are good? How can evil be good?" A few in the class titter. I ignore them.

"I did not say evil was good, but that one cannot exist without the other."

"I misunderstood."

"Do not be ashamed. Not understanding is the way to learning. What were you thinking about?"

"I wrote a song."

"A song. Would you sing it for us?"

The song comes to an end and I wait for Abram. He is smiling and the class is clapping their hands. I thank them and return to my pillow.

"Your song is an excellent description of what we are exploring here."

"Thank you, Abram. I am missing a consideration. I still cannot answer your idea about evil."

"I will come to that. First, one more detail about your song. The melody is skilled and you made my words poetic. I agree there is a point, which went astray in your understanding. I asked you to go to the center of your being and inspect the behaviors that describe who you are."

I sit back. "You are right, and I forgot. I will do it." I may not have understood contrasts well but my song was successful.

Later, Abram gives us a lesson on why to find your life's purpose, the reason we are here in this place. Do I have one?

The family is at the late meal and the loud conversation keeps me from my reasonings. I hurriedly do the cleaning and go to sleep happy and determined to understand contrasts.

· · · · · · · · · · · ·

I wake up fretful, and late to fix the morning meal. I do not wish to face what is next. Kotharat will be angry and I did not do what Abram asked. I push the jumble of my mind aside. Work comes first. I will find something to say to Abram. I am surprised to find Kotharat seated in the garden and not taking care of a sick friend. I bow my head. "Best wishes for a pleasant morning."

"Peace be with you. Elisha. Did you sleep well?"

"I am sorry to have overslept."

"The rest of the family left before sunrise."

I do not see any food and turn to go to my sleep space. I stop and walk to the cook pot.

"You seem disturbed. Can I help?"

She will not have the answer. "I am having trouble with a task Abram gave us and am at odds with myself."

"And what is it?"

I hesitate. Resheph must have told her about our lesson. He tells her everything. "Abram asked us to find our life's purpose." I fill my basin and sit on a mat.

"Your life's purpose?"

"What I am trying to say is I am afraid to make the wrong decision."

She laughs. "You are such a mindless young woman. Even I understand life's purpose is not a decision."

She knows? "It is not?"

"No. Purpose is built into who you are, your heart's desires, your talents."

"I thought about it in the wrong way."

"You are not bright like my son, so you are not able to understand." Scraping my lower lip with my teeth helps control the anger. "Explore who you are and what you choose to do with your life. How you choose to live. You study as Resheph does, so I assume you want to teach or aid those in need. Do you understand?"

"Thank you, Kotharat." I never expected her to help me.

She is cruel on one side and says words to hurt or embarrass you. Then she turns and is kind and helpful. My notions about her are in pieces.

This need to understand who I choose to be is important. Has someone whispered in my ears for ages and I never heard them? Without this understanding, I will not move forward.

Sandalphon murmurs into my ear. "This task may be long and laborious, like birthing yourself into this realm. You must consider yourself a baby."

· · · · · · · · · · · ·

The sun is high, and I leave before Resheph can join me. I need to decide the words to use when I speak to Abram. He will be leaving soon. The question roams around my head and the freedom of being alone encourages me to run toward the groves. I make sure Resheph is not following me. I need Sandalphon.

"Come back to me, please."

The voice arrives inquiring, "Why are you so agitated?"

"I need your advice."

"I am listening." He is gentle. "First close your eyes and connect with God."

"I do not believe in God and prefer my reflection."

"Let me know when you are ready."

I do a short contemplation. "We can begin."

"You need to go back for your tutoring. We can continue along the way."

"I am nervous because I must ask Abram how to fix my troubles. My fear says he will think less of me."

"Abram is a religious man, and he is trying to teach the mysteries of the Holy Spirit to those of your world. God hoped for religion to be a way to share and not oppress. What can Abram teach you about your troubles?"

"How to fix them so I can go home."

"Can you not do this yourself?"

"I do not think so."

"No one knows you as well as you do."

"That is true but I am not clever. Let me ponder on that." I weigh his remark and that much is right. "Perhaps Abram's teachings will give me the answer. One more thing. The others in class are doing far better than I am. Resheph assures me this is not true, but I do not trust him."

"Why do you not believe him?"

"He cares for me, and sometimes he is my protector. He might hide the truth if it would hurt me."

"Say more."

"I have trouble grasping how to do better with Abram's teachings. I do them with my full heart but am not sure my understanding is good enough."

"You said the same before."

"Abram has so much to teach us."

"Like the soul's needs we spoke about?"

"Yes, yes. Like that. I miss the mark. Some teachings fix themselves in my head, but they are not yet a part of me. I cannot explain them to anyone. I am not able to put the ideas together for myself or anyone else. They are a mystery."

"Would you say it is too soon?"

"Please do not say that. I would swallow them whole and have it go through my body into my blood. Become my blood. Then I know they belong, and I can translate them into another song. I need to have knowledge of those sentiments."

"The fact is that humans feel many things but go through your world in a muddle. Put a name to your feelings. Once you do, there will be less trouble composing and your songs will be outstanding."

What does one have to do with the other? I am at the gate to the house. "I decided what I want to do. Teach others with my songs and show them the way to heal and find contentment. This is a worthy undertaking."

"There is more."

"I am afraid to tell Resheph my vision for the future and fear how he will react. I need him to respect what I choose for my life. Women are valued by men as wife and mother and I want that too, but I also yearn to follow what calls me. The passion for music fills my heart the way the passion for Resheph does. I pray he agrees."

"Think about songs and Resheph and whether they are wants or needs."

"Why?" Sandalphon does not answer. "You are not around me anymore." He whispers in my ear. "Do not ignore putting names to your feelings. Your songs will blossom."

I stand outside needing time to be present with my surroundings. Wants. Needs. Name feelings. I open the door.

CHAPTER SIXTEEN

We are on our pillows waiting with patience for Abram. Most of the students whisper and gossip about why he might be late. I do not listen. If Abram is late, he has a good reason. Resheph is chatting with the men. He is even more handsome in the pale light, and my heart opens to him. All I want is to see him, listen to his voice, and watch his every move. Most of all I long to be near him and touch him, though he pretends I am not there. He glances my way often enough not to be an accident. I turn my head before he catches me.

An understanding came to me after I spoke with Kotharat. Abram's teaching is not about good and bad or right and wrong. The contrasts are two ends of the same tree trunk and equal. They exist so we can experience them to understand both. I am pleased with my conclusion.

Abram's arrival interrupts my reflections. He gives no apology. "What came to my attention is your need for an important exercise. Get ready and sit with ease on your pillows. You may also lie down. Close your eyes and take a few deep breaths." He paces across the front of the room. "Imagine you are in front of a large pair of doors. Use your will and they will open. Go inside when you are able."

Abram's voice is so far away I cannot make it out. Behind my eyes are thick, heavy, black, menacing doors of wood. The building is made of stones larger than any in this land. They belong to another time, a time in the future. I pull on the handle with every bit of strength I have and the door opens a sliver.

Flattening myself to get through the opening, the edge of the door scrapes at my back. Murky darkness makes it hard to adjust my eyes. Oil lamps mark the sides of the great hall and light themselves as I pass on my way to an enormous room.

In front of me are uncountable barred enclosures lining both sides of the walls. There is a person in each one. The whites of the prisoner's eyes shine. With deliberate steps I move closer to the first one. Ima stands and stares at me. The next pen holds my father. His head is in his hands. Then my grandmother and Nathan. The other pens are filled with all the villagers including the children. Why are they here? Each confine holds someone who was part of my life.

The prisoners stare at me without any expression. "Why am I here? What does this mean?" Their silence is disturbing. Did I put them in the pens? I need to do something but do not know what. I search for understanding and find no answer. I continue to walk and one word comes to me. "Forgive."

Awareness of time is lost, as one by one, I go to each pen, gaze into the eyes of the prisoner, and say, "I hereby pardon you for any wounds, abuses, affronts, or criticisms you made. If you are able, please pardon me for any difficulties I caused." With that done, I open each pen and set them free.

My eyes close against the strong sun when I walk out of the darkness. The outside air is refreshing. A fascinating freedom is released in me. My heart is settled and I dance with wonder and lightness. I return to class and the colors are clearer, purer, sparkling. Even the faces of my classmates are softer, gentler, happier. Did my face change? What about forgiving Qayin and Kotharat? I am not ready.

· · · · · · · · · · · ·

I now live with the fear of putting people back in the pens. During the next few moon cycles, Kotharat continues to give me more to do and complains about how I do it. I ponder on how to not blame her for the extra work and Resheph for making fun of me. He hears me grumble and laughs. All attempts fail.

"Sandalphon, where are you? I need help."

His colors glow with a strength not seen before. Yellow stands out. "I am here, Elisha."

"I am glad to see you. Two problems need guidance."

"I am aware of that."

Of course he knows. "It is strange to know that my knowledge is now greater than my father and Nathan." We both laugh. "After the exercise about the pens, clarity, lightness, and joy ran through me. Now uncertainty has taken their place."

"What needs explaining?"

"I am afraid to act or speak, knowing one misstep may cause me to put people back in a pen."

"Continue."

"How do I move ahead? I understand we sometimes hurt others and do not realize what we did. I cannot think about it any further."

"A lack of understanding is preventing you from finding a solution. Who do you most need to release?"

The name comes to me right away. "Kotharat."

"She is a proper choice to start. Not too close to you and you do not know her long."

"What am I supposed to do?"

"Practice what Abram taught. Find out if you can release her. Try to come to a better understanding of who she is and why she acts the way she does."

"Sandalphon, you know I tried, but nothing happens."

"We will see, will we not?"

"Is that your last word?"

"For the moment."

He makes me angry. "The other problem is Eve. I pondered a bit more about the connection of being marred to Eve's story. She ate the fruit though that meant death, and it changed their lives. But she did not die, and women need to care about knowledge."

"Is there more?"

"Is that all you can say?" He does not answer. "My thinking turned to the men. Perhaps men decided women could not be trusted to obey because Eve disobeyed God. They assumed they had to control females so they declared themselves in charge." I shrug. "That is what I thought."

"Excellent."

"You mean I am right?" Sandalphon does not answer. "Nathan was treated as the welcomed one and me as one to be dealt with. I became aware of a loneliness and a part of me that shrank inside and was empty. As if I was not a respectable person to talk to or be friends with."

"You are correct, and can you name the feeling?"

"The sensation was a kind of poverty but not for food. What do I do now?"

"Continue your work."

"It is strange to know that my knowledge is now greater than my father and Nathan. Which work?"

"We will chat again."

He is gone leaving me with questions, much to think about, and a task to try. It is a way to help myself and I cannot wait.

. . . .

The evening meal is over, the cleaning is finished, and all is put in place. I excuse myself. "Abram asked me to do some exercises. Sleep well." Vague nods come in response.

My back is against the wall, and the cover is wrapped around me. The lamp is lit, and I welcome the kind of relaxation that makes it easy for my head to roam. Will releasing Kotharat be hard to do? Understanding why she acts as she does will be more difficult.

At this moment I would not choose to free her. She just told me I will do the wash for the whole family. It was fine at the beginning, but in the short time that passed she added many more chores and that gives me no time for my studies. I cannot accomplish what I was sent here to do.

My tribe said, "Every person fights difficult battles to survive." After the pen exercise, Abram also told us, "Focus on the one who hurt you and picture him or her as a whole person rather than just your torturer. He or she also has a life with their own challenges, heartaches, and scars." Then he said, "Separate the act from the person. Remember when you made a similar mistake. Are you better or worse than they?"

I was able to do the work on Eve so maybe I can be successful with Kotharat. I try to find a new way of thinking about her. Do her quarrels have anything to do with me? What if the problem is about her? Her needs, her desires, her fears. That is it. I lie on the mat and close my eyes. I have no idea how long I waited when an idea causes a laugh which comes from deep in my belly. My face is buried in the mat so the family does not hear.

Kotharat is terrified of this Hebrew girl. Terrified I will take Resheph away. Unsure of her hold on him. I found her nightmare and her weakness. Now I can let her go. I let out a huge sigh. My mother would be the same.

· · · · · · · · · · · ·

After a night with little sleep, I woke before dawn. Kotharat added more commands and it took a long time to fulfill them. Abram said he would be late so I stroll to the outskirts of the city and lie on the grass. The sadness is back and makes my head feel like it was bounced around like the ball the boys play with or was stuffed like a cooked bird at a festival.

It is difficult to relax. My questions take turns floating through my head. The opposites we learned, Kotharat, and forgiving. The area where I am is not filled with trees and flowers, yet my contemplation calms me, and somewhere through the meanderings, sleep takes hold.

I wake up and the sun is over the horizon. I am late, too late for class. Abram will be angry. My dreams were of loneliness. I am an outsider again, just like at home. I live with strangers who are Canaanites. Abram teaches. Only Resheph and his family talk to me and they are not friends. There are no kin and no mate to love and share my life. A family is what I long for, but Resheph does not show interest.

My brother will marry. He and his wife will live with the family. My parents accepted the possibility of my leaving for a marriage and becoming a member of my husband's household. Then I was banished and my parents did not know if I would ever come home again.

· · · · · · · · · · · ·

The lane away from the house is made of craggy rocks. A liveliness pushes me to continue though it is slippery. Abba would say, "You should be heavy with child, not climbing on rocks." He spoke with longing for grandchildren I am not providing. I hope Nathan will give him a brood.

I sit on the ground with my back against the last boulder watching the plants try to lift their heads from between the rocks. The sky and the water are bluer. I close my eyes and take in the surrounding scents. One by one the miseries slip away. A gentleness comes over me and replaces the hurts with an appreciation that my family did the best they could.

When a branch falls to die and crumble, it will live again by becoming part of the dirt that feeds the tree. The branch does not ponder. No wins or loses. It is merely a stage of life.

A picture appears in my head. A tree, this one larger than any in this land, has roots deep into the earth and yet it reaches toward the sky. It seems to expand as its silvery branches reach upward and move with the gentle breeze. The pictures continue filling me with the beauty of each thing I see.

"I am happy to see you appreciate beauty and the people who love you. That is a major step."

I sit up. "Thank you for coming to me. It was not as difficult as I thought."

"Congratulations." His voice fades.

I am ready to move on. In the past few minutes several new thoughts came to me. I mull over the sky and water, the hurts that slipped away, the tree, and shining leaves that made me content with the promise of joy.

Why was the branch silvery and what does it have to do with love or loneliness? Ima told me about a stone. She never told me the name, but it wears the same silvery color as the tree. She said, "It is a protection stone for travelers and one of its properties is to make the carrier feel cared for." This is not a warning. It assures me I am protected.

Staring at the water, I know this new awareness will not leave me, never desert me, and will help me be less afraid. My eyes focus on a beautiful cloud when a sound rouses me. It is Resheph. He is sitting nearby, humming and watching.

"Why were you not in class?"

How long has he been here? "I woke up late and assumed Abram would be angry."

"Stupid girl. He would be angrier for not showing up. I can show you now if you are ready."

"Why are you here?"

"Sometimes you are more than slow." Not slow, puzzled. "I brought a tablet for you to learn the reading and writing. Remember?" He holds it out.

I pull it from his hands. "Do you know how long it has been? I waited and you never said we could start. Did you think about how far behind I am? Did you care? Do you want me to fail?" I take a breath. "How did you find me?"

"How do you think? I saw which route you took." He gets up and turns as if to walk away.

There was no way for him to see where I went. "Wait. Do not go."

"I will not stay if you are so angry."

I move as close to him as possible. "I could have been further ahead in my studies."

He stares, his nostrils flaring. "Do not show me your anger." He takes his stone tablet out of his sack and shows me a drawing. "This is called writing."

"This picture of a man with a short tunic?"

"Right. By drawing in this manner, what is represented can be recognized and understood by all. Copy it."

"How marvelous and so easy. I assumed writing would be difficult and I could not do it."

"It is reasonable. Experiment with drawing the man moving."

My focus is on copying it well. "Here it is."

He laughs. "This is so simple. You cannot do anything right. A bent knee is what shows going forward. Now, a woman cooking."

"Will you do it first, then I will know how." I move closer, almost touching. Resheph's glare goes through me. I become a statue with eyes on the tablet.

"Here you are." He twists himself away from me. I copy what he did. He studies my picture and laughs again. "Your depictions are horrible and crude. I am not sure you can improve. How would you show a baby?"

"In swaddling clothes. Will you teach me more?"

"Ask the others with tablets to permit you to watch what they do. Explain you are learning and need help." He is pushing me away.

"Thank you, I will. What more can you teach me?" I move a bit closer.

"I do not have time for you." Resheph gets up and turns toward me. "And do not sit close to me."

"I do not know what you mean."

"I will not let you ruin my life."

My eyes open wide. "Sitting close will ruin your life?"

"Do not pretend. You understand. You heard my final word."

He may think that is his final word.

· · · · · · · · · · · ·

With everything in place after the final meal clean up I am too awake to sleep and go to the garden to enjoy the stars. They sparkle and play go find me, while anxiety fills me to overflowing. "Sandalphon, are you here? I need you."

"Yes, Elisha, but I need to complete a task. Can this wait a bit?"

"It can, but not too long, please."

"I promise."

A stroll away from the house and the cooler air is pleasing to my skin. I have time for quiet consideration. Two suns ago, Abram said, "Resentment is a burden carried in your heart and is a barrier to forgiving." No resentments reside in me.

"Are you positive? No resentments?"

My chest pounds. "I wish you would not do that, Sandalphon."

"You asked me to return soon."

I hide behind a tree. If anyone passes by they cannot see me 'talking to the air.' "We spoke of you not coming upon me with abruptness."

"Does my behavior make you angry or resentful?"

He takes me by surprise. "I admit to having anger and annoyance, but I do not feel resentment."

"Who causes you to be resentful?"

"No one."

"Think back. All the way back to your village and your tribe."

I wish for him to grow a face to peer into, to read what is behind the question. "Qayin? I tried to forgive him and Kotharat during the forgiveness lesson but could not excuse them for what they did."

"Think. What did you resent?"

"Qayin thought he was smarter than everyone else. He wanted my tongue to be cut out and accused me in front of the tribe. I was banished because of him." It is a purge of feelings inside I never admitted were in me.

"I think perhaps you have more to say."

I hesitate. "He pretended to be in charge and told each man and woman what to think. I have so much outrage mixed with the resentment, I am as terrible as he was." I bend my head to hide the shame on my face. I peer at Sandalphon from the corner of my eye. "He was wrong in what he said and made trouble. But I understand now that he spoke truths he was taught by his parents."

The cloud bobs up and down. "Correct. What about Kotharat?"

"Must I do that now? I am not ready, and it will not turn out well."

"You are anxious again. Let us proceed one step at a time. Why are you not ready?"

"I still must live and deal with her."

"I will pretend you said yes, so we can move on. Would you rather stay in your anger and resentment? Forgiving can bring peace. Whether it is your banishment by the council, Qayin as the cause, Kotharat, or dry weather when rain is needed, compassion soothes the beast."

"I want to be peaceful."

"This is one of the tests sent for you to learn and grow. The testing often comes from people. We blame them for interfering, get irritated and resentful, but they are the messengers. Can you recognize this?"

"I think so. You are saying no matter what happens, and though we may be angry, it can come from a person and we need to decide why the lesson is necessary."

"You are ready. Do the necessary work with Qayin and you might choose to think about your village."

"My village?"

"There is work to be done there." He is gone.

CHAPTER SEVENTEEN

The sun rises as only it can in this desert. Heat rippling the air and muting the colors announces a new morning. The family is at the morning meal in the courtyard and the kettle, thick with gruel, is back hanging on the hook over the fire. The ladle, full of the mixture, fills my basin. Dried grapes and a chunk of the delicious bread I baked the way Resheph's father taught me, complete my meal.

There is little conversation. Can it be family troubles or deep thoughts after a dream filled night? If we are alone, Resheph has a special way of sending me a message with his eyes glowing, inviting. If others are present he is distant and mean. My meal done, I rush to complete my tasks.

Resheph is at my side. "Why did you run away?"

"Do you always sneak up on people? You frightened me."

"How could I make noise? I am barefoot."

He makes me feel stupid. "You could cough or clear your throat."

"But why would I do what is not needed?"

"So you would not scare me."

"Why are you scared?"

I was nervous around him the past three moons. "I do not know."

"It is your problem, not mine."

"I guess so." He turns his words around and puts me at fault. "You are quite beautiful."

My heart jumps.

I turn and he is gone. Just like his mother, hostile some of the time, and then, for no reason he is kind. Is that how Resheph shows love? Are all the Canaanites the same?

Morning tasks done, I hurry to class. I am comfortable on my seat, and the class is ready. Abram is missing.

We sit on our pillows, the six of us, waiting. The room is hushed. The one movement you can hear is the shifting of garments against cushions as our discomfort increases. We glance at each other.

Resheph catches my attention and holds me in his presence with the light in his eyes and a half-smile. Abram interrupts our communication, crossing the threshold as if he is completing a foot race. "Let us get ready to work." We shift again, turning our attention to the front of the room. Abram is winded. He arranges his notations on his lap.

"We will talk about love." The men snicker. "If you will consent, I might be able to complete my thoughts." He stares at them. "We will address love of self, love of others, and love of God. They are the same and yet they are different. Does anyone care to comment?"

"How are they not the same? Love is love." The beautiful one taunts Abram with a toss of the head she holds high.

"The heart is the heart, but do you love your parents the same way you love your friends?"

"No."

He caught her again. "So they are different. Can anyone explain?" No one moves. The air is still. "Let us consider love of self."

"That is selfish. My tribe said so." Why do the other students laugh when I speak?

"Let us examine the question. How many of you dislike parts of yourselves and try to change them?" Every hand goes up. Many of them laugh.

"What if I said you are perfect just the way you are?"

"No one is perfect." "What you say is not true." "I am not perfect." "I would not choose to be perfect," are the many strong reactions to his question.

Abram must help me. "How can I be perfect when I hurt people?"

"Do you hurt them on purpose?"

"Sometimes, but most of the time, no."

"Then the hurting is not a part of who you are but a lesson to be learned."

"Thank you, Abram, for a new way to consider the matter."

He turns to the group. "Who among you is angry with yourself for not growing taller, or smart enough, or having a nicer appearance?"

"What is wrong with that?" Yadid asks the question we all need answered.

Abram laughs, and we join him. "You were made by the Holy Spirit, therefore you are perfect." His eyes turn cold. "Do you enjoy feeling bad for what you cannot change?"

"Abram, I am not pretty. Most people say so." My head is down. I do not want to see his face when he answers.

"What people say does not matter."

"It mattered in my village."

"In the eyes of the Lord, you are beautiful." I smile and the men laugh. They may think their scorn was hidden by their whispers, but I heard them.

"What caused your laughter, Resheph?" Abram stares at him.

"Elisha may be pretty but she will never be beautiful."

"Will you?" We laugh at Abram's question.

"I am handsome."

"Are behaviors such as your snide laughter handsome?"

Resheph turns away. "I guess . . . not."

"Does the way you look or the way you act please God?"

Resheph sits up straighter. "I do not care what God wants."

"Then why are you here?"

"Melchizedek said you are a great teacher."

The beautiful one yells out. "He is saying that to please you." She does not like Resheph because he will not pay any attention to her.

"One who is handsome on the outside, may not be attractive on the inside. Remember that I said you have a pestilence in you. Heed my words, young man. I hope you can learn to practice what you gather from this understanding. Abram turns to us. For everyone else loving yourself brings confidence and the willingness to be truly you."

· · · · · · · · · · · ·

We leave class and Resheph walks in a different direction alone. I walk toward the house calling for Sandalphon. I watch the cloud approach. "Is what Abram said true?"

"About perfection in God's eyes?" I nod. "You can trust Abram. You are the one person in this world like you." I sit in the middle of the lane. "Are you all right?"

"I am."

The cloud bends down close to me. "You had better move before someone walks a donkey over you."

I jump up. "This is another lesson that changes my beliefs. Another idea that will take time to reach my bones."

"It is difficult."

"How will I make these lessons mine?"

"Many people complain about parts of themselves, but to God, you are perfect."

I bite my lip. "Did I complain again?"

"I deem it so."

"Sandalphon, who am I?"

"You can be whoever your heart wants you to be."

"You are saying it is my choice. Thank you."

"Well, well. The last time you said thank you was the first time I spoke to you about females. I am glad you enjoy our time. Time is more precious than humans can imagine. It goes fast and life is over. Do not waste a moment."

"I will think on where I waste time, but can I continue?" He nods. "When I lie down and breathe deeply peace comes to me and I do not want it to end. It is as if I leave here and go somewhere else. Up on a cloud or among the stars. What disturbs me is that being there," I point to the sky, "is better than staying here."

"What are your questions?"

"I have many, but that makes me feel odd, the way my tribe said. Is it better in the sky?"

"You are not peculiar. You are lifted to another level, away from the concerns of living in this realm. What happens when you are there?"

"Colors appear behind my closed eyes, purple and green, and I am no longer anxious or unhappy. I have energy and the trickery is, I am on the ground and floating in the air. As if I have two parts of me."

"Do the parts connect?"

"I do not know. Wait." I recapture the moment. "Yes, they do. The ideas I receive are not forgotten. They are helpful."

"How do you explain this?"

"I cannot."

"Remember you are perfect."

Now I am really confused.

. . . .

I wake the next morning and the first thought is I am powerful. Or did Sandalphon whisper that in my ear? Power has meaning and says you possess opinions and use what you learn and observe. How could that happen to a poor female, young and not gifted?

"Yes, Elisha, it is true."

"Thank you for coming. What kind of power can be mine if I will be confined to family life while men make the decisions? How can a woman accomplish anything, even if I live with passion and use all the might in me and be clear about what I want?" My cloud does not move. "I would choose to reach out but do not have many talents. My writing pictures suffer from an unsteady hand and no one can make them out." I sit. "I can sing and am pleased when people like the songs I make up. What I want more than anything else is to create songs with Abram's words. I think it is what I am supposed to do."

"That is a good idea."

I jump up. "Sandalphon? Is that the truth?"

"I always tell you the truth. Otherwise, what am I? You will help others but not in the way you think."

"How will it happen? I am seldom in high spirits."

"Do you remember I said name your feelings?" I nod. "You must do that if you want to succeed."

I stare at the ground. "I am sorry for being negligent, but I did some."

"All will be made clear if you are ready. What is most important is your intention and what you mean to accomplish."

I lift my head. "I did not make up songs because I was not safe enough to do so."

"Hold your intentions in your heart and you will be successful."

"Sandalphon, why will you not tell me how?"

"I cannot foretell the future. You maintain control with free will."

"What I must do is hold my intentions?"

"The hardest part is to keep them clear no matter what happens. You may encounter hardships and disappointments. After you sing, it is possible people in the audience may throw things to taunt you. That can make you feel bad about yourself. If you do not have faith in your gifts you will lose your way."

"What if I am having a difficult time? What do I do then?"

"Ask for help. Trust you will be answered." He disappears into the blue of the sky.

. . . .

I am alone and lonely. Sadness is making its home on my chest. I step out to go to the spring and try to remember what I must do. Walking toward the well, I put them in the remembering place in my head. Name my feelings, listen to my inner voice, and become more aware of when and how I receive guidance. I miss it thinking it is a coincidence or an accident. Oh. Intentions. I almost forgot.

Abram said there is no such thing as chance. It is true that if I were not banished, this journey would not have happened. I would not meet Abram. Not know about learning and growing. Not learn about love. But I still cannot dream up a song, the words will not come and that makes me angry. I try and nothing happens.

Abram keeps us busy and I have no time to think about intentions the next few suns. I am determined to do my work well. I study before the late meal and will do so after we eat even though I may walk home in the black of night.

. . . .

The usual after meal cleanup is over, and I walk down the rocky passageway to think.

Resheph plants himself at my side. "May I accompany you?"

"At this time?" He nods. "Yes, you can save me from bandits." We both laugh. "I need to get some air and think about the teachings."

"I am the same. Perhaps we can think, then discuss it together."

"I need time alone."

Resheph put his hands together and lays his cheek on them. "Then I will be as quiet as a lizard asleep in the sun."

We continue past the rocky area to the grassy terraces. He never came this way before. Said he did not like it here. A quick peek tells me he is content.

I sit with my back against the same olive tree as the last time I was here. The difference is I have a tablet. The scratchings on it are few, but enough to remind me what I want to think about.

Resheph sits behind me on the other side, facing the opposite way. My hope is that having him out of my sight will give me freedom to concentrate, but his presence keeps invading my purpose.

Little by little my wayward head is pulled back to the examination of intention. Absorbed in my thoughts, it takes time before I realize Resheph's hand is on mine, his touch so gentle I did not notice. He strokes my hand over and over. I try to pull it away. "Please do not . . ." He grabs my hand, holds it tight to his chest, and crawls around the tree his body blocking the moon.

He lets go of my hand and raises both of his as if to cup my face and kiss me. His body is straddled over me and pushes my back in to the soil. Before I can fight back, one arm holds me across my neck. I choke. He grabs both my arms and pins them to the ground above my head. He holds them with one hand. What are supposed to be kisses on my face are bites.

"No, no. Please," I scream. "Stop. Do not do this."

One hand continues to hold both of mine, the other one explores every bit of my body. My back against the grass is the one part that misses the probing. He seizes my breasts and I cry out, then lifts my tunic, and strokes me over and over between my legs and the woman part only husbands see. He pulls my hands down and shoves them under my back. He is on top of me, his elbows not far from my shoulders. I gasp for air. His hand secures my mouth, and he enters me with one huge thrust. It makes me scream, but all anyone can hear is a grunt through the fingers pushing my lips against my teeth.

I dig my heels into the soil, determined to push away from him. He is massive against my small frame. I cannot gain ground.

Each thrust he forces inside, each push is more painful than the one before. I am pinned down and unable to twist or turn. My kicks thrash at empty air. I give up. Grunts, like an animal, are the lone sounds. His final stab feels like he ripped me apart. He removes himself, rises, straightens his wrap, and walks away.

I lie on the ground unable to move, unable to think. I try to take in what happened. My chest heaves and it is hard to suck in the air. He ruined me, ruined my life. Whatever I hoped for is gone. I am now good for nothing.

How do I face his family? Anyone. It takes time before I can move. My tunic is torn near my knee. My face must not give away my secret. Screaming, begging, and imploring, made my throat sore, and my mouth dry. My body is soaking wet. He spoiled me, then left me to walk home in the blackness.

I peer at the sky. "You, who claim to be God. You let it happen. Where is the power I was supposed to have? You made me small in stature so I could not fight the slightest man. Why did you not keep me safe? What did I do to deserve this? Now I am trapped with this family, trapped with the man who destroyed my life."

CHAPTER EIGHTEEN

My hands are around my shoulders as if that could hold me together. The smells he left fill my nostrils. Both breasts hurt, marked by his fingers. I taste the blood in my mouth from his hand pushing against my teeth. A sticky wetness drips down my legs when I manage to stand. Did I bleed? "Please, Eshmun, make me as whole as when I was born."

I grab a bunch of leaves to wipe myself. Blood. From the light of the stars I can see the bright red circle shining against the green. The red that announces my position. If I am with child how will I live? The family cannot find out, cannot see me weeping. I hold back my tears and grab a small rock to wear around my neck in the hope it will push the child out before it grows.

Kotharat awaits my return so we can go to sleep. She will scold me for making them wait. I must hurry and try to be ordinary. How do I explain a torn garment?

· · · · · · · · · · · ·

I limp my way back to the house and my head fills with the words I will need. I am surprised that the family is lounging on their mats still enjoying hearsay. I join them and try not to squirm. There was no time to clean myself, to purge Resheph from my body. If I could wish myself back to the tiny hut filled with people I love—but they would not comfort me either. "And what did you do to make it happen," would be Ima's reply.

"I hope you had a pleasant time." Kotharat glowers at me. I nod and run my hands through my hair. "I needed to study. Abram insisted." Resheph appears victorious.

Nikkal watches her brother's beaming face and turns to glance at me. "I am sure the time was rewarding. Elisha, you are pale. What happened to your tunic?"

"My knee got to close to the branch of a bush. I am fine. Tired." My insides want to throw the last meal back into my throat, yet the lump stays down in my stomach heavy like a boulder.

Resheph smirks. "Did you find our class demanding?"

My attention is on the floor. "The whole day was difficult." If I could only scream out what he did. "I could not keep up with the concepts." He tilts his head, his smirk congratulates himself for being so clever.

These people misplaced their hearts, except for Nikkal and maybe Baal. How will I face anyone? Or sit in class and learn with him? Continue living in the same house?"

Nikkal strolls over to me and whispers. "What is wrong, Elisha? You do not seem well."

"Too much to be done."

"Resheph's face said something happened, but I was not sure of its meaning."

Kotharat interrupts us. "What is the whispering? Are you telling secrets we cannot hear?"

"Sorry, Ima. It is girl talk about betrothals," Nikkal sidesteps.

"We went separate ways," I whisper. She knows that is an untruth.

"Is this how you treat a friend?" There is no answer. "If that is what you wish."

"There is no more I can say."

He betrayed me, broke my heart. No man will want me for a wife. I did not one thing, yet I am the one marked, stained, ruined twice over. A female and a harlot. My dreams are gone and what remains is misery.

I wish to pound the earth or fell a giant tree and crash it into pieces. My chest tightens and forms a barrier. Numb from the neck down. My body weeps for me, it weeps in silence and sheds no tears.

Nikkal goes back to her seat. I need to get away, walk, clean, do something. I sit like a statue. At long last they go to their mats, and I scour myself inside and out. Still not cleansed, I head for my sleep space. What kind of powerful God deserted me and agreed Resheph should violate me? Please, let me not be with child. I cannot cry. Every corner in the house would echo the sound. Regret dwells within me.

. . . .

Sleep remains elusive. It is not long before my curtain is rustling. My eyes open. I am so frightened I cannot move and turn hot, then cold. My body shakes. Not Resheph, please. Not again.

"Can we talk," Nikkal whispers.

I sit up with dread. If I say no . . . "Come in." Will she say something to the family? That is my fear. She sits across from me at the far end of the mat.

"I may be younger, but your expression says you met with harm."

I clear my head. "I do not know what you think you see. I am fine."

"You are not fine. How was your class?"

"It was fine."

"Before you said it was difficult." She pauses. "I cannot make conversation alone." I do not answer. "Did you ever go to the Canaanite Temple?"

"Of course not."

"You could not go inside. Except for the sacred prostitutes, women are allowed once in thirteen full moons. They go to pay homage to Baal, one of the fertility gods."

"Sacred prostitutes? Gods for fertility?" Why is she saying this now?

"Some men think it is their obligation to deflower women, so they will not become sacred prostitutes. That prostitution should not happen in a Temple."

Deflower. She knows. "Do all Canaanites believe so?"

"No. It is a way for a few men to have a woman they would otherwise not be able to."

In the emptiness that follows, I change the discussion. "Your religion has many gods, is it better with many?"

"We think so. Baal is the god of thunder and lightning; Athtart of passion, sexuality, and creativity; and there is El, who created all the gods and goddesses. There are many more."

"Do you know of Eshmun?"

"He is a god of healing and the guardian of Sidon. A serpent coils around the staff in his right hand."

I nod. "Your gods are part of a group. They each have separate duties. If they were put together they could make up one complete God."

Nikkal raises her head. "I must admit I never pictured it as pieces of a whole. You do know Abram's father made and sold idols."

"No, I did not."

"Get a pleasant night's sleep."

"It is difficult, but I will try."

Nikkal gets up and walks to the curtain, her eyes red. She turns her back to me. "He is my brother." The words hold the essence of sorrow. She hesitates as if to express one more concern, then disappears to the main room.

We cannot speak of it, but at least someone is aware. I pull the sleep cover over my head. There is a rumble of upset in my stomach and my head is pounding. My eyes close and a giant animal with Resheph's face is before me. A beast, not a person. The swine who reduced my life to rubble.

. . . .

Four moons passed. Sleep evaded me a good part of each night, and my few dreams were filled with being violated. Mine and other women. Forcing me to live it over and over. Each time I woke up in a panic needing to scream. Tired and shaky, I cannot feel my fingers, my toes, my body. Mine is a mutilation not visible, a wound that is mine alone. A wound that shouts, *I have no future.*

A rock lays between my breasts, or is it a monster? This is not a time for learning. I cannot concentrate. The family must not know I am avoiding Abram's class. I still must go to the well.

For the first time, I try holding one jug on each side but they are too burdensome on my bones. About to move them to my shoulders, I see a bird perched on the ground lapping up water. Its feathers, a yellowish brown and black, are at rest. The longing to take wing fills me once more, to be anywhere but here.

Poor bird on the search for provisions. But I am not like this bird, not free, always searching for how to be. I have no way to spread my wings and take to the air. And where would I fly? I can escape in my head and sing like they do, but I do nothing. The bird flies off and I picture my heart gliding along, higher and higher until we are out of sight and nestled on a fluffy white cloud.

. . . .

I finish all the work Kotharat gave me and leave as if going to class. Instead, I go in circles, nowhere, just wander the outskirts of the city praying those who are friends of the family do not see me. What did Resheph, that bastard, say to them?

I go down the path to the place where Resheph taught me writing and lie down, napping at times, crying in between. Peace is gone.

The sky is filled with clouds playing hide and go seek with the blue of the sky. The sun is at its high point.

"Sandalphon, please come to me. Resheph is a brute, not a man. Why did my intuition not tell me? Why did I not recognize the kind of person he is?"

"Yes, Elisha? There are questions?"

"I was blinded by Resheph's comely features and ignored his faults. Nikkal warned me."

"You prefer to ignore certain instincts."

My lips push against my teeth. "What does intuition have to do with Resheph?"

"You did not pay attention when you knew Resheph said he never went near the terraces."

"Oh."

He bows toward me. "Good. Recognition. Awareness provides you with the ability to identify danger and be sure of decisions. You will be confident inventing your ballads and sure of who to befriend or leave behind."

I will not cry. "So many feelings are mixed, so many reactions I have not yet named. I do not choose to mark them. That will make what happened real. All I feel now is agony."

"Time will heal. Back to the problem. Intuition is real and ignoring it as you do does not help you progress."

"Did I make it happen or agree to it in some way? Could I have done more?" I moan.

"Think. I already gave you my answer. Make your way back to class." The cloud flutters as he floats away.

Resheph is strong and I loved that about him. He turned that love against me. I hate being a woman. A weak woman. Will he try again? If anyone finds out, or if Resheph speaks . . . no one will find out. I will make sure. He robbed me of safety and confidence, and other things I have not yet named. A shiver comes with a memory. While I fought him and screamed with pain, my body liked it after he entered me. Even my body betrayed me.

I lie down and inhale deeply. This time it is different. My shoulders are back against the soil and my hands are turned upward. Thorns seem to jab at the center of my palms, but do not hurt. The pricking ceases and I am peaceful and healed. At least for now. "Thank you, whoever you are."

It does not last. Pictures of Resheph moving above me run through my head. Men are strong. Women cannot stop the violation. I swear no one will ever harm me like this again. I look down at myself, at this body, this thing I hate, this thing that deceived me. I hate me.

CHAPTER NINETEEN

*I*f Kotharat finds out I was wandering, I will be in trouble. I go to class the next morning. At mid-day I return to the empty house. I had to be away from Resheph. Seeing him makes me want to crumble into pieces and bury myself in the soil. Hurt myself so I know I am alive. My arms want to pound the earth, break something, or throw a cook pot. How do I stay away from the beast? Was I stupid to go to class? I cannot accomplish anything, but Abram might be upset if I do not come back.

Two date cakes and I am back in my seat. The only empty pillow is one I avoided. A disagreeable muddy brown. I stare at Abram while he speaks and hear but one word, home. The thought makes me shudder. I do not have one. I thought I did. Where do I find another? I trust Abram . . . Abram. A small ray of hope warms me.

I fidget waiting for the class to finish. My future depends on this. I must be careful of what I say. The other students leave. Resheph is gone. I cringe at what I must do, but it cannot wait. My stomach is wrung out like the wash but cannot be healed by hanging it in the sun. I force myself forward. My hands are steamy. My insides are screaming. I am at the front of his bench.

"I am sorry to bother you, Abram, but may I speak?" The tremor in my voice betrays me.

"I have been waiting."

"There was some trouble."

"Yes, child. Your face and wandering attention told me something was wrong."

I hesitate. How do I say what I need? "I have difficulties with the family that took me in."

"I am listening."

I fight back the tears. "It is difficult to speak of and I am so ashamed."

"Did you bring it upon yourself?"

I study his face. Can he tell I might be with child? "I do not know." Tears escape.

"Tell me."

"I am thankful for finding Resheph's home. I did everything they asked and they were pleased. Resheph's mother added many more things to do. I did not mind, but it was not what we agreed on. It tired me and left no time to study."

"But you do well in class."

I shrug my shoulders. "My work is not adequate. I am anxious all the time and worry constantly."

"Why do you doubt my words?" He studies my face. "What are you not telling me?"

"I will say no more." He remains silent. Have pity, Sandalphon, it is the shame making me lie again. "Resheph leers, tries to catch me unclothed and touch me. He creeps up and it is not in jest. He has been helpful, but that is a trick to make me think the other things he does are innocent. I do not feel safe."

"Safe. Is that the sum of what he has done?"

I do not move. "My future is now in question."

"Why is that?"

"I am afraid to live in that house any longer."

"That is a bit severe. Is there more?"

I can no longer hold it in. "Oh, Abram. He followed me the other night. We were each going to work on a lesson." I take a breath. "He did what should not be done to a virgin."

"What do you need from me?"

"If . . . maybe I could live somewhere else," my voice trails off. "I am sorry to ask so much. I will go." I turn to leave.

"I did not say it is too much. Let me consult with some people and I will try to find a solution."

I walk back toward him sucking the knuckle of my finger. "Thank you. Abram. You asked us to be merciful. But how can I do that with such a deed?"

"It will take much time before that will happen. We can be generous with the person for their frailties because everyone suffers from them. As for the deeds, forgiveness may or may not come later. Can you try?"

"I am not sure."

"Hiding from what occurred does not permit you to heal. When we no longer avoid our reality and choose acceptance, peace has a pathway to healing. Then hurts will slowly dwindle. Take your time. It will come."

His gentleness warms my heart. "What about now? How do I live with this family, go to class with Resheph, be near him?"

"You are in a difficult position. If someone has taken advantage of you, it is not your fault. The indignities you carry are not yours. Let them go and I will try to have an answer soon."

My arms go around his neck and I hold on tight. He puts his arms around me, offering safety, support, and love. I could stay in these loving arms forever. I would go anywhere with Abram.

• • • • • • • • • • • • •

Walking out the door my legs falter. The front of Melchizedek's house offers a place to pause. Home. Was it ever a welcomed word? I would like it to be. Sandalphon takes his time setting down as if to assure me of his gentleness. "I must make my way to Kotharat's. I need to be sure Resheph is not near."

"You had a difficult time."

"I am so glad you are here. Will Abram help?"

"He said to wait."

"If I must leave, what dangers will I face?"

The green in his cloud throbs. "I cannot foretell your future."

"I must go as soon as possible."

"Do not rush the steps. Allow them to unfold and have love in your heart."

I stand and move away. "Love? What will I do if I am with child? This is too hard."

"Take a deep breath." I do as Sandalphon asked. "Will a discussion of Eve be too difficult? It might help with your thinking."

"I am too upset to listen."

"The story of Eve has been misjudged in your realm. Lilith, was Adam's first wife and appeared to the couple as a serpent."

"Lilith?"

"She was jealous of Eve, the new wife, and tried to entice Adam to come back to her by tempting Eve with the fruit. Eve bit into the fruit and they were banished from the garden."

I turn to the cloud. "And Eve was blamed."

"And so may you be blamed for what happened. For this couple, that was the moment they received the knowledge of good and evil."

"That is a gift?"

"Lilith did not know her actions would cause the couple to walk hand in hand, as Sarai and Abram do. No longer innocent, they were exposed to pain and pleasure, the contrasts we spoke about. You too, have left some of your innocence behind and are becoming conscious of the realities of life."

I turn away. "Am I supposed to thank god for being damaged? For being blamed? How does this help? My life will never be the same."

"Neither was Eve's. Find peace. You will also find a way." The green in the cloud swirls as he disappears. Why must we learn with pain? One concern is not gone, my blood flow has not started.

Preparing the last meal of the day gives me no time to think. With that meal done I excuse myself and fall into an exhausted sleep. My dreams are filled with demons and strange creatures chasing me, trapping me with nets, and taking me to a different land.

· · · · · · · · · · · ·

Six cycles of light and dark pass and at dawn on Abram's request, I am on a donkey going to Sarai's tent. I lied to Resheph and Kotharat and told them Abram gave me a special task to be done at a place of my choice. My excuse is somewhat true. Abram's servant introduces himself as Doron. He stays at my side. There are no worries, Abram's servant keeps me safe.

Each lurch of the animal makes me cringe. Of late I jump at almost anything. The sun is at its peak as we draw up to the one tent as far as can be seen. Sarai's servants surround me. They lift me from the animal and escort me to the entrance. I see Sarai and the same feeling strikes me as at my first meeting with Abram. She shines, twinkles like the stars, a most magnificent woman, ageless in body and face. More than that, the air around her sings of peace and joy. I cannot move.

As if my reaction is well known, she takes my hand and sweeps her free one toward the tent. I barely nod. With her arm around my middle, she moves me inside and points to a mat. I sit. She hands me a goblet. I drink. She sits next to me. I stare. She waits.

My fingers move over the mat's suppleness. It is unlike any other I sat on, soft and made of lamb's wool. My fingers wish to dig into it but I cannot command them to do so. Time passes.

"Welcome to my tent."

She spoke in the softest voice I ever heard, yet she startled me. I manage to swallow. "Thank you, my lady." My tone is that of a child. I clear my throat and wait.

"You may call me Sarai. Abram told me you must leave Urusalim for your safety."

Did he betray me? I did not ask him to keep my secret. I stare at the vastness of the tent and its pretty blue and white stripes.

"If you do not want to speak of it . . ." Her voice trails off. It is soothing, but waves of disgrace move through me. "I hope I was not insensitive," she adds. "Abram suggested you join us. We go to Kiriath Arba soon. I thought it was best to meet and get to know each other before the trip."

Go with them. Kiriath Arba. My head bobs up and down. "I would like to go." I force my lips to turn upward.

"Ah. There you are. Now I can say welcome."

I turn away. "I am sorry. Your presence is so strong it took me by surprise."

"And you have had a challenging time."

"That, too. Also, Abram speaks of you as his crown, his princess." What will it be like with the two of them in the same room?

"We will get along well." She sounds sure.

"I think so, too." I smile. "At least I hope so."

"Hope is grand and so is knowing. Be sure of your knowing even if you are not able to speak it."

"Thank you." I sit up tall. "I am sure we will get along."

"Elisha with the sad eyes. Remember you are God's child and worthy of a valuable life. Abram's servant will return you to your quarters." She rises. "It is settled." She moves toward the outside. "When Abram is ready."

I follow her. "Is there nothing more? No questions?"

She turns back. "I have all the answers needed."

We say our goodbyes, and I climb on to the donkey. My wish

at this moment is to be in this woman's presence. She is different from any other female I have met. The donkey rocks, and I call out, "Until the next time," my spirit soaring.

On the way back my attention darts in many directions. How do she and Abram understand people so well? What will it be like doing their cooking, baking, and cleaning? To wash and fold their clothes with loving care? Will she like me, treat me as she did before, putting me at ease?

One thing that disturbs me is the god issue. Abram prays to the Holy Spirit so Sarai also must. Will she try to change me? Even so, I want to be with her. "Please," I pray, "make this happen for me. I wish it more than anything. Please let me live with Sarai and Abram and have them be my teachers. And—keep me safe."

What if she is busy and ignores me? What will I do farther from my family? Did Abram tell her my secret? There are no answers, yet peace envelops me and my heart soars with a joy I had forgotten. The last time it lived in me was long before the council fire.

. . . .

I am at the house and the family is enjoying the evening breeze. I want to retire to my mat, to be alone. It finally feels safe to go to my sleep space. I stand and wetness runs between my legs. I race to my curtain. My body announced my woman's cycle of the moon. I use some leaves to clean myself. I will clean the mess again later when they are asleep.

. . . .

Many cycles of light and dark have passed since I spoke to Sarai. I wait and wait for an answer and continue living with Resheph. Thoughts of hurting him roam in my head and bring unrest. Sandalphon's muted colors signal his arrival, but I must finish the cleaning.

"Are you troubled, Elisha?"

"The family is outside. Can I clean while we talk?"

"Of course."

"I have been thinking about my parents. I want to go south with Abram and Sarai but is that what I should do? Go farther from home?"

"I do not make choices for you but can help with questions. Do you wish to change your circumstance or stay where you are?"

Questions. Always questions. "What are you saying? How can I stay here after what happened with Resheph?"

"That sounds definite."

"Nikkal does not know all that happened. She is my friend, but she may accidentally tell my tale." I move away.

"What disturbs you?"

"Sadness, shame, and anger at Resheph." I did not mean to say the words and hide my face in my hands. "I was sure I could make him love me. Baal Hadad is speaking to two Abbas for Resheph's betrothal. I cannot live through what will come. The celebrations, the ceremonies, the excitement and joy. If they could know the truth about their son."

"Then tell them."

"They will not believe even if proof is in front of their eyes. He is the son who can do no wrong, the one who is worthy."

"And your anger?"

"I am not angry. I am upset."

"Because you are angry?"

I lift the broom and shake the dirt into a pile. "Are you saying I should be angry?"

The cloud bends. "I am saying you have the right to be. Did you forgive him?"

I sweep another area. "Ima taught me women do not get angry."

"It might be too soon for forgiving. What is next?"

I shrug. "I must decide and send a message to my parents."

"Remember you have choices. You can go home. You have leaves to choose from."

I stop sweeping to look at him. "It is right for me to observe this woman who brought heaven down to earth in the way she leads her life. She can teach me much before I return to Shechem. Abram said he would keep teaching me if he is not too busy taking care of his holdings."

"It is your choice."

"If I go home, I will be unacceptable again. All that will happen is more unhappiness, more disagreements, and shunning or banishment."

"It is your leaf to eat."

"The outcome has been taken out of my hands."

"Are you convincing yourself?"

I do not answer and turn toward the trees. "What I wish is to be like a daughter and help the couple. I love Abram already and his woman is special. That could be my repayment for their kindness. Not in the way of a barter, my actions would come from my heart."

"That is a wonderful idea. Remember the healing of the hands you enjoyed? Why not try doing that after you wake up? And one more issue. You asked me to pardon you, and that is not within my power." His voice trails off and the cloud dissolves.

I would love to do for Abram and Sarai what I cannot for my own parents.

. . . .

Sandalphon was right, the palms up contemplation is a wonderful way to welcome the morning. I walk the winding path toward the spring. If Abram and Sarai will let me go with them, I will be the best helper and say nothing. I will learn everything, think things through, not depend on others, and do whatever is necessary for them to know I am worthy.

The well almost in sight, Resheph comes along on his way to class. I shiver and the need to throw up grabs at my stomach. My heart tells me to send him away but then I might not have a home. Choices, choices. I hate being caught between two things. The elders gave me no alternative when I wanted to stay, and now Resheph stands beside me and I wish him gone but dare not speak the words. "What is wrong with you?" he asks.

His voice is muffled, and his observation disturbs me. "Nothing."

"You jump at the slightest sound as if danger is ahead."

Who is slow now? The threat is you. "There is no danger."

"Say what is wrong."

Wrong? Does he think what he did is right? He knew what he intended. The thoughts make my teeth clamp together. First he assaults me, now he is trying to befriend me as if nothing happened. If I were a man I would . . . "Nothing is wrong," I repeat through gritted teeth.

"Do not hurry. Your tasks need to be done. I will tell Abram you will be late."

If I could hurt him . . . but I can't. If only my abba was here. He would cut off his organ.

. . . .

The filled jugs stored, I am on my way to class. If Abram betrayed me I know of no way to make it different. I will not deny him. I love the man. How should I be in his presence? Treating this as a challenge will help me get through. I must trust that what should be, will be.

The class is excused, and Abram signals me to wait. I have an excuse to not walk home with Resheph. Does he have an answer?

"First let me say you are welcome to come with us to Kiriath Arba."

I break into a big smile. "Thank you, Abram, thank you."

"We will be leaving soon, so gather your things. I will inform you of the meeting place and time."

"I will be ready." I turn to leave.

"Wait. There is some unwelcomed news. Please sit down. A messenger arrived. Prepare yourself." He takes a long pause while my insides turn over and quake.

"Your father passed on."

His gentleness does not soften the blow. The scream from my belly soars through each part of me and exits my mouth. I pound the floor with my fists. This cannot be. Not yet. I am a mess of grief, agony, heartache, and anguish. My insides yell, *He is no more.* "Are you sure? He is too young."

"That is what the man said."

My abba is no longer here. "My abba," I shriek. My fists pound the floor. Tears flow. Abram sits with me until I calm myself. "How do I deal with this searing pain?"

"Pain is as sacred as the most benevolent gift."

"I was right?"

"Yes, my dear. Remember our talk in class about the Holy Spirit providing for us to learn?"

I sit up in front of him, my head on my knees, tears still streaming. "Then the pain serves me?" I look at Abram.

He nods. "Pain is a lesson, forcing us to consider obstacles. If we did not have pain could we enjoy its relief? It gives you the time to reflect by slowing us down. Pain teaches patience."

I look up. "Patience. Another thing I must conquer."

"Patience is vital and is first learned during the nine full moons in the womb. Think of a child when they learn to eat and crawl. How many times do they fall before they walk? They have patience and determination. While the child gets frustrated, the youngster returns to the task composed and single-minded."

"Thank you, Abram. I hope that understanding will make tolerating the pain easier." He makes a tear in my tunic. "Now they will know I am in mourning."

· · · · · · · · · · · ·

Abba is gone, never to hold me or catch my eye and smile. I walk to the center of the city. How do I make the pain better? My heart is sliced open and there is no way to fix it. There is nothing to fill the empty space or take away the pain. Do I go home? By the time the messenger arrived, the funeral rites were over. Mourn with my family? That difficult time is also finished.

I sit on the grass and the sobbing returns. This time body-wracking cries. I hold on to my knees and the tears are in charge. I do not care if the family sees red eyes.

I am still not settled but am at the house. Kotharat yells at me before I am at the cook fire. "What is your excuse this time? You are not here, and you should be. Is it my task to make the meal? No, it is yours," and on and on, with me a sleepwalker unable to understand, and her not bothering to look at me.

"Elisha, what is wrong? You were crying."

"My abba passed."

She catches sight of the rent in my garment. "I will carry on preparing the food. Take a drink and have a respite." Life with Sarai will be better.

CHAPTER TWENTY

Sleep did not come, and I choose to not go to class the next morning. Abram will understand. I leave the house and walk as if in a dream. I wander the city, trying to settle my head and decide if I listen to it or my heart.

What can be accomplished if I go home? I will lose the chance to be with Abram and Sarai. How guilty will I be if I do not? This is my chance to learn more. Going home, I lose that.

I walk in a different direction. After inspecting all sides, the truth of wanting to go to Kiriath Arba becomes clear. I yearn to go home, but not yet. They cannot help me, nor I them. The grief is mine, to be dealt with alone.

I wander the outskirts. There is a future. A new life with Abram and Sarai. That warms me. The smell of cook fires and food being prepared hovers around me. I walked the time away. It takes a while to retrace my steps and return to the house. The sun is halfway to the horizon. I complete the chores and decide that after the late meal is the time to speak to the family. I am not looking forward to a confrontation with Resheph.

. . . .

We are sitting in the glow of excellent food and an evening cool for the desert. "Elisha. What is wrong with you? You could not stay in your seat all through the meal."

"I am fine, Kotharat." Her voice makes something in me change. I am ready. Nikkal notices. Her eyebrows are raised.

"May I speak? There is news." The stares they send give me the message that nothing I say will be of any importance.

I turn to Resheph. "I will be leaving soon."

"What are you talking about?" Kotharat yells. She sits up straight. "No one wants you. Where can you go? You are making a fool of yourself."

I walk to her and look straight into her eyes. "I am going to a place where I will be treated with respect and love."

Kotharat crosses her arms. "As usual, Elisha, you are tiresome. I for one do not care to listen to your fantasy."

"Ima, let her speak," says Nikkal, ever the rescuer.

"I am joining Abram and Sarai when they leave for Kiriath Arba. I will be living with them."

Resheph's face is red. "That is an outright lie." His voice is cold and filled with loathing. "I would hear about such a thing."

"I do not believe Abram has to share his plans with you, Resheph." He thinks he knows everything. His eyes examine my smiling face. His sneer says he would like to shove a knife into my heart. My hand goes to my mouth.

"Stop right here and becalm yourselves. If Elisha was invited, we will find out soon enough." Baal never stepped in before.

"That is my point." Resheph's fist is tightened. If he was closer, it would be in my face. "I would know. She is a liar."

My tone is the sweetest I can make it. "I know what you can do. Why do you not ask Abram?" Resheph's stare is filled with hate.

I stare back. How did he make his way into my heart? He cared for me so little, and I would have given up much for him.

Nikkal comes to give me a hug. "I wish you, on behalf of my family, a satisfactory trip and much happiness."

"Thank you, Nikkal, it is much appreciated."

"When do you leave?" There are tears behind her question.

"Soon. A few suns." I lay on my mat and enjoy the perfect evening. It washes away any bitterness.

· · · · · · · · · · · ·

The past six suns were difficult. Tension ruled the house, and I was anxious to be on my way. My responsibilities are completed for the last time, and I am behind my curtain gathering my belongings. The arrows did their duty and the tan tunic is beyond repair. Repeated washings brought it to an end, but it is what I have. My brown tunic is not much better. Will Sarai permit me to weave a new one? Kotharat claimed her loom was not available. Was she afraid for me to dress better? That did not stop Resheph from deflowering me, did it?

The last time I saw Abram he assured me, "You are not to worry about any supplies. My servants will oversee all provisions and make sure you are safe and well." As if I thought otherwise.

The sack Ima made is all I have. Still useful, I pick it up and my hands spread the bottom wide enough to store my remembrances. Except for Abba and his leaving us, I do not think of the family as often anymore. They are distant in many ways.

Eshmun is wrapped in my poor tunic and goes in first. The tunic underneath should offer some safety from breaking. My most precious possession, the stick doll is next. I wrap her in some flax cloths. That is all I can claim in the world. The sack is lighter on my shoulder than on the last journey.

The shawl guards my head from the sun as I make my way to the breach out of the city. I arrive to see six donkeys loaded with provisions and Abram's belongings. The servants are lined up, prepared to leave.

"Hurry, hurry," they call.

Abram approaches from the other side. "There you are. We are ready. Give your sack to one of the servants, and he will pack it on the donkey." He turns and walks away. "Sarai told me you may share her tent," he calls over his shoulder.

My moment of joy is interrupted. "Good day, Doron. You took me to Sarai's tent. Do you remember?"

"Of course, I remember." He bows in front of me, as if I were one to have servants. For that tiny moment, I am a wealthy landowner with many men to order around and Sarai's tent is my home. I will never feel richer than this. The notion leaves me breathless.

"Forgive me," Doron says. "Abram is in a hurry." He pulls the sack from my hands and runs back to store it.

We start for the south. Abram wants to reach Sarai's tent before nightfall. It is the same trip I made to meet Sarai, but the donkey's plodding does not agree to moving with swiftness. We arrive before the evening meal, eat a light repast, and sleep on the ground outside of Sarai's tent.

· · · · · · · · · · · ·

The next morning it is hard to estimate what is behind me. The line of donkeys grew until the end is out of sight. The men worked through the night. How rich is Abram? I wish my family knew what a splendid life I am about to enjoy. They would be proud.

We eat another spare meal of bread and fruit. I get to the front and Sarai is climbing onto her donkey. A young woman walks toward Abram with a grace unknown to me. Her color is different from anyone else. It is like olive oil shining in the sun, combined with wood of a somewhat darker hue. Her eyes are black and colored on top and underneath with a substance of green. They seem to look as if they turn up at the edges.

Who is she and why does Sarai agree to having a beautiful young woman so close to Abram? My village would be shocked. The woman purses her full lips at the servants, then turns back to stare at me. Her hair, curlier than mine, is as dark as a night sky with no stars.

. . . .

This next part of the trip will take at least three suns. Lined up, we begin the journey. Sand from the donkey's hooves blows in every direction destroying my dream of enjoying the hills and valleys around us. We walk with eyes down, mouths closed, our heads protected with shawls for the women and layers of cloth for the men. The wrappings are no defense. Sand fills our noses making it hard to take in air. There is no way to make conversation, and my head chooses to jump from Abba, to leaving Resheph behind, then to learning with Abram and pleasing Sarai.

. . . .

We reach Kiriath Arba, and my excitement grows. Our arrival falls on the eve of the time ten full moons ago when I arrived in Urusalim and was threatened with stoning.

"Elisha," Sarai calls. I join her and the olive skinned young woman. "This is Hagar, my handmaid."

We bow our heads. "Happy to know you," I offer. Hagar does not answer. Not very welcoming. What is a handmaid?

More oil lamps than could be found in five of my villages light the tremendous blue and white tents that are up in the air. The tents were woven from goat's hair. In our tribe the women weave the cloths for the tents and also repair them. The men prepare the cook fires. At home that is also the women's work. This couple has helpers to do everything. What will I be charged with?

"Elisha, all we have for the late meal is bread and fruit. It will have to do. Let us prepare that. The morrow will be better." Sarai helps me with the preparation, Hagar sits and waits. The four of us sit on the grass and pick at the provisions.

"The men are taking care of everything. I am a lucky man." Abram smiles.

Sarai smiles back. "We are lucky in many ways."

"You are right, Sarai. Many ways."

While we eat, the men unpack and put things where they belong. Sarai's tent is larger than Abram's and bigger than three of our huts. It can hold more people than twice the fingers on both hands. This country girl now lives amongst riches beyond anything I could have imagined.

Something about Hagar bothers me but I am not sure of what. We share a second spare meal in the tent's surroundings, and I am glad when Hagar goes to her own shelter. The servants hang two animal skin curtains for sleep spaces and arrange small slabs of hardened mudbricks in every corner to hold the oil vessels. Three men bring in something large and heavy with pieces of carved wood on the bottom of its four sides and ends that seem to be claws.

"Sarai, what is that?"

"Hagar's father, the pharaoh, gave Abram this gift meant for sitting. Royalty uses them in Egypt. Their name is chair, and this belongs in Abram's tent." Her hand signals the men to remove the object.

Hagar is a princess. "To you, Sarai, this is not unusual. To me it is a wonder."

She shakes her head. "I understand."

The men bring in jugs and pitchers of all sizes and store them in what I assume is the vegetable keeper. Is she hostess to these men and their families? Are they visitors? Shimmering pillows made from rare cloth are strewn about the dirty floor. They are precious and should not be there. I sweep up and put them to the side.

"We had a difficult trip and are tired. I hope you both have a good night's sleep." With that, Abram goes to his tent and we retire.

My sleep space is larger than at Kotharat's and contains a soft mat like the one I sat on at the meeting with Sarai. A mudbrick slab is also mine. My stick doll goes on top of it. Eshmun stays in the sack and goes on the floor behind the slab. I recline on my mat. Sadness beats against my breast. I should be content, but my family will never know about my new life. I, from a small village, with two torn garments to my name, must fit in with these people and their riches.

. . . .

Excitement wakes me too soon. I fly off my mat and run outside, curious to inspect the new surroundings. Abram's land spreads like the desert, as far as can be seen. Not like Shechem, built between two mountains, or flat like my village, but a bit of both. Other parts ripple with endless risings and fallings.

The rumors that Abram was given gifts by the pharaoh must be true. The fields are filled with his servants, male and female. Asses, oxen, and camels wander everywhere. Many herdsmen and shepherds are caring for the flocks. I shade my eyes and Doron, the servant who took my sack, is working with a group who may be digging for a new well. He seems to be in charge. Some women are weeding the vegetation. Children are frolicking and yelling to each other, having fun.

My first task is the meal. Sarai is awake. "Is there anything special you want me to prepare, Sarai?"

"We are still not organized so it will be bread and fruit."

She and Abram eat with no conversation. They are prepared for the efforts they must put forth. We finish eating, and they are ready for visitors. The servants sent out a signal that they are home and people lined up well before dawn to consult with them.

My next task is the preparation of an offering for Abram and Sarai's guests. We never know how many people will come, so I prepare as much as I can. On my way to the bushes of pomegranates, I wave to the people who wait for their turn. I notice smaller tents around the outer limits. The women are outside sweeping up and tending the family plantings. They must be homes. More men are cleaning and fixing something so far away I cannot make out what they work at. Abram's wealth surpasses any in Canaan.

The fruits I find are luscious and larger than any at home. It may be the weather in Kiriath Arba is better for their growth. After bringing as many as I can to the tent, I remove the tops. My mother said the preparation must be done with great care.

My hand is in the air, the blade is ready, and my heart almost stops. Which way do I cut? Do I go across the middle or from the top down? My insides turn over. This task may be a disaster. This is my chance to learn from a woman. I must do what she asks and do it well or she can send me back to Urusalim.

What is wrong with me? I did this every morning at home. I slice across the middle. Wrong. Sarai will be here any moment. I cannot let her know. Gathering up the remains, I run behind the tent and toss them as far over the bushes as I can. The morning is cool, but I am dripping and though my stomach is empty, I vomit over the shrubs.

The remaining fruits are cut up and down where the yellow shows. Ima explained that they do not get cut all the way through. The seeds are squeezed out and after draining they go into the chopping basin where my muscles are tested by the pounding.

The wheat, already ground, is in a jug, and I make the cakes and put them into the tabun. The juice sits and the seeds fall to the bottom. The cakes ready, water is added to the juice which is poured through a flax cloth into a large pitcher. We now have juice and cakes. The offerings are ready. The morning disappears like the light that flashes in the sky during a rainstorm.

The next important thing to do is setting up a working tent. The utensils and jugs are washed and stored. The vegetables are cleaned and put into the jugs. Cooking and baking is next, then the sweeping and making everything neat.

. . . .

Five suns passed, and I am now used to the chaotic early routine. Sarai invited me to join her for a respite. The sun is almost at its peak. She is tranquil and it is safe to ask about the vegetable keep. "You always find enough food for your guests, though you began with little. How does that happen?"

"Who told you that?"

"Hagar. She came to fetch the dirty garments and wash them."

"An interesting question and something I do not ponder." She is quiet for a moment. "I trust."

"What do you trust?"

"Not what. Who. I trust that the Holy Spirit provides what is needed."

"All we need?"

"Most of our thinking is concerned with finding answers. We look outside ourselves because we do not trust our own guidance. We have knowledge inside and must learn to use it."

"Like the times I go in a certain direction or make a decision, and I am right?"

"From what you said, I think you use your insight but have not learned to trust it from the bottom of your heart." Sandalphon said the same. "We need the connection to the Holy Spirit, and also the deeper knowing of ourselves." Abram said the same.

"One more thing, if you do not mind."

"Go ahead."

"I have but two garments and as you can see," I get up, hold out my arms and turn around, "this one is not presentable. The other one is even worse. May I weave cloth for new ones?"

"I do not weave or sew." How do they make things? "A servant of Abram's has a wife who is wonderful with the loom and needle. She will make some tunics for you."

"Thank you, Sarai." Those men are servants, not helpers. And the women, too.

Two suns later, the first experience of Sarai's efforts to help the women set the pace for me. The work is hard, but what becomes clear is that no matter how difficult, it is important. I am helping them and they make me feel useful, safe, and protected.

Sarai comes into the tent. "Your tunics are almost ready. They will be here later." A woman arrives when my work is finished. "Is anyone here? There you are. Your tunics." She turns to leave before I can offer her anything. My arm is caressed by the softest linen. There are three, one yellow with green embroidery, the other green embroidered with blue and white threads, and the last is turquoise. I am the most fortunate person in all Palestine. How did she make them so quickly? I fold them carefully and place them on my slab.

I am surprised when Sandalphon arrives. "It is good to be useful. More important is to be yourself."

"Why?"

"I must go, but it is important you know that."

He left before I could ask if Abram told Sarai my secret.

My work done, I go to my mat for a respite. Eyes shut, my attention turns to staying still and waiting. Whatever or whoever helps to heal me kneads my palms like they are making dough. When my reverie is over there is a message. *You do not trust,* it tells me.

"That is true. Why?"

You lost trust after those of your village turned against you, then you were betrayed by Resheph. That is what makes you suspect your secret might not be kept.

"But I try."

Ask for guidance without expectations. Make note each time you are answered. Ask for different things. Observe what comes to you, then do it again. Play like a child, make it a game. There is one thing. If it is not the right time, what you want may not come to you.

Play like a child. I trust Sandalphon, Abram, and Sarai more than anyone else.

"Someone said I am angry. Please help me understand why I never feel it." I wait. About to give up, a new thought crosses my brow. "Why do I cry?"

Crying may be the way you hide angry feelings.

I cry a lot. Was I angry each time?

CHAPTER TWENTY-ONE

The sun just made its appearance when Abram comes running into our tent, his hands on his chest. "Sarai, Sarai," he calls. We both rise from our sleeping space. My sleep cover around me, I run out to find her in her under-shift. Surprised, I turn my head away.

"The Holy Spirit came to me last night."

Sarai's hand goes to her breast. "Quick. What did he say?"

This is personal for them, but where to go? I back toward my sleep area.

"Do not go, Elisha. Your ears may hear this. The Holy Spirit said, 'Fear not Abram. I am a shield to you and your reward shall be great.'

"'Lord God,' I said, 'what can you give me, knowing I shall die with no one to carry on my teachings?'" Sarai nods. "The Lord said, 'Ishmael shall not be your heir.' Then he took me outside and showed me the stars. 'Count them if you are able. Your offspring shall be as many.'"

Sarai is confused. "Who is Ishmael?"

"The Lord did not say."

"Oh, Abram." Fear covers her face and her eyes are wide. "Did the Lord say when we might see our young?"

Abram hesitates. Sarai's face perks up. "No. He did not." Her shoulders drop and she tries to hold back her tears. I am sorry for her. She is older, but am I not the same? She has Abram. I have no one.

. . . .

Seven moons have passed. Abram was away in Beersheba longer than usual. Sarai is finishing her morning cleansing. She comes to the cook area. I smile at her and return to preparing the morning food. I no longer have to grind. A servant does that. If I had my harp, my hands would no longer hurt when I played it. Reasonings came together and I need her opinion, but I learned not to speak. Not until she has eaten the first meal. I work until she is ready.

"Sarai, may I ask a question?"

"Of course. You need no permission. You watched me eat and waited. We must prepare for the women. Let us talk while we finish the offerings."

Embarrassed I turn my back, measure out the flour, and begin the mixing with water. "I came to realize I must change to grow, but how do I think about it?"

"You cannot have a new future by holding on to your old ways. You must decide to change by making different choices. Altering your life is not comfortable to do. You go into unknown places you do not wish to go to but must. You found that on your journey with physical difficulties. Now you must face the difficulties from the sensitive parts."

"How do I start?"

"Choose one new behavior or way of thinking. That will become comfortable and you choose another. This is not a process to be rushed." Sandalphon said that. "Doing something in a new way once does not make it yours. You must do this over and over. What else did you consider?"

I sneak a peek at her as I add the fermented dough to the mixture, cover the basin so it can rise, and set the mixture aside. She is smiling. "Can you say more about life giving us what we need to grow?"

"The Holy Spirit makes sure that what we need is put in our way. Then we choose to do what is in front of us, or not."

Holy Spirit again. "Thank you. I misunderstood. I must get to the tabun."

Listening to Sarai and being one of those who receive her loving way of teaching, makes me think that if she knew my secret, she would not treat me differently. My heart still recoils.

· · · · · · · · · · · ·

Sarai and I are ready to prepare for the days visitors when the flap of the tent opens. Abram returned from doing business. He is holding two basins in his hand. One white and the other black. Unlike wood, they shine in the sun.

"What are these, my husband?" Sarai reaches out to touch them and Abram makes a ridiculous face and hides them behind his back.

"A merchant spoke to me on the passage home. He makes these basins of clay on a new sort of wheel. I am not sure how it works, but they are beautiful and smooth." He puts them in her hands. "Be careful, they can break, but there will be no more particles from wood to worry about."

"They are beautiful but must be expensive. What about the washing?"

"They can be used without worry."

She holds them like a baby. "We will try one at the next meal."

The sun is high and I cross the fields to gather vegetables for the evening's repast. The children are playing running games. I watch them for a while and decide to introduce myself. They see me and their faces change. They stop their play as if they did something wrong. "Peace be with you. My name is Elisha."

They smile and tell me their names but there are so many I cannot remember them. "I did not mean to interrupt you." There is a tune in my head trying to come forth, but I am not able to grasp it. "Say 'peace be with you' to your parents, from me. I live with Sarai." That was silly. Everyone must be aware of that by now. On the way back to the tent the tune from long ago evades me, and I give up trying.

Sarai surprises Abram by serving him the late meal in the new black basin. He is pleased.

· · · · · · · · · · · ·

Many full moons pass, and the unbearable sadness descends again. It leaves when I am excited at something new and reappears too soon after. It never stays away. I miss Nathan. Abram reminds me of him. They are alike, always busy with the animals.

Almost every day, Sarai sits with a group of women. Listening to their conversations, I try to learn her special way of treating them. Like Carnia with Pinchas and women of my village, their lives are centered on pleasing their men with no concern for themselves. The meeting over, Sarai's choice is to enjoy a respite on our mats outside. The air is drier and cooler than usual, and the scent of flowers is enjoyable.

"I miss my family, in particular my brother, Nathan."

"Oh, Elisha. I am so sorry. Do we keep you from going home?"

"No, Sarai. I am not ready. I have been away a long time and it makes me sad."

"I do not know what to say. You are sad quite often."

"It is the way it is."

"Would it help if we discuss it?"

I shake my head.

The quiet is broken by the noise of children yelling. Some rough play is going on. Older boys are frightening one of the younger ones. That child is on the ground. I run across the field and pick up the little one.

"What are you doing? That is not nice. He is much younger than you."

"You are not our ima."

"No, but your ima would say the same. She is not here. She is working for your food." Their faces lay bare their shame. "Do not do that again." A memory flashes across my brow so fast I can catch just a bit of it. I am playing with a group of children near our hut. I go back to Sarai.

"What happened, Elisha?"

"I am not sure. It is not the first time I went to them. Something about rough play bothers me. I had a snippet of a memory but could not catch enough of it to remember more. I have no idea what it might mean."

"It will make itself clear."

"What did you say, Sarai?" I try to give her my attention.

"About your sadness."

"Oh. I never spoke to anyone about that."

"Your parents never asked? Surely they knew."

I shrug my shoulders. "No, never. There is little to say. It began as a child."

We take in the sun's warmth. She turns toward me. "Returning to what we were saying, I have been wanting to tell you how grateful I am you are with us, Elisha. I do not know how I managed before you came."

"Thank you for your kind words." I enjoy her remark.

. . . .

I have not tried to create a song or sing since Urusalim. That makes me sad. My songs are a need, not a want. My time is spent observing Sarai and being in her presence. I am able to ask her anything. I love to hear the nurturing words she speaks to Abram and see the devotion she conveys to each person with every glance.

Two moons ago, I questioned Sarai. "You pour your love on everybody and all you touch. My parents were unable to express what was in their hearts. How do you and Abram do that?"

"The Holy Spirit made it clear to me that the most important thing is to love without conditions. Abram and I married, and we promised to love each other that way."

"Tell me about your wedding."

"We lived in Mesopotamia. Our betrothal was different. Abram and I had the same father. We are not brother and sister because we were born from different wombs. Terah, our father, questioned Abram from sunrise to sunset, to make sure it would be an acceptable match. He realized how much we cared for each other, and he agreed. The papers were signed, and we were betrothed."

"Not very romantic."

"It needed to be in writing." I nod. "The celebration was held after the harvest. People came from all over the land, too many to count. There were happy homecomings, and music played for seven suns. We danced and sang, fell into bed, and did the same over again. Food and wine overflowed, and it was joyous."

"Seven whole suns? In my village, the celebration is two."

Her face lights up. "Dawn proclaimed the end of all festivities. We were ready to retire. Abram took the corner of his mantle, held it over my head, and led me to the bed chamber. He vowed that unlike others, he would never take another wife."

"And he has not."

"That is true." Pain clouds her face and I wait for her to continue. "Though that night we promised each other a large family. Many years have passed, and I have not been able to give him one child."

"Oh, Sarai, I am so sorry. I did not mean to make you unhappy."

"It is something I must live with." She goes into the tent, and I hear her crying.

My tears flow for the husband and children I will never have, but my teacher showed me how deep love can be. I want to be like her, pour compassion with the ease she pours wine, teach the way she does. She shows me what to strive for, not to mimic her, but to express myself in a new way. I respect and love her, but still cannot bring myself to tell her my secret.

· · · · · · · · · · · ·

It is difficult to appreciate how much time passed. The sun and stars are in the same place as when God spoke to Abram about stars and children thirteen full moons ago. I am busy preparing the ingredients for the mid-day meal and Sarai returns to the tent. She is hurried, breathing hard, and almost turns over the jug of flour.

"Stay here in the tent, Abram and Hagar will join us soon."

"Of course." The cakes are prepared, and I ready the libation. My head spins with possibilities, not the least of which is the realization she treated me like one of the family.

Once they gather, Sarai becomes the envoy. "Please sit." They make a small circle. I pick up the cakes I made with grapes and figs and bring them over. She waves them away. Before she speaks the gaze she and Abram share could make the sun stand still. It is filled with love and resignation.

"Since we are getting old, my husband and I came to a decision. We came to this land of Canaan thinking that living on holy ground we would not remain childless. Ten years passed since our mission began and still no descendants." Hagar shifts in her seat. "The Holy Spirit spoke to Abram of children but it has not happened. We decided to move on."

She turns to Abram. "I hereby give you, Hagar, my handmaid to carry our child. Hagar, as an Egyptian princess, you are an appropriate match for the father of the Palestinian nation."

My hand goes to my throat. It is not my concern but giving

another woman to her husband is against the desires of wives. My mother said God's plan is not to have more than one wife to one husband, unless the wife is widowed.

Sarai beholds each of us. "My womb is empty, and we cannot wait any longer to fulfill God's promise of many nations. According to custom, Hagar will bear the child on my knees, and the infant will be Abram's and mine."

For the first time, the strength of an army in a woman is before me, in Sarai. My heart is torn for her loss, her sacrifice. For the face she puts forth. Living with her and Abram, I saw the openness with which they honor each other. How many times did she shade her eyes and scan the area to find Abram working in the fields? He sensed that she needed him and would turn to wave, his face a broad smile. Their love made the air between them shimmer.

Tradition permits Hagar to sit on the lap of Sarai as Abram releases his seed. This shows that the child will belong to them under the law, and Hagar is a substitute.

· · · · · · · · · · · · ·

For many moons, I deal with my own monsters. Each dream is of Abraham invading Hagar's body. Every morning I wake, and my body remembers Resheph. I grow cold, unable to move from stiffening and needing to scream. Will it ever finish? It is countless moons since it happened.

The wait is all Abram and Sarai talk about. Sarai is different. "Are you not well? You drop utensils and jump at the slightest sound. I am concerned."

"The consequence of this impregnation has great meaning. I am irritated because I am not sure of which outcome I desire. If she is pregnant, it proves my inability, but if not," she pauses, "we cannot reproduce and fulfill the Holy spirit's edict to increase our tribe."

I am surprised she confides in me but do not show it. "Are you saying it could be Abram?"

"It is possible."

"Where I came from the blame was always put on the woman." I try to choose my next words with care. "You say that whatever happens is God's will. Now more than twice the age span for marriage, I no longer expect a child in my future. You and I share the understanding of deprivation. But I will move on and do the work I am meant to do."

She watches me a long time before she replies. "You are gaining in understanding and the ability to choose your words. You came far in a short time. You are wiser than you ever admitted to yourself." My cheeks are hot. Sarai is as wise as the ancients. People tell of her wisdom being evident as a child. Hagar said it was one of the things that made Abram love her.

· · · · · · · · · · · ·

The evening meal is not far off, and I overhear Abram and Sarai right outside the tent.

"Abram, all I wanted was to give you a son."

"Oh, my beautiful Sarai. Your words say you are a failure."

"My beauty did not give me a child. I would make myself unattractive, scar my face, give up joy, if that will make me conceive."

"You would still be beautiful in my eyes."

"My husband, you are the greatest gift God could give me."

I dash to the opposite end of the tent before Sarai returns and settles herself.

"If I am not too forward, Sarai, how did you and Abram come to this decision?"

She sits on her mat and pulls the covering over her legs. I continue preparing the meal.

"This was the most difficult decision of our lives." She stares at the tent, her brow creased with pain. "We spoke about my inability to conceive even a daughter. Abram asked me to trust God. I told him I could no longer trust the Holy Spirit would provide. Abram was shocked. 'That is the first time you ever spoke such words,' he said. I told him Hagar should be our substitute."

I shake my head. "If that is the end of the story, he gave no answer."

"I needed none. He agreed without words."

"My heart goes out to you for the sacrifice. You are indeed a lucky woman to have a man of such understanding and loyalty."

"Abram knows me well, in any of my moods."

If Sarai spoke out in my village, she would be banished for being insolent and disrespectful. We now share not trusting God. How can anyone give away their strength of mind to something they cannot know or see?

. . . .

Rain threatens the morning. Sarai agreed to have me listen in on her group. There are more women than usual and they sit in a circle inside the tent. Some are calm and others fidget. All eyes turn to me then to Sarai. Are they grumpy because they see me as a mere servant or stranger?

"As you see, there is a visitor. Elisha requested that she sit with us. She is aware of our talks and has had her own problems in her life."

Some of them chuckle.

"Thank you for having me," I offer.

"Last time we gathered," Sarai considers each woman, "we exchanged thoughts about an emptiness inside that some of you have. Does anyone want to say more?"

One woman leans forward. "I do." Sarai nods. "My husband does not speak unless it is to order what he wishes and tell me how

I am to do it. The women have wonderful chats about our children, keeping up our tents, the weather, and what we will do if there is time for enjoyment."

Sarai nods. "At least you have that."

"But he never talks, Sarai. He is like a ghost, never revealing what he dreams, what he needs. Beside food of course." The others laugh, and I join them. "I do not know who he is. Who lives in that body. How he sees himself. He makes me an outsider, alone, and not good enough for him to talk to, yet he is there beside me."

"Any comments?" Sarai folds her hands and waits. They shake their heads and are quiet. Some lower their eyes, wanting to say something, but afraid.

"It is not in your power to change him. We can change only ourselves. That is the work that needs to be done. Did your anger stop you from asking questions or telling him how much he is appreciated for what he does?"

"I think I forgot, I was so furious."

"Try again and listen to his answers. Make yourselves a couple that shares, not sits there and stares."

The woman glares at Sarai. "What good is that?"

"It may give us answers. Also a bit of flattery can go a long way. Give it time and it will happen." The woman nods.

The next one told of beatings for the slightest violation of her husband's rules. Another of a coming marriage with a man she never met. Yet another in love with a man her father will not allow her to marry. Then came stories of broken bones, bruises, being beaten until they miscarried, and one whose husband took the baby and gave it to a traveling merchant and his wife.

Next were tales of being ignored and not useful no matter how much work they did, and virtuous only for taking care of their homes and making children.

The stories of emptiness, abandonment, and desolation birth a sisterhood. As we listen to each one's anguish, we laugh and cry.

Sarai gives the women encouragement and reflects back to them their ability to listen and love.

When they are complete, Sarai goes to the tent opening. "It stopped raining. We can go outside for our ending." The women draw pictures in the damp sand representing their regrets. They make a ceremony of walking in a circle to see what each one drew. With arms raised and hands open, they consent for the wind to blow the pictures away. They return to the tent with their faces radiant. The gift is not just from the experience, but also from Sarai's words and kindness, from her ability to make them feel accepted by the way she beholds them.

They pray and bless each other for their lives as women. The group ends with a joyous dance. "Goodbye, and thank you for allowing me to join you," I say as they leave. Sarai says her farewells and whispers something to each woman.

They are gone, and we decide to recline in the cool breeze. Their tales were not easy to hear.

"As a child, my dreams were filled with finding a man who would look at me with love in his eyes. His father and mine would bargain for a bride gift. We would have brilliant children and be happy. That is what lived in my heart," I muse out loud.

"That is true of most females."

"What did you whisper in the women's ears?"

Sarai smiles. "It was something personal to let them know they were heard."

"The women back home and the ones you speak to never realize their dreams."

"Alas, not. They carry heavy loads, the rules of their communities, the instructions of their husbands, abandonment, being hurt or ignored. Their hearts close to the beauty inside of them, and they become what is expected. They bury themselves in what they are told is their obligation."

"I listened to their stories and my heart was stirred. I long to help or at least cry for them."

"We cannot take their troubles away, but we can try to help them carry their burdens."

I turn to Sarai. "That is true. Something you said is troubling me. Can we speak of it now? If you are too tired—"

"I can always listen."

"You told me the story of your wedding and said you could not give Abram even a daughter. Why did you say it that way?"

"A son is important to a man. Children are known through their father's name. But a male carries on the father's work, while the female goes to her husband's house."

"My thinking caused me to question that. Does it not demean a female to be considered disposable?"

"It does for some. The female must build a relationship of mutual respect for herself and her husband."

I shake my head. "That is not fair. It places the burden on her. Men do not listen. They are in charge. You are aware of that."

"You are right. I do not have the answer. It can be done and perhaps it will happen in the future. I am fortunate. Abram is a unique man. Now I need some stillness."

She goes back into the tent and Hagar appears as if from nowhere. Her face tells me she is up to her tricks. "Who do you think you are? Sarai?"

"So, you eavesdrop also?"

She continues as if I did not speak. "It is obvious you would delight in becoming Sarai and do you desire her husband, too? You are not clever enough and your faith not as divine. Do you think she will allow you to teach her women? You are an uneducated inferior from the country, too afraid to speak up and too foolish to have the right words."

She disappears as she arrived. She is wrong, but her words hurt.

· · · · · · · · · · · ·

When the next group is complete, we relax in the sun. "Sarai, I am thinking about the women."

"The women were able to conquer their fears through female companionship and hope. A settlement comes anytime we can understand ourselves a little more."

I bite on my lower lip. "I will try to work on that."

"Trying is not choosing. Decide what you will do."

"You told me that once before, but I can hear you now. Those women's lives are hard. It is easy to appreciate why they have trouble with gratitude."

"But Elisha, the most unfortunate person can have something encouraging. It can be difficult to find, but there is the sunrise, the sunset, the stars or being alive to suffice. What if I propose we be grateful for things which make us angry?"

I sit back. "Why?"

"What if someone cheated you? What could you find to be grateful for?"

"I would be indignant."

"Could it remind you not to be like that person? Not to cheat, not to do wicked things?"

"I could be grateful for the reminder. Sandalphon said that gratitude is important."

"We can be offered many different leaves." We stare at each other and then share a good laugh. She remembered what I told her Sandalphon taught me. Sarai continues, "We must choose which ones to eat. Lessons become a sort of loving relationship like we have with friends, or between a man and a woman."

"I would not know."

"I am sorry, Elisha. I did not mean to hurt you. Perhaps in the future. You are still young."

"I am no longer young, nor a flower to be plucked, but I am content. Sandalphon said females are marred before we are born. His meaning was clarified by those women's stories. They helped me recognize what being damaged means for a female's life. Thank you for agreeing to have me listen to the group."

I wait as she hesitates. Will she question my words? I go into the tent to bring her something to drink.

I come back and Sarai is laughing. "I love using leaves to describe making a choice. You help in a way that allows me to do my work with no difficulty. I appreciate it."

"My wish is to ease your burden."

I can no longer hold my tongue and turn to her. "Why does Abram not teach me? Did I do anything to anger him?"

"I do not think so, but you must ask him."

. . . .

The visitors never stop coming. Some days Sarai has different women who come alone. I prepare their drinks and cakes and clean up after they are gone. She just ended another group meeting, and I go into the tent and hand her the persimmon tea she loves. "Thank you, Elisha. I did not expect this to be such a difficult meeting."

"I could not avoid overhearing some of it. This group was able to name what their inside feelings were. Sandalphon said I need to name mine to make my songs better."

She takes a sip. "He is right. Until we know what we feel, we do not know ourselves."

"Is that what brought the women the peace and joy on their faces?"

"We are grateful any time we find joy. I must rest."

Her gentleness with this difficult topic leads me to think that if she knew what happened, she would not judge me. She walks to her sleep space, her steps difficult as if she has taken on the burdens of the group. She said the desire to focus gives her energy. Is this group different or is Hagar, that viper, the problem? I need to decide about my secret and understand what Hagar already knows about me.

Could I have been asleep all this time, unaware of what was going on? Men are educated and do what they want. Women tell of assaults and attacks and being made to obey. They numb their feelings to escape the pain and go on. Some husbands confuse them by making them do something and then punishing them for it. I had Sandalphon and Nathan to lean on. They have no one to help. How will Sarai move them from bitterness to compassion?

I am not like those women. I will never succumb to a man.

CHAPTER TWENTY-TWO

The next morning, I wake while it is still dark. The memory of my harp makes me want to cry. It has been so long. My harp was a need.

The cloud sets down near me. "You are right. Your passion for what you are doing and learning makes you feel more than you are used to. It drives you to find, to go, to understand."

"Sandalphon, I am so glad you are here. You have blue in your cloud. It is beautiful."

"I want to say that you are doing extremely well. You will not be needing me for a long time and I must move on to others. Remember to speak up, wrap yourself in love, and ask your heart what to do."

He is gone before I can speak. My passion is music, and I have ignored it. There is a small place, very private, not too far away that I remember seeing. I run to it and hope no one will hear me. While the sky grows hazy and dawn colors begin to show, I sing undisturbed and it brings peace, a smile from the inside, and the finish is a readiness to do my duties with enthusiasm.

Almost back at the tent I see someone walking toward me. It is Sarai. Why is she up so soon? "Sarai, is something wrong?"

"Someone woke me with their singing. Was that you?"

My insides turn cold. I cannot lose her. "Yes, sorry I woke you. I did not know you could hear. I will not do it again."

"You did not wake me, and I would like to hear more. You have a splendid voice."

"Excuse me, but what are you saying?"

"You sing and the music moves through you but it also goes out for others to take it in."

I want to chew my hair. "You are sure I did not wake you?"

"I am sure. Collect yourself and listen." I drop onto the sand ready for a tirade. "Though we do not think about it, words express both ideas and feelings."

"Words? Feelings?"

"That is why they are important. They help us to understand and think." My insides are twisting, swirling. "Music helps to rouse the heart and inspire it. Tunes must be chosen to reflect the feelings of the words. They work together and the hearer can experience a release leading to an understanding and perhaps their own creativity."

"Is that true?"

"Would I tell you otherwise?"

Heat crawls up my face. "I am sorry to . . ."

"Do not be ashamed." Sarai laughs. "It is a surprising concept for you. Now, will you do what I ask?"

I am ready to run. "The offerings will be ready as fast as I can make them." I turn to rush to the cooking area.

"Stop! I meant for you to sing as much as you want, all the time, anywhere."

I turn to her. Tears are in my eyes. "Yes, I will obey." I scuttle away. Freedom to sing, to compose. I could not have asked for more.

· · · · · · · · · · · ·

Two suns pass and Hagar decides to parade herself around the community. With his hands clutching Sarai's waist, Abram succeeded in inseminating her. To Sarai, this proves beyond any doubt, that she was the problem.

It is soon after the morning meal, and Hagar is yelling as she walks. "I am more of a woman and more blessed than Sarai. I am pregnant while Sarai cannot manage this simple duty."

Sarai continues to treat her well and induces the women to call on Hagar. Hagar's air of superiority and the words she spreads causes a cry of indecent remarks toward Sarai. While Hagar spreads her venom, goading the women toward her thinking, Sarai is gracious, at least to the outside world.

Hagar takes to speaking with the noblewomen visiting Sarai. I heard her say, "Do you wish to have as a leader this unworthy woman who cannot conceive? If she were righteous, would she be barren?" Another favorite was, "What do you think of a just woman who could not become pregnant for her many years with Abram, while I became pregnant in one time?" She boasts to any who can hear and does all she can to defame Sarai's unsullied name.

· · · · · · · · · · · ·

The dry season is upon us, and I am at the well. Hagar sneaks up behind me. The jug is filled to the top, and she jiggles my elbow from side to side so I am wet from head to toe. She whispers in my ear. "I know. It is Sarai you love. You watch my every move when I am cleaning and folding her clothes." Her implication is outrageous. "I told you I would be Abram's and you have no chance."

I turn to face her. "You are not his wife. You are a mere surrogate. You are also a viper, but you will not bite me." I cannot hold back and throw enough water to drench her. I refill the jug and smile all the way back to the tent.

Whenever Hagar catches my eye, the message in her stance says, *You poor thing, you lose, and I win out.* But she does not come near me.

We three are often in the tent together. Sarai might ask, "Hagar, have you done the washing?" Hagar would not answer. "Hagar, have you done as I asked?"

"Yes, Mistress, I became pregnant just as you wished."

Sarai does not fuss and fume in front of Hagar. But when she leaves our tent Sarai shows her fury. "How did I become reviled in her eyes? Should I get drawn into speech over the words of such a wretched creature?"

"I am sorry, Sarai. Is there anything I can do?"

"There is nothing to be done, Elisha. At least, not yet."

We are alone in the tent preparing the meal and Sarai scrubs the two basins so hard they could break. Another evening she stirs the pomegranate drink with such vigor it turns over and drenches the floor. Problems, mine or others, big or small, make me feel powerless. How do I offer her comfort?

Abram worries about his wife and is cranky with Hagar for the trouble she is causing. He questions me when we are alone in the tent. "You know Sarai well. What is wrong?"

"I am not positive, but I am somewhat certain she blames herself for not conceiving."

"It was my conclusion also. Thank you. I will speak with her."

"Abram, may I ask you something?"

His look is filled with curiosity. "Of course, you may always ask."

"You said you would continue to teach me and it has not happened. Do you not wish to do so?"

"Oh, Elisha," he laughs. "How can you think that? I assumed you would realize it is more important for you to learn from Sarai. She can teach you in a way I cannot as a male. She tells me you are doing well."

"Thank you, Abram. Now I understand, and my heart is settled."

· · · · · · · · · · · ·

The first meal was over a while ago, and I am alone in the tent. Sarai went to Abram and did not return. I take a long time making the breads so I can wait for her. They are almost ready when she appears and seems more resolved. I am relieved. "Many things Abram revealed have quieted my concerns about Hagar. We will see what the future brings."

The future is no better. Hagar's words bite like a snake. No sign of envy or anger is displayed by Sarai. Hagar remains poisonous and arrogant. She does not realize how this couple is different. Sarai and Abram discuss business and personal concerns. They consider themselves equal partners. It does not take much more time before Sarai can tolerate no more. She engages Abram in another discussion. What would my ima think of her taking the lead? Sarai is in Abram's tent for a long time. She returns smiling and the tension is gone.

Before the sun goes down, Hagar quits her tent.

· · · · · · · · · · · ·

It is dawn. It rained during the darkness and the grass will be wet, but I go out on a search for the next meal. My apron is filled with lentils and barley when I hear the children across the field making raucous noises as if they are fighting. I drop the corners of my apron and run. The children are in a circle and their heads are bent. There is a different young child in the middle. I watch them draw closer and closer chanting the familiar na, na, na, na, na, na. They are hitting the child with their hands.

"Stop, stop," I yell. They do not hear. I reach the circle. "Stop," I scream. "Do not do that. Stop, I said." I attempt to separate them. Tears are in my eyes. "You promised not to do this. You are terrifying her. Look and see what you do to her?" The child looks like me. "You do not like being afraid, so do not scare anyone else."

"Elisha. It is not a girl."

How can it be? The children must think I am crazy. "My mistake. Promise this hurting each other will never happen again." They nod.

I walk back across the field baffled. Not a girl. With each unsteady handful of lentils and barley I place back in my apron, the chant pounds in my head. My whole body is wobbling. I drop the few vegetables I pick up. Why do I keep going to the children? That little boy looks nothing like me. A picture forms and I close my eyes.

I am in the middle of a circle. The children close in on me. My arms are raised to protect my head and face. They are beating me with sharp rocks. They shriek and the na, na chant is in my ears. Their fists fly over my stomach and head, trying to reach my face. I cry. They hit me with their hands, then with fallen branches from a tree. I squeal with pain, afraid they will not stop until they kill me. A woman comes to my rescue.

I never told anyone. I forgot. But I remember now. Being overpowered. Sure I would not survive. That was why I was afraid of my friends.

I tug at my hair trying to decide if I should chew when my cloud settles down right next to me. "That was a difficult memory. They did not treat you well as others have also done."

I hold back tears. "Sandalphon, you came back. That is true. At times, life has not been easy."

"Did this teach you anything?"

"Teach me? No." He does not say a word. "I guess it should have, but I do not know what."

"You pretend to protect yourself by not thinking things through."

"I am too upset to think. Please help me." Again he does not speak.

I take time gathering up my apron and collecting more food. "Did the children hear the villagers say I was evil and not wanted?" He will not answer. I must think. "I was an example of what could happen to them. That made them afraid. They decided to solve their anger and fears by beating me."

"Excellent. There are different paths in life. One is fear, another is love. Show love for others and yourself, for living in fear is most painful."

"Thank you for my lesson," I call after him.

CHAPTER TWENTY-THREE

The first meal is finished. "Sarai, are you ready for a question?" She nods. "I woke up to a picture of you ready to light a lamp."

"Picture? That is strange."

"It made me remember that in our village the smallest thing was precious. We lit oil lamps if it was too dark in the hut and on the Sabbath. I understand that you and Abram are able to have anything you need, including oil, but why do you light the lamps every night?"

The smile embraces her face. "They are a symbol of God's light and how it shines down on us. He answers my prayers, provides me with oil, and gives me the strength to stand beside my husband through every test. It is the chance to bow my head in thanks."

"I wish I were . . . No, I want to be as trusting as you. I am not sure God is there, and have a difficult time believing it is he who gives me what I need."

Her hand is on my shoulder. "When you do, you will find the joy that comes with appreciating it."

"I hear you, Sarai, and I promise to think about—do it." I said that to please her.

The sun is not quite high and Hagar appears, dusty from her travels. We are astounded. Abram takes her to his tent and speaks to her at length, then comes to us to recount her story.

"Hagar went into the desert on the path to Shur. An angel appeared when she stopped at a spring. He decreed she must submit to her mistress. 'Return to Sarai without fear, and I will grow your descendants so that they shall be counted for a multitude.' Then he said her son is to be called Ishmael." Hagar no longer spoke of the Holy Spirit. She calls her god El Roi, the Seeing God.

My heart goes out to Sarai. Hagar will have the son Sarai wants. Will they fight over the child? Hagar's presence continues to brings chaos and disorder. She complains about discomfort from the pregnancy to any who choose to listen. It was not difficult having to do Hagar's chores as well as mine while she was gone but having her back meant I could take care of something I want to do.

When I have time alone, I go outside. The men built an altar for Sarai, and I want one of my own. I wander around Sarai's tent and then Abram's. There is nothing of interest, so I move farther away. A tree branch fell in the night, and I break off a stick that resembles an arrow or a flock of birds flying. I stroll until a rock small enough to fit the palm of my hand sparkles in the sunlight. Picking it up, a carving of the sun is on its face. I carry my treasures back to the tent. I add the arrow and sun rock and stare at the new collection.

The display makes me happy, different, transformed, accepted. I understand with sharpened awareness that I do not value Sarai as I used to. She will not judge me. My shame rules me. Not sure I can speak the words, I feel more a woman of courage.

. . . .

Hagar continues badgering Sarai. Abram cannot help. One evening as the preparation of food is underway, Sarai finds some peace. She helps prepare the food as she used to, and we are ready to eat. The women are calling for help. Hagar is ready to birth Ishmael. Sarai with her strength and nimbleness is faster to her tent than I am.

Hagar is squatting over the hole and breathing hard. The women gather and are on every side to support her. The birth is quick and easy. Sarai washes the baby with warm liquid and salt. The oil to soothe his skin is rubbed all over and he is wrapped in strips of swaddling. She hands the bundle to me, and I raise my eyebrows in question. She answers with a nod toward Hagar, and I put the little one to his mother's breast.

I watch the two women. Sarai comes to Hagar's side. "We have been blessed with a healthy baby boy." Sarai shows no hint of anger or jealousy in her voice. At the age of eighty-six, Abram has his son. The oil lamp that burned down in celebration of the birth goes into my apron to become part of my altar. No one else wants it. We leave the new mother to care for her child.

I add Ishmael's candle to my collection and wave the flames over my head the way Sarai does for Shabbat. It does not matter if my prayers are perfect, what matters is the intention, but I am still nervous. "Dear whoever you are, please help me to be a better person and tell me if I should be composing. My last attempt was not adequate, but as of late the urge to make up songs and sing came back. Is that what I am supposed to do? Please let me know and I am grateful for your help."

· · · · · · · · · · · ·

Through the years of watching Ishmael grow up Sarai changes. Did Abram see it? She moves through her daily work like a soldier in armor, sludging through the desert sand. As if her heart was removed from her chest, and she is to blame for the happenings with Hagar. Her head hangs as if to say, *The Holy Spirit will never allow me to conceive.* Her light returns when she sits with the women who come for advice. When she does not feel well, she has gained enough trust to let me meet with them. Sandalphon told me that if I was a gentle speaker like Sarai the women would be more attentive. He was right.

Hagar decided she is now a prominent person and develops an unsuitable haughtiness. She wishes one and all to acknowledge her status as higher than Sarai's. She condemns Sarai for not having a son by parading Ishmael everywhere.

Sarai returns to dullness. She fulfills her duties, but during our time alone she lets down her protection. "I do not know what to do. Abram is growing closer to Hagar. She is the mother of his child. She is back to her old ways of defaming me and urging people to think of her as his wife."

"Can you speak to Abram?"

"Abram makes sure to listen to my complains and do not suffer too many indignities. But that is all."

"Is there anything I can do?"

"Thank you, Elisha, but no there is not."

I decide to speak up. "Sarai, I know how difficult it has been, but I see you wavering. You say you walk with your God, but there is a part which disregards him with dullness."

"You misunderstand. God is always in my heart. I never ignore him. Inside us there is a place in the pit of our existence meant for healing. It is the same place where we attempt to settle and reconcile our problems and resolve feelings about the people concerned."

"I think I have been struggling to do that since I left my tribe."

"It often takes a long time."

I go to sleep, thinking Sarai and I are not so different. As people, all humans share some similar experiences and feelings, but I do not believe in the Holy Spirit.

CHAPTER TWENTY-FOUR

Everything is cleaned and put away. Abram left at dawn for Beersheba. These days he goes there often. There are no groups or women coming. After attending to my altar, my heart encourages me to unburden myself. Sarai is thoughtful and I am not sure of how she is feeling. My insides are curdling, but I must speak now. My body is tense, and my stomach is angry at the meal I forced into it.

I gather the courage and determination to approach her. "May I please speak with you?"

"Elisha, why so formal? Many moons passed since you asked me like that. Your face is ashen. What is wrong?"

"This is the most difficult thing to speak of."

She takes my hand. "We have plenty of time. Shall we rest?" She pulls me to the mats.

I swallow hard. "You spoke of a healing part. In my belly, I know I am not whole. I hope that by speaking of the problem, I can be."

"You do not have to whisper. Whenever you are ready."

"If I do not say it now it may not happen." Sarai remains silent. "Long ago I went to speak to Abram in Urusalim. I tried to avoid telling him everything that happened to me. He pushed me to say it out loud." My chin shakes so hard that my words are garbled. "The son who lived in the house, he . . ." My tunic is wet with perspiration. "I was a virgin and he spoiled me forever."

Sarai's fingers cover her mouth. "I am so sorry, Elisha. I have appreciated for some time your sensitivity and deep-seated hurts." Her compassion warms me.

"He went to class with me, Resheph. I am surprised I can speak his name. He would be nice, then turn mean. Young and uneducated in these affairs, I was afraid to challenge him for fear he would toss me away. My heart told me he could change, and we would be happy together. I loved him and thought he loved me. I was so wrong."

"Elisha," Sarai's voice is hushed and filled with tears, "there are many ways we can be betrayed, but this is horrifying and the most unbearable."

"It is still hard to speak that word. Under the pretense of working on one of Abram's assignments, he reached around and held my hand. He held it so tight I could not pull away, and then he did it."

"Dear girl, you are brave for telling me. Thank you. You hinted at this once before. Your honesty touches me. What can I do to help?"

"I do not know. Your kindness is enough for now."

"I am here any time you wish to talk, or if you need anything else from me. Will you permit me to hold you?"

She reaches over, and I throw my arms around her. It takes time to weep away the many years of self-imposed silence.

． ． ． ． ． ． ． ． ． ． ． ．

I wake before dawn, leave the tent, and my go to my corner to enjoy the stillness. I hope to find a new song. Abram is walking from the horizon toward me. By now I know his disposition. He spoke to the Holy Spirit on his way back from Beersheba. I hurry inside to let Sarai know. She waits for him at the entrance to his tent.

I cannot hear the words that pass between them and busy myself cleaning. I am about to put the broom aside and find them coming into our tent.

"Elisha, please join us. Abram has news to share."

His face radiates joy. I put the broom away, and we make ourselves comfortable on the mats.

"I am blessed. God spoke to me again. He declared me a prophet, and I threw myself down on my face. 'You shall no longer be called Abram,' he said, 'but your name shall be Abraham. I will maintain an everlasting covenant with you and your offspring throughout the ages.' Then he told me, 'Such shall be the covenant you are commanded to keep. Each male among you shall be circumcised, and throughout the generations every male shall be circumcised at the age of eight suns. My covenant shall then be marked in your flesh.'"

"Abram. You will cut your foreskin? How will you suffer the pain?"

He voice is gentle. "My name is now Abraham, and the Holy Spirit will help me to counter that with my love for him. But there is more to be told." We sit back and watch his face. "As for Sarai—" she sits up, her back straight—"God said, 'She will be known as Sarah. I will bless her and give you a son by her.'"

"I am now Sarah." She brings a shaking hand to her forehead. "A son by me?" She holds up her hand as if warding off any more information.

Abram shakes his head. "It is true. I laughed, and the Holy Spirit assured me, though I will be one hundred and you ninety, we shall be parents."

They are both deep in reflection.

Abraham stands. "I will gather the men for the ceremony. Please prepare libation and water as you would for a birth."

We gather the available jugs and heat the liquid. The new names are strange, they do not yet fit. I am curious why new names were given. I want to ask her, but the time is not right.

. . . .

Many full moons passed when removing the sand at the entrance to our tent, I hear voices in the distance. I turn to see and three men are approaching. It is late, yet Abram has guests. He meets them at the Terebinth tree.

"Sarah, Abraham has visitors."

"Visitors?" She goes near the tent flaps and looks out. "I do not know these men."

We watch. Still young in his build at almost ninety-nine, Abraham kneels before each man and washes the visitor's feet. Then he ushers the three into his living quarters.

He entertains them while Sarah and I hurry to prepare food and drink. A servant roasts a lamb. Sarah carries the flatbread, curds, and fig cakes we made to Abraham's tent. I am surprised when she reappears and waits hidden in the flap listening to the conversation. She runs back to me, her face red, one hand flailing in the wind and the other covering her mouth to keep the laughter from spilling over.

"What is so funny?"

"Those men," she has trouble getting her words out. "They said a moment ago," she pulls me into our tent, "I am going to be with child, and he will be born within the year. It is the funniest thing I heard in a long time."

"But Sarah, your Holy Spirit told Abraham it would be so. Do you not trust?"

"Can you imagine me with an out-sized middle? I am a shriveled old woman. It is ridiculous. What am I to think? I will speak with Abraham after the men leave."

The three men go on their way and Sarah goes to Abraham. She returns in a few moments and is still laughing. "Abraham said he does not understand why the men said that. He also questioned how it will happen since we are both past our prime. It does not make sense."

"Does it have to make sense if it comes from your God?"

She continues as if she did not hear me or ignores what I said. "As far as Abraham knows, the covenant is the one made near Shechem. He was quite sure that was the one. We will wait for a sign."

Could I allow a God to run my life? But everywhere I go it is God, God, God. Sarah appears to be losing her convictions.

· · · · · · · · · · · ·

There were two women's meetings, one early in the morning and another that finished a few moments ago. Sarah is tired, but peaceful in the fading warmth of the sun. I sit next to her. "Sarah, I wanted to ask a question, but the time has not been appropriate. May I ask now?"

"Thank you for your consideration. Things have been difficult. Please speak."

"Why did your God change your names?"

"Most people think names are a thing so others know how to get your attention. They are not. A name influences the potentials of its bearer. It can change your life."

That is why Sandalphon instructed me to call myself Elisha. "Does my given name, Galina, mean courage?"

"No. It means God is my salvation."

I gasp for air and cover my mouth with the palm of my hand. If Sarah is right, her God has been taking care of me all along. That is the most ridiculous thing she could say.

· · · · · · · · · · · ·

Ten full moons later, Isaac is born. He is a beautiful baby and Sarah cannot stop laughing. The birth brought a joy which comes from a place deep inside. She is holding her tiny bundle and watching his every move.

"The birth made me realize that this is God's way of showing he speaks to women as well as the men. That he speaks to each one of us if we listen." I try to take what she said into my heart.

Abraham and Sarah are charmed by their infant and spend much time with him. I too am held captive by this miniature of Abraham. He is a new experience for all of us.

The next morning, I am outside finishing the baking and Hagar catches me by surprise. "I watch you cradle Isaac in your arms. Do you wish to be his mother? You will not, nor will you be Abraham's wife. They belong to me. You will see. In the end I will have them both." I dare not let Sarah know, but I pray for her.

· · · · · · · · · · · ·

I finish the sweeping and go to my altar. There are new questions and new reflections. How was it possible for Sarah to conceive and give birth to a child at her age? This never happened before. Did a God truly order it? If so, he is the most powerful God ever. If all this is true, how do I make amends for shoving him away? I imitate Abraham and lie down on my face as he did.

"Dear God, please do not punish me for not accepting you. As a youngster I wanted to do the opposite of my parents because they were not nice to me. I loved Eshmun because he was small and not pretty, like me. He was my only friend. When my parents turned to you there was nothing to hold in my hand, nothing to see, nothing to comfort me. Abraham and Sarah have shown me your power and the love and faith people have in you. They agree to monstrous things you ask of them and carry them out even if it means death. But I was too frightened to accept that. Though I am still afraid of what you might ask of me, and I am not sure that all comes from you, I am prepared for you to be my God. I pledge to follow you for the remainder of my life and to do as you ask. Thank you for giving me this chance. I am your servant, Elisha.

"Oh, I almost forgot. I promise to listen for your guidance."

. . . .

Four suns pass when just after dawn Sarah and I are watching Isaac in his cradle. She is doing her utmost to rock him to sleep. "Since birthing my son I have been thinking about creating."

I perk up. "We never talked about that."

"As females, we create life. Creating means a moving onward, a growth and the coming of something new and different. There is fulfillment in reaching a creative dream."

"That reminds me of composing a song."

Sarah smiles. "Exactly. It happens whether it is birthing a child, composing a song, a better way to purify the tent or cook a respectable meal. The soul is creative and helps us grow. If we do not honor our creativity, it will not develop. Then something inside withers away."

I put my arm around her. "You have birthed many things, but this child is your greatest accomplishment. Do you think achievements will come my way?"

"I was born to teach by helping women with words, you with songs."

"Thank you, Sarah, sometimes I forget that. In Urusalim I had trouble composing."

"Why?"

I get up and move away. "I am not sure. I think it was because I was filling myself with new learning."

"Why do you make up songs? Do you wish your songs to be sung, or for people to recognize your talent?"

"Sandalphon asked me that a long time ago and I did not know the answer. I want to make up songs with Abraham's teachings and your wisdom to teach others. Composing and singing make me happy, though some people say my songs are not good enough."

Sarah turns toward me. "Do not concern yourself with what others think. It is your soul that needs to be pleased. Your purpose is different from mine. For countless moons I did not know where Abraham and I were headed. My faith carried me. Enjoy having your faith do the same."

My soul and my music are connected like Sandalphon said. "Thank you for reminding me."

What I forgot to say to Sarah is that it is one thing to be with child. We have some understanding of how that happens. Where does the marvel of how it forms into a human being come from? And is the same true for my songs?

The verses I write will begin with Abraham's teachings and Sarah's wisdom, and arrive as a poet would shape them. They will flow into my head in a flash like a panthera after his prey.

· · · · · · · · · · · ·

If the women come for their group or Sarah is busy or tired, she gives Isaac to me. "Thank you, Elisha. I will not tolerate that woman, the Egyptian harlot, being near my child." Playing and cooing with him is the best part. I tickle him or twirl him around and make him laugh. Those times are great fun, and when they are done, I go to my retreat and write more new songs.

The encounters between Hagar and Sarah grow more and more bitter and come to a climax. Hagar chose to block the entrance to our tent and taunt the women as they arrived. Sarah sends me to ask Abraham to come to her as soon as he is complete with his business.

Before Abram is fully in the tent, she speaks. "I am upset by Hagar's actions toward me," she begins. "They are more detestable than before. God declared nations will grow from your seed. The covenant with Isaac began on his eighth sun of life with the circumcision, though he had no understanding of it. Ishmael was circumcised at the age of thirteen aware of the meaning."

"He is also my son."

"Yes, and God said he would have a nation of his own. I demand the mother and son be sent away. Ishmael should not enjoy Isaac's legacy."

"I feel much distress from your words but will take it into consideration."

Sarai still surprises me every time she lays out her needs to her husband with such firmness.

Later in the evening, Abraham comes back to our tent. "I sought God's instruction. He told me not to be tormented and to do as you wish. You are right, there are to be two nations, but the covenant is with Isaac. That is the promise the three men spoke of."

Isaac was growing into a strong boy able to run like a wild deer and shoot a straight arrow. Ishmael had also blossomed but was a wild animal, always on the move, preying with a need to conquer, destroying everything he touched, running away when called, and in trouble all the time. He and Isaac were true brothers, though the elder often took advantage and made the younger cry.

Before dawn Abraham calls Hagar and Ishmael out of their tent. The entire community is present. "I hereby release Hagar and Ishmael from any form of slavery. I declare this to be right and true forever. All those within hearing are witnesses." Abraham presents provisions for their journey. He is pained. His first-born son disappears from sight.

. . . .

The next dawn brings a dream message. It is time for me to approach Sarah. I find her in the tent preparing for her women's meeting.

"Sarah, I am called to go out and sing my songs for the people, if they will have me. I wish to travel and spread the teachings and join my family once more. Then I would be content."

"Elisha, I too have considered your need to go home. You have become a daughter to us, but we have kept you too long."

"No, Sarah, not too long. I would not be able to do this if I had not spent this time with you and Abraham. It was a blessing."

"Make yourself ready. I will inform Abraham on the morrow."

I am relieved she understands. "One more thing. I want to thank you for what you have given, all you taught me. Your caring ways made this possible."

"I do not know what I did, but I am happy for you."

· · · · · · · · · · · ·

The sun is barely up and we have not washed our faces when Abraham rushes into the tent. Sarah goes to him. "What is wrong?"

"Isaac and I must leave before the next sunrise." He runs away without explaining. Sarah runs after him and does not come back. She returns to the tent the next morning her face drawn. Did she shut her eyes?

"What is happening, Sarah? I never saw Abraham like that. All the color in his face was gone."

"He was so unsettled that I went to him. I stood outside, not sure if he needed me. I knew by his stance that a voice spoke to him."

"A voice?"

Sarah is pacing. "God came again. Abraham would not tell me what was said, but it had something to do with Isaac and he was frightened. I went into the tent and laid down next to my husband. His quivering arms held me tight." She turns to me. "I asked what was wrong, and he lied to me for the first time. I knew it from the way he avoided looking at me. He claimed it was sadness.

"I knew not to question and stayed there until dawn. He ordered two servants who would go with him to prepare the donkeys with provisions." She grabs my shoulders. "Again I asked where he was going. He said he was given a ritual for Isaac to be carried through with haste. And he would be back before the Sabbath. He did not say 'we' would return." Sarah throws her arms around me. "I was distraught and came back to our tent."

I hold Sarah through her numbness and tears. She lays her head on my shoulder. While Abraham arranges his preparations, we mindlessly watch the insects crawling and the sand shifting with the wind.

"Sarah, do you remember the time we talked about a peace which comes with the connection to God. That it is unlike any other understanding. Being in safe hands. You thank God for what happens, what you receive, because you and He are walking the same path."

She moves away. "Why are you saying this now, during my great sorrow?"

"Because of your sorrow. Are you walking the same path now? Why do you say you are not safe? Do you believe God would have harm come to Isaac? He is innocent. Oh, Sarah, I cannot imagine what you feel."

"I hear your wisdom, but right now I cannot receive it. I have not lost my faith or my trust, but I am just a person. My heart is torn open with dread and alarm. Your words were heard and I will ponder on them. But I am not able to do that now. I love you for trying to help but I must do what my heart tells me."

"You do not hear me or what I am saying. Those are your teachings. You say God takes care of everything. Your heart can be tranquil if you will let it. You are forsaking the Lord. I love you, Sarah."

"Abraham and Isaac are out of sight." Sarah is trying to get my attention. "Let us prepare to leave."

Where are we going?

CHAPTER TWENTY-FIVE

We climb on the donkeys, signal away the servants who come to accompany us, and urge the animals forward. We stay out of Abraham's notice, though he is so intent on his mission, he never looks. Two cycles of light and dark, and we are at the foot of a mountain. Isaac is tethered to an altar and Abraham is bending over him. As we watch Abraham straightens up. We see him reach to one side and remove a blade from its holder. He raises it over his head.

Sarah is about to scream. I put my hand over her mouth and point to Abraham. "He stopped and is studying the distance. Something is changing." I whisper. "Abraham is watching the trees. They refuse to bend in spite of a strong breeze."

"Elisha, something is strange." Abraham's donkey backs up and becomes as stiff as a walking pole. He is gazing at the sky. We see nothing there.

The sky fills with a brilliant white light and silence spreads through the area. Abraham raises both arms. We cannot hear his words.

"God," Sarah murmurs. "You gave me the ability to conceive this child, how can you now take him away? Are you gnashing your teeth at me for banishing Ishmael? For Hagar? Do not make me lose my son. What have I done to displease you?"

Her hand goes to her mouth. "Wait," she whispers, "two angels are at Abraham's arms. Raising them. Away from Isaac." Chills run through me. Abraham drops to his knees and appears to praise God. "It is over," she declares.

We get back on the donkeys and urge them to go fast. Out of earshot, Sarah cries out, "Why, dear God, did you do this? A prank, a cruel punishment? For what? To tear my heart out? To bow down to Abraham? I do not understand."

We push the animals to get home quickly. Once in the tent I hold Sarah as she cries and screams at this injustice of God's desires. We cannot sleep. We eat little. She is listless, and my heart goes out to her.

Light turns to dark, and the second time it does, we hear noise. Isaac is running and yelling, "Ima, Elisha." Behind him is Abraham's servant, Doron, with the donkey.

Isaac falls to his knees, grabs Sarah at the waist, pulls her close, buries his cheek into her stomach and cries. We exchange glances over his shoulder. Terror is in Sarah's eyes.

"Where is Abba?" she manages to ask.

"He goes to Beersheba to plant a tree. His hope is that the number of people he brings into his way of thinking will grow as big as its many flowers."

"Take your servant and go to your father's tent. Make yourself clean. We will do the same. Then we will listen to your story."

Isaac gives me a long hug and runs to his tent. We are past the tent poles when I take hold of Sarah and we dance around. "They are safe, they are safe," we cry together, then rush to get a meal ready. "Please let Isaac tell his story. We cannot tell him we were there."

"I do not wish to lie."

"Just do not say anything."

Isaac repeats what we already know. "Please Ima, do not be afraid."

"You are here, my son. No need for worry." She smiles. "I am sorry you were frightened."

"I tried not to be. I knew Abba would take care of me but drawing the knife..." He crawls to Sarah and throws his arms around her.

....

We wake early. No work will be done. We will celebrate with singing and dancing and eat all the sweet cakes we can hold. Later, in the dark, Isaac goes to his tent. Sarah and I walk farther away to talk.

"What do you make of the story, Sarah?"

"It sounds as if Abraham received another message. This time not to kill Isaac. I do not understand what it was about."

"Abraham lied to Isaac and made him carry the tools for his own death."

"Otherwise Isaac might have suspected. Abraham did not know God would stop him."

I nod. "Why do you not trust it was a test? What else could it be?"

"Perhaps it was meant to prove Abraham's strength, his loyalty, or his willingness to do what is asked. I cannot assume to know what God wants."

"It is not a question to be answered. In all honesty, we must be thankful they are well."

"I hope Abraham comes back from Beersheba soon. Elisha. Please stay with me until he does."

"Of course, Sarah, I could not leave you now."

We never had answers to any of the questions.

CHAPTER TWENTY-SIX

Shortly after dawn, a few moons after Isaac's return, I am in my corner. Now that Sarah can ask Isaac for help, I am free to hide and create. Satisfied my new songs are suitable, the first meal needs attention.

When I finish that, baking the date cakes is next. While they cook I walk around the tent. There is nothing much to see until I get to the back. A glistening fluffy white cloud sits on the top. Its purple and green colors gently sway back and forth. Sometimes Sandalphon has those colors. I turn away, then back, to make sure I am not fooling myself and race back to rescue the cakes. Too late. They are burnt. Is Sandalphon an angel?

. . . .

Abraham does not return. Sarah's face confirms her concern. Isaac is young and mends well. Sarah grows more despondent the longer she waits and does not mention my going home.

She is on her mat outside the tent. "Sarah, we need to talk about Isaac. He is not happy sleeping in his father's tent with the servant. He might be more comfortable if he could be close to you until Abraham comes back."

She is surprised. "You are right. I was thinking about my husband and not my son. If he comes into my tent, will you stay in Abraham's?"

"The call is growing stronger. I need to move on, sing my songs, and make for my village. I must try to get home before my mother passes."

Her arms are around me. "It is wrong of me to keep you, but I will miss you so, my daughter."

"As I will miss you." We hold each other for a long time.

"Begin your packing. I will arrange for a servant and a donkey to accompany you."

"Thank you for your generosity."

"What generosity when you have given me so much."

She called me daughter once before but this time she said my daughter. That makes me so happy I want to cry. They are so kind. They gave me the chance to find out who I really am. I must spread Abraham's teachings and Sarah's wisdom. I pray to be up to the task.

. . . .

How to tear myself from people I love. Three suns later, at dawn, Doron is loading provisions on the donkey. He will be my escort until the trip's end. His name means the gift and is appropriate. I observed his caring and vigilance in his ministrations to Abraham and the animals, but this is the first time I notice how the sun makes yellow streaks in his light brown hair.

"Doron, with the two of us and one donkey, the return to Urusalim should be quicker than the trip to Kiriath Arba. True?"

"The journey should go with some swiftness," Doron agrees.

Our trek begins with a magnificent blue sky and light winds. Will Melchizedek help me with my plan or am I making the biggest mistake of my life? I want to chew on my hair and cannot with Doron so close. We do not go very far when without warning, a wall of dirt is upon us. The winds turned strong and there was no time to put up the shelter. Tree branches are tossed from side to side. In one moment brightness turned to blackened night.

Doron pulls a cover from a bundle on the donkey and we lie down and use it as a shield over our heads. That makes it difficult to breathe. Doron's presence keeps me calm, though sand and dust fill the air. We raise the shield to catch some air, but our nostrils fill with the rubble. Dust forces our eyes closed, makes them blink and sting as tears mix with the dirt and leave grimy streaks on our faces.

Nostrils and ears are filled with flying sand. Like a fire from the driven sands any bareness burns our skin. When the storm is over, we are swathed in a crust of silt from head to foot. We wash as best we can and have a quick meal. I search the field for aloe to soothe the burns. Exhausted, we decide to sleep, hoping the morning will be more pleasant.

· · · · · · · · · · · ·

The sunrise is especially glorious. With Doron standing guard, I wash in the nearby stream. The warmth of the sun and water brings relief and one of my songs to my lips.

Doron is talkative while we are at the first meal. "My parents passed long ago and like you, I was born Hebrew. I chose to be in service to Abraham. I met the lady who became my wife." His face changes. "We never had children."

"I am so sorry."

He tries to gain his composure. "My wife passed, and I did not marry again. That would not be fair. My life was devoted to Abraham's needs."

"I understand." Meals give us the chance to hear each other's stories, we have no idea how long we will wander.

"Elisha. I must ask this. Why do you write songs?"

I look into eyes darker than my brother's. "When I was a child my abba gave me a harp and the songs came to me. Now I want others to understand Abraham and Sarah's words. Passing the knowledge on helps me believe I am accomplishing something."

He leans his head to one side. "What about your own words?" I do not answer. "How do you feel when you sing? What happens to you?"

I get up to wash my hands in the stream. "I do not follow the questions."

"You change. Your face lights up and your body becomes fluid in its movements. You bloom like a flower. You are enchanting to view and the sound is healing."

"I sing a song and the feelings in it fill me. I get lost in the expressing of it."

"I am happy for you."

He asked me about my own words like Sandalphon. He said my singing is healing. That makes me think about Eshmun. I search through my sack and find the statue was left at Sarah's. It was behind the slab and I forgot it. Another child will play with it like I did.

The sand is still flying though much lighter than before, and we plod through the dust as fast as we can. The wind picks up again and Doron puts up our small tent. We choose not to chance trying to cook outside and eat a meal of cold food near the flap so we can see. Doron sleeps outside the entrance. The noise of the wind does not allow either of us to get much sleep.

By the second evening, the wind blows with malice and I insist he rest inside. He assures me we will not lose our shelter. He stays at the tent flaps, as respectful a distance as the tent will permit, but my old fears of being badly treated take hold and my eyes do not close.

The winds are less frantic as we reach Urusalim. My stomach leaps all over. We come nearer and I shiver. Am I dressed properly? My fingers fix my hair in place. I remember the location of

Melchizedek's house. My future lays in these next few moments. Will he remember me and what will he think of my plan?

Doron and the donkey wait at the side of the house. I close my eyes and ask for help.

"I am with you."

"Thank you, Sandalphon."

I knock on the doorpost and it seems like many moons until it opens. Melchizedek's face breaks into a warm grin.

"Elisha. What are you doing here? I am glad to welcome you. Come in, come in."

I did not expect such a warm welcome from a man I knew little. "Thank you, my lord."

"Please sit and share the news about you, and Abram and Sarai." He signals the servant who brings fresh water and dried grape cakes.

"Thank you. May I ask for water for the servant, Doron, and a donkey waiting outside?"

"Of course, of course." He nods to his servant.

"I did not think you were aware I went to live with them."

"Yes, Abram explained your difficulty." My face flushes. "Many things have been spoken in my ear and it was told to me in confidence."

I nod. "They are both well. God has given them new names. They are now called Abraham and Sarah."

"How wonderful."

"A great number of things happened and it is hard to know where to start." I offer a short review of the history. "Abraham is now in Beersheba making a sacrifice. Sarah and Isaac are in Kiriath Arba awaiting his return."

"What about you? Why are you back in Urusalim?"

"I came to ask for your help." His carriage is still imperious, his eyes soft and kind. "I wrote songs with Abraham's teachings and Sarah's wisdom. My dream is to use the songs to teach their way of thinking to the people."

"What a glorious idea, but it cannot be done. Women do not travel this land alone, and I do not know of one who sings."

"I walked alone from my village to here. The servant, Doron, promised to stay with me until I reach home."

"That may help but you are not married. I do not think an unmarried woman will be acceptable. But . . . can you sing one song for me?"

"It would be my pleasure." I stand in front of Melchizedek and pray it goes well. "The song is about how not forgiving those who hurt you will tear through your soul. It ends with the idea of forgiving for we are all flawed and do similar things." The song over, he is smiling.

"Thank you, Elisha. It is wonderful. What is it you need?"

"Would you have a way to gather people so they could listen to a few of my songs? I need to find out their responses, then I can decide if I should continue."

His hand is on my shoulder. Unlike our first meeting, I do not shrink away. "And afterward?"

"I want to travel through villages and towns, whoever will let me sing as I make my way home."

"I understand. It would be suitable to start with a small group."

"Yes, that is what I tried to say."

"I will let you know in a few suns. I cannot promise anything."

"Thank you for your willingness."

He scratches his head. "Wait. Where will you stay?"

"Abraham's servant will take care of that."

"If you have any concerns, call on me."

"Thank you. I will."

We say goodbye, and Doron has the donkey ready to move on.

"Where will we stay tonight, and do we have food left?"

"Do not worry, my lady. The tent is safe and provisions are plentiful."

I look at Doron. "I would like to make camp near the boulders where the flowers struggle to open. Happy times were spent there."

For the evening meal we sit between blooms in their fullness and those who spread their seeds and are ready to die. If this plan does not succeed there would be a kind of death for me, a loss of my dreams and my hopes. But I will not give up and allow it to stop me. I will move ahead no matter the consequences. According to Melchizedek, I am to do what no woman before me has done.

· · · · · · · · · · · ·

Doron is setting up the small tent near the plantings. "Come and see," I call. "The moon is right overhead."

"It is beautiful," he says but does not turn his head to look. Men. Too busy to enjoy.

"We may have to be on the move before we choose if the village people come. What do you think, Doron, will it be comfortable enough here?"

"We rise before dawn."

During the trip from Kiriath Arba, Doron developed into a friend. We speak as comrades and share our history. I am comfortable with him. "If we need provisions, we can go to the market in the morning. Is there anything to offer in case we must barter?"

"Yes, we were provided with much." I am well taken care of. Unlike the trip from my village to Urusalim, someone shares the burden. So many years ago, innocence was the one thing I could claim for my own. "Do you like adventure, Doron?"

"I was never an adventurer, except for the times I accompanied Abraham. But those were his undertakings. If I may say, your company is far more enjoyable."

That surprises me. "Why enjoyable?"

"Abraham's interests centered on business. He came from Sumer where he learned to argue for benefits and wares. I was not always comfortable with his schemes and we never had any time for conversation."

"He can drive an unbending bargain. Sarah said so." We laugh. "I am weary. Let us ready for sleep."

With the dust settled, the stars gleam and offer to light our way to dreams. Dreams. This could be the end of mine. I fall asleep quickly.

· · · · · · · · · · · ·

Melchizedek's messenger seeks us out the next morning. "Please come to the house on the morrow at sundown and be ready to perform."

The messenger refuses our offer of water. I thank him and turn to Doron.

"What is it? You are as white as the sand."

I stare at him. My fingers are so cold they do not bend. Ripples of alarm tear at my chest. "His words made it real. The entire trip depends on this. If I fail I do not know what I will do."

"You speak of failure, but you have not begun. Of course, you are nervous."

"It may not discourage me, but it can get in the way of the singing."

"Not if your efforts are on why you are doing this and what you wish the meeting to bring. Picture yourself singing for one person who is taking to heart the lessons in your songs because of this gathering. Is that not what you wish for?"

How did this servant gather his wisdom? His eyes are large and shimmer, their darkness is like a deep hole. "You astound me. How do you know this?"

"I saw how people acted when I used to play the lyre for my father. He sang in our village."

"You play? But you are a servant."

"It was a long time ago."

"Is your instrument here?"

"It was my father's gift and I always carry it with me."

I carried my harp but it is gone. "Do you not understand?"

"Understand what?"

"We could both take part in the presentation. You could accompany me and play songs of your choosing."

"Are you sure?"

A warm light turned on inside me. "I am. It is what we need to do. Like someone arranged it this way. Unless . . . did Sarah or Abraham listen to you play the lyre?"

"No, they did not."

"Then it was meant to be. We must practice."

"There will be enough time."

My heart is lighter and concerns drop away. I can meet my new challenge. "Do you think you could know three or four songs in time for the performance?"

"I am a fast learner. I am sure I can."

"What about playing something of your own?"

"It has been a long time. Let me see what I can ready."

We work into the evening and through the next morning. He is quite brilliant at the instrument and by afternoon we are content the presentation is as polished as we can make it.

At sundown, we knock on Melchizedek's doorpost. "Pardon me, Elisha, but is there a reason for the servant joining you inside my house?"

"Yes, my lord. He informed me he plays the lyre and we rehearsed my songs. He is a wonder at the instrument and if you wish he can play something of his own."

"Ah, I understand. Welcome, it is Doron. Yes?" Doron nods. "Please make yourselves comfortable. The guests are almost finished with their meal."

The far end of the room is filled with voices exchanging the happenings of the community and the politics of the city. Not one raises his head at the noise of our entry. We sit near the entry door as far away as we can for the smell of the food makes me nauseous. Or is it the lack of interest from our audience? Of course, no women are here. Do they not enjoy music? They could bring their wives.

A few men are turning their conversations into an argument. They call Melchizedek over. There is more discussion. Will they not let me sing because I am a woman with a man's name? My sponsor smiles and nods with reassurance and goes back to his seat.

We wait. The stillness is on the outside. We cannot fidget, someone might see. We glance at each other, then turn back. My mouth is dry and my thoughts race. I focus on what Doron said and push the fearful ones away. They keep coming back. I try to fight them but am not successful. My stomach flutters and I am ill enough to leave. Too late. Melchizedek is announcing the entertainment. The little confidence I had is gone.

The room is quiet, the men's attention is on me, and I must begin.

"Good evening, my lords. My companion, Doron, and I have prepared some music for your pleasure. My songs are not known. The fact is, this will be the first time that anyone outside of family and friends will hear my compositions." That brings understanding laughter.

"The words are based on the teachings of Abraham and Sarah, and I hope you take some pleasure from them." The decision to speak brought calmness and the time necessary to prepare.

The small concert goes well, but the end brings stillness ruining the afterglow Doron and I share. With a short time to prepare, our performance was perfect. We wait and wait. Not one person responds. I cannot stand still and grab onto Doron's arm. "They do not like our music." The heat of embarrassment creeps up to my face.

Melchizedek is relaxed and slowly begins to clap his hands. The others hear him and at a snail's pace, join him. The longer they applaud the louder the sound grows. Doron might cry were he not a man.

Melchizedek notices our faces and comes to us. "Gentlemen," he turns to the group, "you heard a presentation pleasing to the ears and uplifting to the spirit and soul. Elisha and Doron would love to sing in your villages, communities, and cities. While Elisha and I take time to talk, you can make arrangements with Doron." Doron catches my eye and shrugs his shoulders enough for me to see.

Melchizedek pulls me to the back of the room. "No business is done with a woman. I should not have to say that. I would have intervened on your behalf, but now with Doron here, I chose to appoint him."

"I had not considered the business part. Thank you. He will manage well."

Melchizedek eyes are set on Doron and the visitors. "He gives the impression of being different from most servants."

"He is. He played the lyre to accompany his father. He could have earned his keep with music but chose to serve Abraham."

"I am happy you have such a man to watch over you. Let me find out how he is getting on."

He approaches the group around Doron. The men part with deference and give him space.

There is a lot of nodding of heads accompanied by smiles. Are they pleasing him or interested? As I wait, the old feelings return. The men came together and have no intention of agreeing to let us entertain. I turn my back and head for the door.

Doron runs to stop me. "Where are you going? The men are waiting for you. They wish to congratulate the woman who wrote the songs. Many have expressed interest. Come."

He drags me back to the gathering. There is much bowing and acknowledging. Some wish us well, others extend their appreciation for what we did. With so many men talking at once my head is filled, and I depend on Doron to remember the information.

"Doron. I am exhausted. Is there any more business you need to complete?"

"The timing is perfect. Let me say goodbye. I will be right back."

I am at the door and turn back to find where Doron went. The men are watching me. I bow my head, mouth a thank you, and smile.

We are not out of hearing and my tongue can no longer be held. "Tell me. Tell me what they said."

"They enjoyed our music but do not know if they wish us to perform. If so, they will make sure they have a home for us to stay in and food prepared."

"You confuse me, that is not what you said before and we do not eat much." Doron laughs. "You are a bad man. Say the truth."

"Each person there stated they will have us come. We need to decide the details and make a plan of where to go first and so forth."

I hold my fist close to his face and laugh. "You are not teasing me now, are you? Every man?"

"I would not tease for something so important."

"But you just did. Doron, what would have happened if the men had to speak to me?"

"What a curious question. Of course, they would not. They would leave."

I want to chew on my curls. "That makes me angry."

"That is how it is."

I throw my arms around Doron and hug him. I pull away. "We do not know each other well, but I am so cheered at the possibilities I had to share my happiness."

"I too am happy. To be able to play my lyre again, and with a talented singer, fulfills the dream I had as a child." Now that it is done, I pray we will please the people who come to the concerts.

Before I fall asleep, Sandalphon's cloud arrives. "I am surprised and happy you came to me once more."

"You are coming into the most wonderful part of your life, free to be who you are. Free to explore what amuses you. Allow yourself to enjoy this time of creativity. Love it, speak it, write it, sing it." He disappears.

CHAPTER TWENTY-SEVEN

We eat a large meal and decide to take a walk before beginning the plan for our journey. On the way back we cannot help but start. Doron begins. "The most southern point is Beersheba and the northern is Shechem, quite a long distance for walking."

"But Doron, we can go slowly. We have choices. And do not forget that once we are in an area, surrounding communities may also choose to have us."

"What you say is true and you also said you are anxious to get back to your village."

"We are provided with the opportunity to do something important, to spread Abraham and Sarah's teachings. I think we should obey. Unless you must return quickly."

"Sarah granted me as much time as necessary to accompany you home. And if we go to Beersheba and Kiriath Arba, we can visit them."

"An excellent idea. I cannot wait to share our great fortune. How lucky we are you traveled with Abraham and know the countryside. I would not be able to even think about it. What about provisions along the way?"

"I think provisions are what the gentlemen meant by food."

"Oh. I was so foolish after the concert."

"The excitement was so great clarity was not possible. I must admit, the evening was delightful."

Is he toying with me? His face shows innocence. "Let us get to the business of our travel."

By the peak of the sun, we have our plan. Doron scratches his head. "If you agree, I would like to suggest we leave now. The journey will take three suns to reach Beersheba, and we would like to spend some time with Abraham. The gentleman from that city assured me they would be ready whenever we arrive."

"There is not much to pack. I like your idea."

"We have ample provisions to Beersheba and beyond."

It is not long after the height of the sun that we are ready to say thank you and goodbye to Melchizedek. He wishes us well, and we are on our way.

We go an adequate distance and after a decent night's sleep eat a simple first meal and move on. At our next stop Doron prepares a tasty mid-day meal. When we finish, the sun is halfway to the horizon. We put things in order and repack the donkey.

"Doron, I know it may delay us, but I am very tired and do not choose to continue."

"We will stay here and proceed leisurely."

We explore the countryside, find water to wash and swim in, cook on small brush fires and chatter without stopping. The way we share reminds me of Abraham and Sarah's way of speaking with each other. We fall asleep to twinkling stars and wake to the rising sun. It is a time of peace, comfort, and freedom.

My sleep is still restless.

. . . .

We arrive in Beersheba and Doron finds the way to our host's house.

"Can you see, Doron, the bottom of the house is made of stones. I never saw that before." And the holes to see out of are covered with wood. Why did they do that?"

Before he can answer our host appears, and as if I am an important person, welcomes me with a low bow.

"Please, my lord, raise yourself. I do not deserve this honor."

Our host leads us through two big rooms, the last one larger than the first. "Welcome to my home. My name is Palluw."

Doron bows his head. "I remember, sir. Thank you for having us."

"I arranged for one room but must ask if you are wed." He looks at me.

"We are not, my lord. We have a tent and shared it with ease. We do not wish to disturb your household or cause embarrassment, but if we are together we can work on our music."

He thinks about it. "If that is your wish." He leads us to the rear of the house and ushers us into another room, a small one for servants.

I point to a strange object on the wall. "Pardon me, my lord, but what is this?"

"It is a lattice window. It can keep the sun out." He closes it. "Or open it to let in fresh air."

"Window." I pronounce the strange word. "What a wondrous thing. I wish my parents could enjoy such a window." That is why the outside wooden holes are closed. They are no longer needed.

Palluw is not comfortable. "I will leave you to settle yourselves. I hope you will partake in the evening meal. We can settle our business afterward."

We unpack our few belongings and lie down for a rest. When Palluw calls, we walk up steps on the side of the house to a flat roof covered with clay pressed down with a stone roller. It is smoother than the floors at home. Silk pillows for seating are in a circle for ease of conversation.

I wait for his woman and children to join us, but no one appears. It is strange for a man to live alone. The coolness up so high is delightful. A breeze comes through the surrounding trees carrying a fresh scent. Most of the time the wind is light, then it blows harshly and I need to wipe hair from my face.

Servants climb up and down the steps, bringing a feast of dishes and libations. The aroma of roasted lamb with heavy spices and the milder scent of fish with vegetables accompany the hearty lentil soup and fresh baked breads. Sweet cakes of figs and dates are still warm from the baking stones. Goblets of wine stay full throughout the meal. At home we have wine after we eat.

The servants clear all but the libation and cakes. "Now that we have filled our bellies it is time to concern ourselves with your visit." Palluw leans back. "We did not know when you would arrive, so no time has been set for your presentation. However, the public was notified, and they await the news. How soon can you be ready?"

Doron's expression asks me to speak. My wide eyes tell him no. "We can be ready after a respite, my lord. Or if the time is proper," Doron offers.

"Very well. By the third moon, arrangements will be ready. In the meantime, you can relax and enjoy some of our city."

I turn to Doron. "That leaves us time."

He nods. "We would like to have a visit with Abraham. Can you show us the way to his house?"

Palluw laughs. "Abraham dwells in his tent."

I join in his laughter. "Come to think of it, I never saw him in any other shelter."

"He lives on land outside the city and comes here often. I will let him know you arrived."

"Thank you," I bend my head.

Palluw glances at both of us. "Is there anything further you need?"

Doron smiles. "Not at this time."

I stand and Doron joins me. "I am ready to retire. It has been a long trip. Thank you again for your hospitality."

Doron sits again. I climb down the steps wondering why he stayed behind. It is not long before he comes into our room.

"Why did you stay? I am ready to close my eyes."

"Because of his remark about marriage, I did not think it proper for me to leave until I was sure you were ready for sleep. And it gave us time for men's talk."

"Good idea." I nod and turn over.

· · · · · · · · · · · ·

We enjoy the morning meal under the trees shading a part of the rooftop and decide to take a day of rest. Abraham contacts Palluw to say he is awaiting us. We send the messenger back saying it will be the following morning. We fill the time with walking through the city, then do our practicing. We relish the wonderful food the servants provide for the mid-day meal and enjoy another respite. We end with a walk around the countryside and back to the house.

The evening meal is superb, but the walks tired me. "Please excuse us, Palluw, but we must practice before we sleep. I hope we do not disturb you."

"Do not worry, Elisha. All is well."

· · · · · · · · · · · ·

The next day Doron and I set out for Abraham's tent right after we finish eating. We are both refreshed after a good night's sleep. It is a long walk for most, but not for us. We come near, Doron calls out his name, and I land in Abraham's arms for a great hug.

"Come in, come in. The sun is high." Abraham opens the flap to the tent. "I will bring drinks for your dry throats."

We wait for his return. Hagar is handing us Sarah's favorite pomegranate juice. The shock of her standing there silences me. It makes so much sense with his many trips here. It is difficult to find my tongue, but I must not embarrass him.

"Hagar, it is nice to see you," I manage to say.

Abraham ignores the surprise written on my face. "Elisha, enjoy your drink."

We chat about our trip from Kiriath Arba to Urusalim, our meeting with Melchizedek, and the small concert that brought us here.

"I see no sign of Ishmael. Where is he?" I ask.

Abraham shakes his head. "He is visiting Hagar's family."

"And Sarah?" Doron stares. "I thought she would be here."

"Do not worry, she is well. I have much business here. Is Doron taking care of you?"

"He is wonderful. There is nothing he cannot do, including playing the lyre."

"Doron." Abraham's scolds him like a little boy. "You did not tell me."

"I was too busy taking care of your other needs, Abraham, and I had not played for a long time."

"I am a lucky woman. Doron now accompanies me in our presentations and plays some of his own music."

"You two make a sure match."

I shake my head. "You misunderstand, my teacher. We are not betrothed or joined as husband and wife. We make music."

"I am disappointed. I hoped that by putting you together, which I suggested to Sarah, we achieved something beyond friendship and business."

My cheeks flush, and I smile not knowing what to say. Doron hides his face by considering the floor.

"Nothing is going on you say? I am not sure about that."

I make sure to laugh. "Please, cease your rattling. There is nothing to tell. I promise."

Doron joins the conversation. "That is the truth, my lord."

"I am sure it is. Do not call me my lord, Doron. You are no longer a servant."

"I promised to return."

"Wait and accept where life takes you. Then decide. I will not free you now, but in the future?"

"Thank you, my lord."

Before we leave, we explain the arrangements for the concert. "I will not miss it."

We wave our goodbyes. "We will meet again soon."

We are out the door. Doron stops me. "What do you think of that?"

"He changed the subject when I mentioned Sarah. Do you think she knows?"

"I do not think so. We will not mention it."

Poor Sarah. He broke his promise. An unusual silence takes over during our return to Palluw's house. Neither of us wishes to return to Abraham's remarks. Is something brewing between us? I never considered that and shrug it off. Abraham is an old man and his mind strays.

The evening meal is not comfortable. Palluw does the talking. He gives up. "Are you two feeling well?"

I laugh. "Yes, Palluw, we are fine. Tired from the walk and thinking about the morrow. The nervousness has begun."

"I sympathize and will leave you to your business."

There is no heart in our practice this night. Our conversations are formal and distant. Even with the window wide open, the room feels stale and airless. I remove my garment as fast as I can and pull the cover over me as soon as I lie down. Foreboding fills the air. The practice did not go well. It takes a long time to fall asleep.

CHAPTER TWENTY-EIGHT

Doron and I are glum and irritable since the visit with Abraham. It is nearing time for the concert and we argued over everything since the first meal. What song to start with, when to be there, and what to eat beforehand so our stomachs would be settled. Most of it was nerves for the presentation, but the rest is the nearness to each other. For me, it is also the possibility of his pressing me for my secret if we become more than friends.

We reach the gathering place, and I stay far from Doron. The breathing practice helps to settle me. The audience gathers, some sitting on the ground, others standing, all catching up on the latest news. Palluw quiets them and introduces us.

The presentation begins with "There Is Always Plenty" and ends with "How Can I Say I Forgive You." In between, Doron plays two or three known songs mixed with a few of his own compositions. The audience reacts well and applauds with vigor. The concert ends and they are smiling. We meet many of the guests and receive praise. Some bring gifts of the fig cakes I used to live on. Doron goes to make plans with our next host. Abraham waits with patience for us to complete our business.

"Elisha, I am astounded. Why did you not sing these songs while in Urusalim?"

"I did, but they were not acceptable."

"Ah, yes. Now I remember. Whatever you did to change them, keep doing it. They are wonderful."

"I was worried you might not approve."

"Why would I not?"

Tears come to my eyes. "Thank you. You were a father, a teacher, and a guide to me."

He nods. "And you took my words and made them poetic like the work of Gilgamesh."

"I wrote them in homage to you and Sarah and the marvelous things you did for me. Out of my love for both of you."

He holds me in his arms, then moves me away to see my face. "Go, my daughter. Your work is waiting. You have my blessings."

He called me daughter. I watch him walk away. "Thank you. I will do as you ask." There is no mention of Hagar.

Palluw joins us. "The concert went well and I am content." His face shows complete satisfaction.

"Thank you, my lord. I am glad you are happy. I now hope the venture will go well."

Doron grows near and overhears us.

"Why would it not?" He is more positive than before. "We have something to offer."

"Poo, poo. You never know what might happen," I respond.

Palluw rises from his mat. "I am ready to retire."

"We are also ready."

. . . .

We sleep well that night. In the morning we eat an enormous meal and are packed and on our way to Ein-gedi with the promise to return. The promise is made because it is expected.

The tension between Doron and I lessened but is still obvious. He takes care not to touch my hand and walks far ahead of me as he leads the donkey. Conversation includes only needed responses. Ein-gedi is not too far, and we expect to arrive in a little more than two suns.

. . . .

The journey goes well, and we settle down outside our small tent for the evening meal. Visitors arrive. Doron is concerned and whispers, "Go, stay near the donkey until I find out why they are here. If anything happens get on the donkey and run for your life."

I move closer to the animal and pet him while trying to listen in on their argument. "Elisha, please come here," Doron calls. He turns back to the men. "I must call on Elisha to settle this. These are her concerts. He turns to me. "Explain to them that we cannot sing for their villages because we are expected in Ein-gedi."

"Good evening, my lord, what is your concern?"

"A warm welcome to our composer." I bow my head. "Word spread of the concert in Beersheba and Abraham's presence there. Every village near here wishes you to do the same for us."

"One moment, sir, let me speak with my musician." I pull Doron out of earshot. "I fail to understand your displeasure. This is something we must do. My purpose is to spread Abraham and Sarah's words as far as I can. Do you not agree?"

"And what about those who are waiting?"

"We ask the villagers to send a messenger explaining the delay."

"What if the next village is angry when we do not appear?"

"Doron, we do not have to treat this like a business. We will calm them and explain and if they no longer want us, so be it."

"I do not agree. Are you sure it is what you wish?"

"I am sure."

The families in each village contribute to our housing and food. Many times we are given so much, we must return what is left or overburden our donkey. I do not know how many villages we stopped at before we reach Ein-gedi and the same thing happens on the way to Gerar.

We look forward to a leisurely walk to Kiriath Arba, but that is not to be. We perform in what seems like hundreds of small villages. There are many more full moon cycles before we reach Sarah's tent and darkness is getting ready to close in.

Doron waters the donkey, and we go to the front of the tent. "Sarah," I call in a gentle tone. "Sarah, are you here?"

She runs into my arms. We hug and cry, examine each other, then hug and cry again.

"Come in, Elisha, you too, Doron. The wait was too long. Excuse my tears. I worried something happened to you." She brings us each a large goblet of libation, then joins us on the mats. "Tell me of your travels. I cannot wait to catch up with your adventures. Have your drink and let me call Isaac. He is in Abraham's tent."

Doron whispers, "I still do not understand. Can you explain your purpose?"

"I have nothing more to say. We made no promises and Abraham's words and Sarah's wisdom need to be heard."

Sarah comes running into the tent. "Isaac cannot wait to see you both and asked that we wait so he can listen to all the news. Your arrival was expected many moons ago. I heard from Abraham after he attended your concert. He said you and Doron were wonderful. How is he?"

Having to answer her disturbs me, as if I am lying. "He is well and involved in business as always." I smile.

"He needs to return home. He has been away too long." Sarah rarely complains.

Isaac comes in. "Elisha, Doron. What a surprise." We embrace each other and take our seats.

"You are a young man, Isaac. I am so happy to see you."

"You changed also, Elisha. You became an adult."

"It happens to every one of us sooner or later." They appreciate our joke and it breaks the tension of Hagar hanging in the air. Questions fly, we talk over each other, sentences are left hanging, we laugh a lot yet manage to catch up on the news.

"I am proud of the work you both are doing," says Sarah. "Songs with Abraham's words."

"And your teachings," I interrupt.

"What a blessing." She turns to Doron. "From the length of time it took to get here it seems you are well accepted."

Doron's eyes are fixed on her. "How are you Sarah?" he inquires. I note the glance between Sarah and Isaac. "I am well." Isaac examines the floor as if it is a beguiling woman.

"I am glad to hear that." I study Sarah's expression. Her smile was not real.

"How long will you stay?" she asks.

"Not long enough. One more moon and we must be on our way."

"I am disappointed, but I understand. You and Doron settle yourselves in Abraham's tent and Isaac will stay with me until you leave."

"It is not necessary," I assure her. "I do not wish to disturb Isaac. I can stay with you."

"It is obvious you have become close companions. Isaac will sleep here."

She reacted the same way as Abraham and knows me better than my own parents. Sarah is hiding something about her health. I will get the secret out of her.

· · · · · · · · · · · · ·

As soon as the sun rises Doron wakes me. I try to open my eyes. "Where are you going? I can hardly lift my head."

"Sarah said Abraham is in Beersheba. I want to make sure the cattle are in favorable health and taken care of as I instructed." He joins us for the morning meal and disappears.

I turn to Sarah. "He is checking up on the running of the business. He feels responsible with Abraham gone." Or is he using that as an excuse to avoid me? "Are you well? In all honesty, well? We spoke last evening and I felt something was wrong."

"I am fine. There is nothing to worry about." Sarah never evades matters that need discussion. "Isaac has done so much to make the herds larger. He is betrothed to Rebecca. I am so excited and cannot wait for their nuptials."

"Sarah, that is wonderful news." She avoided my question. "Do you like her?"

"She is a wonderful young woman who enhances Isaac's essence. She is delicate with dark hair and eyes and a soul that shines with joy."

"I am pleased for all of you." She does not bring up Hagar.

Our visit is short and the leaving distressing. Doron acknowledges that as well. His slumped shoulders give away his feelings. Will I ever see my beloved second mother again?

· · · · · · · · · · · ·

Back on the trail, the area grows more remote. Sadness prevents conversation until we sit to eat.

"Was all well with the animals?"

"The men are reliable and doing as I asked."

I reflect on our meeting. "That was difficult."

"What was?"

"The leaving Sarah and Isaac, of course, and knowing I may never see them again."

"I was hoping you might be referring to the remark Sarah made."

I look away. "Which remark?"

"Becoming close companions. Added to Abraham's comments, it warrants consideration."

"Do you give it significance?"

I turn to watch his expression. "I would rather you answer first."

"Yes, I have."

"And?"

His face tells me what I want to know. "I think they told us what we have been avoiding telling each other."

In one graceful movement Doron pushes the food away and is by my side. He takes me in his arms. His lips graze mine with such tenderness only the shivers that run through me can assure his mouth is real.

"No, Doron. No, I cannot." I push him away, scramble up, and run toward the donkey.

He runs after me. "What is wrong? Tell me, please. You feel something for me."

"I do, but I cannot." I walk around to the donkey's other side.

"Do you not trust me?"

"I trust you. It is my problem." I go back to the mat.

"Anything that troubles you concerns me." His words stop me. "I care about you. My feelings are sincere, and my wish is to know who you are."

There is no place to put myself. "You would not choose to have knowledge of this."

"I do but will not insist."

He is so sad, so alone, so disappointed, my heart breaks. I cannot . . . "Please, leave me alone." He walks away, slumped shoulders and head down. I will not let him leave like that. "Wait. Please sit. I cannot stand and speak the words."

I am on the ground next to him. He takes me in his arms and strokes my hair. I am safe. Really safe. The happenings in Urusalim. Kotharat's meanness, Resheph's crafty ways, the Sacred Prostitutes, the violation, the lie to Abraham all spill onto his welcoming chest.

I sit up. "I think about how he attacked me and it still seems like it is happening now. I scrubbed myself inside and out, over and over, but could not wash away his smell. I did not trust love would come to me again."

His answer is to pull me closer. The strokes of his hand on my back bring tears. Doron does not move, does not pull away. The tears grow less and I lift my head. I reach up, pull his head down, and fix my lips on his. There is urgency in my blood. His insistence matches mine.

Doron introduces me to the essence of making love, the basic animal urge, the depth of the feelings, the pleasure, the glow afterward, and the sweet lingering scent of my lover. We hold each other, my head on his chest.

"I have been long overdue to the experience of love. There is no one I would rather have as a tutor. The way you are looking at me right now makes me realize that you are the first man, except for my brother, to peer into my heart. It was as if not just our bodies came together but my soul became one with yours. Knowing each other as we now do, I can accomplish anything." I kiss him on the lips again, savoring the sensations running through me. "I love you."

"I know, and I love you too."

CHAPTER TWENTY-NINE

We set out for Lachish with the sun well over the horizon. At every turn, a messenger appears from another village and asks us to entertain. Most of the communities are nameless, so keeping track of them is difficult and finding them even more so. No name is something they have in common with my village. Most of the men are planters and elders greet us and are in charge, like at home.

"Sometimes I wonder what they would think if they knew my tribe banished me."

"We are here to do our concert," Doron reminds me, "not to become friends and share our histories."

"You are right. But it feels like a lie."

"Shall we leave this as a truth unspoken?" I nod.

"Elisha? I have a question for you. When we stayed with Sarah, you were different."

"Different?"

"Yes, comfortable as if they are your family."

"They were my family for an uncountable number of full moons. Leaving them was hard. I never had my own home."

"There is more than that."

"A part of me is barren, like Sarah was. My heart is filled with love not given to a husband or child. I used to dream of how I would play with my little ones." Doron lowers his eyes. "Loneliness was always a part of me whether alone or with others, even with Abraham and Sarah. I never thought about the loss until Sarah had Isaac. Then I understood what a woman is meant to accomplish, what was never going to be mine."

Doron runs his hand through his beard. "I am sorry and wish I could have filled that place. One thing I need to make clear. I have no interest in marriage or children."

Disappointment fills me. The tiny bit of hope that survived, dies.

. . . .

Whether a village or city, we are welcomed by crowds with greetings, food, and drink. We stay in someone's home and are given provisions to continue.

"This wandering takes us far from our destination. It seems we will travel for a lifetime before we reach my village."

"Do you not enjoy my company?" Doron grins and has a twinkle in his eye.

"For a long time, Nathan was the one person I could speak to. Now I have you and nowhere in the world is there a place better than right here." I kiss his cheek. "You made this a glorious time in my life. I am with the man I love, doing the things I love most. This journey is tiring, and I hope we never grow stale."

"Music and being together will never wear out." His smile is broad.

"You restored my trust in people. For the first time I am equal with a man, like Sarah. The wonder of it is that I can be me, all of me, and I no longer am a dependent girl-child. Thank you, Doron."

Things go well in Lachish. And that is repeated in the many villages where we perform. Then we move north to Beit Lahm. We arrive in the evening. After watering the donkey and unpacking the few things needed for the concert, we partake of a tasty meal. Tired from our trek we excuse ourselves and are on our mats ready to sleep.

"The next large city after this is Urusalim," I muse. It may take four moons for the donkey to plod that far. "I would like to stop and visit Melchizedek. He made this possible."

"Of course we will. As we move closer, perhaps we can find a messenger. Then Melchizedek will be aware of when we arrive."

"No, Doron. We must find a messenger. He is always on the move and might not be there."

We do not come across any one willing to do it. We reach the house and Doron knocks on the doorpost. There is no answer.

"We missed him, Doron. What shall we do now? I told you he might not be here."

"What was I supposed to do?" He glares at me. "You did not find anyone."

"Do not blame me. You did not search to find one."

He turns away. "I did not because you said you would."

"Yes, I know it is always my fault." Despite what was predicted, we are getting tired and a bit stale. "What do we do now?"

"I have an answer." I follow behind him bubbling like stew, letting him find the solution. He comes across a gorgeous setting not far away. Or did he know about it from jaunts with Abraham? "Doron, I am sorry I got angry. Melchizedek is important to us."

We take two suns of leisure walking through the countryside to admire the foliage, warming ourselves in the sun and making love in the grass. We eat as soon as we are moved to, and sleep when we are tired. Our time there is divine and at the end, energy and joy return.

We make our way back to the house and Doron knocks on the doorpost again.

"There you are. I expected you many moons ago. I was concerned at not hearing anything. Beersheba is not near, but not so far. Then I received news of the many communities where you performed with much success."

I give him a big hug. "We must apologize. We could not find a messenger. Every city, town, and village wanted to have us. Word travels like the wind and no village wishes to be left out."

He precedes us into the house. "But that is wonderful. What an accomplishment."

"Poo, poo," says Doron.

"What is that?"

"My lord, the saying is to ward off evil. We still have a long way to go and I do not care to reverse our agreeable fortune."

"Please sit." He calls the servant. "Please bring food and drink." He turns back to us. "Did you see Abraham and Sarah?"

We sit across from him and Doron signals me with a look that warns. "We saw Abraham in Beersheba," I tell him. "He is still involved in business dealings." Doron's nose flares. "Did you know that he is there with Hagar?" Doron's eyes glare like a sharp blade.

"No, he never said anything. I am surprised."

"We had a wonderful time with Sarah and Isaac. Sarah is lonely and although she did not say it, I think she is not well. It was difficult to leave her."

Doron takes my hand in his. Melchizedek notices the movement. His only reaction is a tightening of his cheeks as if to control a grin.

"Doron, do you agree?"

"Yes, my lord. She did not seem to be as well as she used to."

"I am sorry. I will send a servant, and we will find out if anything is wrong."

"Thank you, my lord, I will rest better with knowing." My second mother is ill.

· · · · · · · · · · · ·

Melchizedek has much to do, and we spend time together only for meals. In between Doron and I walk through the city. "This house is where I lived."

"The one with Kotharat and him?"

"Yes. Come, we will walk around to the wash stand. No one is home at this time." The sight of the courtyard makes me want to throw up. "This is where we cooked, washed, ate, did everything. Let us go."

Resheph walks in. I grab Doron's hand. He should not be here if he is still studying. "Resheph. I hope you do not mind, my friend wanted to see where I used to live."

"That is fine with me." One eyebrow is raised, and a smirk is on his face. "Pleased to meet you." He nods to Doron.

"Thank you. Elisha told me about you."

The corners of Resheph's mouth turn up. "I am sure she did. And you, Elisha, what are you doing back in the city?"

"We are here to thank Melchizedek for the success of our concerts."

His voice changes. "Success." He hesitates. "Congratulations."

"And you, Resheph? Do you still study?"

"Of course." He turns his head, confirming my guess. "I am glad for you. We must be on our way. Regards to your family."

We are away from the house and Doron stops. "Did seeing him make you sad?"

"Yes. He is the same. Superior and untruthful. The father was not nasty, just distant. They were not loving people, except for the daughter, Nikkal. She was the kind one who understood that the lack of love breeds anger and shame."

"Like in your home?"

The shock goes through to my bones. "My parents did not put love into words, but the caring was real. It was in the covers my ima stayed up the whole night to weave. It was in the small size water skin Abba made for me. No, my home was different."

"Were the results not the same? Do you not suffer the same feelings?"

My feet pound the earth as I walk away. "They did the best they could. Doron, I do not wish to discuss this with you."

"Who else can you talk to?"

I stare at him but will not say more. "I am not sure I want it to be you."

· · · · · · · · · · · ·

Melchizedek returns and we have a delicious feast. "I am sorry to say my messenger was not able to confirm Sarah's health. She refused to discuss it."

I smile. "Thank you for trying."

Sipping the libation loosens the men's tongues, and they talk until dark. I listen but cannot join them. Melchizedek describes the new class he is teaching and the work he is involved in. I nod so he knows I am listening. Doron describes some places we visited and the reactions of our audiences.

"My dear friend and teacher," I interrupt, "we must leave on the morrow. I, for one, need some sleep before we start out again." I give him a kiss on the cheek. Doron stands and joins me.

"Yes, we both need rest."

"May I offer you provisions?"

Doron bows his head. "Thank you, my lord, but our hosts have been too kind. Our animal carries as much as he can."

"You are well taken care of. I will see you in the morning."

"Are you all right?" Doron speaks as soon as we are out of hearing.

"I am now. You brought up those feelings and I could not say a word." We go to our room. "I was a lost child," I whisper, "left alone because they were busy in the house and fields. The worst part was the whispers of being peculiar and doing evil. It drove away friends.

I wandered by myself. The empty part in me needed to be filled. I was angry and resentful of anyone who was hugged or kissed." I go to Doron. "I thought something was wrong with me because the tribe said it was true. I was ashamed. Is that what you want to hear?" I throw myself onto the sleep mat and turn away.

He turns me over and puts his arms around me. Our love-making is different. We finish and he holds me while I cry the feelings out. I do not tell him a gateway closed. My blood did not flow the past three moon cycles.

• • • • • • • • • • • •

We are on our way right after we finish eating. The concerts in the cities of Gilbeah, Gibeon, Gezer, and their surrounding areas go as before. We enjoy our hosts and the audiences show their appreciation. Once those appearances are over, everything changes.

We do the concerts in the surrounding communities in the same way, but the audience reacts differently. They yell out, "You could not study with Abraham. You are a woman." Rotten flowers fly at us. "How can we be sure those are his words?" Rotting vegetables join the flowers. "You are a liar." "You are a harlot. That man is not your husband." Sheep dung misses us. We evade the stones they throw.

Doron has his arm around me as he pulls me from the gathering and heads back to the safety of our tent. "What happened? Why do they say such terrible things, Doron? They do not challenge you. I feel dreadful, like I did something so wrong I should be punished."

Doron examines my face. "Your expectations of yourself are out of proportion. You cannot change people."

"Did I not sing well? Did I mix up any of the words? Was I not loud enough?"

"Your singing was beautiful."

"Then why were they so furious. Did they not understand?"

Doron stares at me. "Do you expect to make them grasp the teachings?"

"I thought they would want to. That they would recognize Abraham's and Sarah's wisdom."

"And is it your fault they do not?"

"If I am not doing it right, then yes."

"Tell me the mistakes you made."

His request surprises me and I push him away. "I did not make any. At least I do not think so." I watch his face.

"You did not. Are you one who makes sure you predict yourself a failure in case you are not perfect?"

I look into his eyes and remind myself he loves me and is trying to help. "I think I always have been. Bad feelings happened each time the tribe reminded me I did not marry, or that I was odd and no man wanted me. Abba said I could never learn to cook, and Ima said my breads were hard enough to grind the flour. Nothing I did was valued, especially my singing, and then there was the humiliation of not being a son."

"If a child is different or criticized, they feel shame. Shame is one of the most painful things we face."

I am curious. "Were you different?"

"Perhaps not in the same way as you were. But I had my share."

The tone of his voice makes my heart reach out to him. "Now hush and let me hold you." I climb into the heaven of his arms.

···········

The following morning as we move toward Mizpah, I decide to discuss my plan with Doron. "There is something we must speak about that may affect both of us."

"I am grateful to have something to occupy me as we plod along."

"I wrote another song. With my own words."

"Wonderful. What is the problem? We can add it to the program."

"What if you are not pleased with it?"

"Sing it for me."

"I would rather we practice it first."

He ties the donkey to a tree, gets his lyre, and I sing the tune. He has a big smile for me. "It is perfect. Now with the words."

"I would rather you consider the words at the concert."

He inspects me and his brow creases. "You are being very mysterious."

His request brings back the fear of the past few days. What might happen because of my words? Will we get hurt? Will someone else? I am afraid. I need his opinion. I relent and sing the words.

"Are you ready to be stoned to death?" I do not answer. "It is a wonderful song and I appreciate the desire to speak out, but you know as well as I it will bring unrest. The women may applaud but they will suffer later."

"I agree. That is what I struggle with. The words need to be heard. It is time men learn to accept women as having intelligence and able to do more than keep the home and have children. You treat me as equal."

"You say that you are not able to speak your mind. I can assure you that indeed you do."

That makes me angry. "What about the words? Should I add some that tell men what they do is wrong and hurtful?"

Doron's face is red. "Do you want to die on the spot?"

"It is the truth and they do not recognize it. We were students of Abraham and Sarah and learned how to talk to each other."

"That is true. Why do you say women are nothing if they cannot share their ideas, that they have been shamed into silence?"

"Because that is the truth. Many women are beaten for speaking their thoughts and opinions. Would you like that to happen to you?"

Doron sighs. "I understand what you are trying to say. It does not change the truth of our society. You may not survive."

"There are women who do not wish to survive living this way."

There is a heavy silence. What is he thinking? "How did you treat your wife?"

"You and I are different. We are on a difficult journey."

"That is not an answer."

He stares at me. "I was not a good husband. Then Abraham taught me."

"Go on," I urge him.

It takes a long time before he speaks. "I beat my wife. That is how it was in my family. My anger went into the beatings. She cried and I ignored it. It continued through the years of our marriage." There are tears in his eyes. "I think it killed her."

"Oh, Doron, I am so sorry." I kiss him, then hold him in my arms until he stops crying.

He sits up. "You and I share the chores as well as being partners in music. It is an equal relationship. But I do not know if men are ready to hear what you have to say. You could be stoned, hurt, or killed, without any concern for me."

"This has nothing to do with you."

"I think it does, unless I am no longer your partner."

"But you are not me."

"So I do not count? They do not see me?"

My head is in my hands. "That is not what I mean. I wrote the words."

"They do not know that. What if they think this song was my idea?"

"That is ridiculous. Men do not speak that way, do not think that way. Including you."

"How do you know that?"

"Because you are a man." We study each other and break into laughter. "Let us pack up and get away from here."

His face shows concern for me. "Can you accept the consequences?"

"Does it matter? If it needs to be, it needs to be. I will tell you my plan and then we can decide. After Mizpah we go to Ai, Bethel, Gilgal, and the surrounding communities. I would like to try the song in a few of those." He has no response. "Then I want to make it an important moment in Shechem. That is the final concert, and when we finish, we go to my home and will not be performing anymore, so it will not matter."

"What if the reactions are harsher than what happened before? What if you get hurt or worse? A large enough stone can break a bone."

"You are concerned for me, and I for you. This is something I must do. I wish to have you by my side but if you choose not, I will value that."

He snorts like an infuriated animal. "I will be by your side. I am not in agreement with what you wish to do. There is only misfortune ahead."

"I understand and trust this is meant to be."

"I hope you are right."

I will hold my head high and not show my fear.

CHAPTER THIRTY

The first attempt at presenting my song is on a perfect evening in Ai, also known as the White City. Our audience does not approve of the words I sing. The women can recognize some of what is said but have no idea why I chose those words. Change is not in the women's thinking. The men understand but laugh, they see me as a woman who does not grasp how things are done. No rocks or vegetables are thrown and there is no violence.

By the time we reach Bethel, word has spread. They wait for our arrival. Men pursue us from the time we reach the outskirts of the city. My hands go over my ears. I do not wish to listen to the horrible names they call me, but they cause no harm. They surround our tent as if to keep us imprisoned but do not cancel the concert. We do not sleep well.

The buzzing in the audience is the loudest of the entire journey. Doron's suffering is obvious. His words sting, and he paces like a caged animal. I pray under my breath.

After the first few songs, the crowd settles down and begins to enjoy the presentation. We are closer to the end and the buzzing can be heard again. I wait until quiet comes, then begin my song.

When I finish singing, there is not a sound. The quiet is strange and scary. One woman stands and yells out. "Thank you. Yes, that is the way of our lives," before her husband pulls her back into her seat, stands over her, and smacks her face as hard as he can.

Chaos breaks loose of its chains. We grab our things and run to the tent. We are lucky that what they throw falls short. We reach the tent and fear an invasion of our private space.

We begin to pack and our names are called out. One man steps forward of the crowd and pulls the tent flaps open. "We demand you leave now. If not, we cannot assure you of the ending."

Doron nods. "Give us a few minutes to collect our things and we will be on our way."

During an unnerving quiet, we throw things into the sacks. The men do not move and they offer no provisions. Doron does not speak. Our host stands near, making sure the men know he encourages their demands.

With the donkey packed, we whisper about how to do the leaving and decide to walk bit by bit and smile. As we proceed they turn as one to watch us. They follow us until we are at their border and that is when we pick up our pace.

Doron's whole body is tense. "I do not appreciate being in this situation."

"Does everything in your life need to be comfortable?"

"I enjoy peace even if you do not."

"If we only have peace nothing will change. No one has enough pain to do something."

He crosses his arms over his chest. "You need to live your life in whatever way makes you happy."

"And you?"

"I will do as I must."

Doron walks to the other side of the donkey. He grabs the reins and moves on. I follow behind him the entire way to the next city.

. . . .

The sun makes the old city shine. This area is called Hill Country and is one of the largest city-states in Canaan. The city of Shechem is protected by two mountains. Mt. Gerizim is on the left and Mt. Ebal on the right. We approach through the ridge route, which in the end passes through the city center. The massive wall of stone in front of us used to be their fortification.

"In a way the wall contains a beauty of its own, though the reason for building it was because of bloodshed," I ponder.

"I find it amazing. You twist words and make a poetic way to describe carnage, as if it is a necessity in the lives of the inhabitants." Doron's tone carries bitterness though not quite as cutting as before.

"Are you not aware each city-state was always at war with other states? How many times did the people rise against the government's constant demands for men and sons to join the military and fight?" I am near tears. "Send support. Send your sons. That is all we heard. So many died."

Doron is surprised. "I did not realize the northern area had the same problems we did."

"This is the most interesting city we visited."

"We have not seen anything yet."

I do not hold back my retort. "My instincts tell me so."

His reaction is what I expect. He huffs off toward the town center. We provoked each other the entire trip, and I am no better than he. I follow Doron at a distance. My intuition only works sometimes, but Doron has something that takes him right where we need to go. I catch up to him as he is knocking on the doorpost of our host's house.

"Good evening, sir. I am the singer—"

"Come in, come in, I was expecting you."

Doron tethers the donkey. We introduce ourselves and learn his name is Oren. We walk into a house like that of our first host. The flawless weave of his garment declares he is another man of wealth. During the journey, we stayed in huts and sometimes a small house. Oren's spacious home goes beyond our first host Palluw's splendid one.

"Please make yourselves comfortable." He walks to the rear and speaks with someone. By the time he returns and is ready to sit, the servant is pouring drinks.

"Welcome. I am pleased to have you in my home."

Oren chooses to get business out of the way, so we chat about our concert and choose to wait at least two moons before performing. We need some distance from each other. Oren tells us the organizers will be informed, and then they will decide timings.

The servants present a wonderful meal. On the trail, we ate the same things, so I relish the spread before us. Our choice is of fish or lamb with a dish of mixed vegetables in a somewhat spicy sauce. Three breads, one made of barley, one of wheat, and one of combined flours served with curds and honey complete the main presentation. The flavors of breads are some I never had before. Cakes of dates, figs, or dried grapes overflow the serving basin and are accompanied by pomegranate tea sweetened with honey.

"The breads are different from those at home. How are they prepared?"

"The barley flour has fig juice instead of water," Oren tells me. The others have cumin or olive oil mixed into the dough."

"I would not have thought of that. They are delicious."

Oren bends toward me. "Enjoy them."

I end the meal with toasted lentils and honey in honor of beginning my journey home. We are tired and our need for rest shortens the evening.

After the delicious morning meal, we take the early part of the day to visit the altar Abraham built so many years before. It is new to me, but I recall the stories my family told.

"Doron, we are so close, can we go up the mountain? I want to see my village from there."

"Are you sure? The rise is quite high. It could be a difficult trek."

"I am sure. Something tells me to." We reach the peak, get close to the edge, and look out. The sight is breathtaking. Before us are the two mountains whose tops are in the clouds. They have many different trees blooming with both vivid and muted flowers. Between them is flat ground. The houses down below are white and yellow and are sprinkled throughout the area. "Doron, can you see a small village over to the right?"

"Is that the one? Over farther."

"That is possible. If so, it is much bigger, and I do not recognize the large building. But I think that is the hill I climbed to listen to the men's meetings. I wonder if my special bushes are still growing." My frown turns into a chuckle, becomes laughter, and then turns to joy. Being here, near the clouds, close to the stars, makes me feel light in my being.

· · · · · · · · · · · ·

On the way back we walk along the Route of Springs. "Doron, count and see if there are more than twenty as the stories claim." I run like a youngster would into the ones that spray the highest. Doron finally laughs, and I am happy to hear that. "Did you count? How many?"

"I did not. I am not a child."

"You also do not know how to enjoy yourself."

For me, delight is the tonic which does battle with the fear of not living long enough to find my purpose. I will find that here, in my old village.

The city of Shechem is much like the other cities. Long winding streets, flat roofs with stairs on the side, people who welcome us as we pass, and gardens of vegetables and flowers.

"I like this place and am happy we stopped here. The people we pass are kind."

"We will know that after you sing your song."

"Why do you bring that up now? We are enjoying ourselves."

He blocks my way. "What do you accomplish by going against the grain of the people?"

He means the men. "Is this because the idea comes from a woman? You who grasp so much, why do you not understand?"

"You are going against an entire society and no benefit will come of it."

I walk around him. "So, should I not speak at all and agree for injustices to continue?"

"You will not change anything so why do you wish to suffer the indignities?'

"Someone must."

Doron throws his hands in the air and walks away. I follow a good distance behind him back to Oren's house, hoping things will get better.

The air is full of tension at the evening meal. I do not know what Oren thinks. I hope he is not upset. "The food is wonderful," I smile. "Thank you for another special meal."

Oren beams. "The offering was made with loving care."

"I can taste that."

Doron does not speak. We excuse ourselves to get ready for the concert. The setting is a short walk away, nestled into the mountains and wrapped in the familiar smell of the olive trees surrounding them.

I sit at one side of the area cleared for us and Doron is at the other. I will not allow him to upset me before I sing. It is enough I already have twinges in my belly. The cause is my family. Are they here? Did they receive notice of the event? I hope not. There is no guarantee of a positive finish and do not want them to be embarrassed. I want to chew my hair.

The concert goes well. The audience enjoys our songs and applauds with generosity. I step forward to announce my last song, "I Am a Woman." There is rustling from movement in the audience and I wait for quiet. I nod for Doron to begin. His face is ashen. By the second verse the gasps, grunts, mumbles, and murmurs by now familiar to my ears begin in earnest. I force myself to ignore them and continue to the end.

The crowd stands as one and the condemnation begins. The men drag their women toward the stage and threaten me. I force a smile to remain on my face and stay there until I choose to bear it no longer. I throw the shawl over my head and walk back to the house. It is done. There are no regrets and no reproaches.

Doron returns to the house a short while later. "Oren asked us to be on our way in the morning."

"I am not surprised."

"Why did you run off?"

I smile at him. "I did not run, Doron, I walked. My work was done."

"What work? Enraging the people? I cannot defend you and do not know what you think you are doing."

"Doron, you did not value my plan. I do not expect miracles. My work is to use words that plant seeds for change. There is no justice for women. We are disposable in ways men are not. Our strengths are not considered important. This may not change for many years. I am aware of the difficulties, but I must say it out loud."

"You have wasted your time and your talent."

I smile. "That is how you choose to see it."

"That is how the whole world would see it."

"It is done. So be it."

CHAPTER THIRTY-ONE

I slept well. I do not know about Doron. Morning musings consider the idea that there may be a gift in failure. At first it is a crushing of hopes and dreams. But then it is the beginning of new possibilities. Sandalphon gave me my name and blessed me with strengths. I learned courage through experience. Though sad and tired, I will gather my energy and rise with enough vitality to use more words.

Doron wakes up and we lie on our mats. The atmosphere is different. Decisions are in the air.

"It is time for me to go home. After all these years, I will be with my family again."

"I know."

"Doron, is there nothing more to say?"

"What would you want me to say?"

"That you will join me in my village."

"I will not."

Tears come to my eyes. "I was hoping with the performing behind us, you would."

"My decision is to return to Abraham. I am still his servant and feel it is my duty."

"Abraham said you could be free. You care for me, I know that. Why can you not accept me as I am?"

"I do care and that is why I cannot accept what you did." He takes me in his arms and his lips nibble at mine. Passion returns and we make love one last time.

The donkey packed, we partake of the morning meal then say our farewells to our host. We stand at the gate not knowing how to part or what to say.

"Take care, Doron. I wish you well."

"I will. I wish the greatest contentment for you."

With that he pats the donkey on his rear and they walk away.

I am alone again. A sack of rocks is on my back. The hopes and dreams of a life with Doron disappear with each stride in the opposite direction. It was all for nothing. My song was not successful. My music and my love are gone. My heart is shattered.

Do I want to go home? Alone? Face my mother without Doron to comfort me? I want to go in another direction but there is no choice. What will life be like? Each step makes the stones heavier. I double over in pain. The radiant blue sky brings no balm. I force myself to stand and focus on what is ahead. How will I find me? My purpose? When my skin no longer fits this village.

Sandalphon whispers in my ear. "This is the time of your life for you to enjoy your own companionship. That is one way to know who you are."

He is right as always. I will be home well before the sun goes down. The surroundings bring back pictures of my life there. The damp soil, the greener trees with their scents of olives, come alive once more. It is time to return, to settle things with my mother and my tribe.

. . . .

Despite the heaviness of my steps, the walk home is shorter than I expect. Abba died and I had word, but nothing since then. I race ahead at the chance Ima might still be there.

My village is in sight. There are three times the number of huts, and where the Council used to gather around the fire stands the large building I saw from the mountain. If this is where the meetings take place, I would no longer be able to eavesdrop. I laugh to myself and take in the scene with the pride of one born here. The sight of familiar things helps me enjoy the moment.

No one is here to meet me, they have no idea I am coming. The new homes make the landscape confusing and it takes me a while to find our hut. A group of children surrounds me before I can call out to Nathan.

"Who are you?" The young man is a smaller Nathan, the tallest of the brood, and I assume the eldest. "You look like my Abba."

"I am your abba's sister, your dodah Elisha."

"Stay here," he commands the other children. "I will find Abba," he tells me.

I want to say, "yes, my lord," but to him it would not be funny. Strange to think of my brother as Abba. The young ones take frequent peeks at me.

"You do not look like our abba," says a small boy.

"Yes, she does. See her eyes just a little darker?" comes from a young girl.

The littlest one, another girl, pulls on my tunic and holds her arms high for me to pick her up.

"What is your name, little one?"

"I am Rena." Her voice is high and more piercing than I expect.

"Were you told how precious your name is? It means song of joy."

"Abba said so. He wants me to be like his sister. She sings pretty tunes."

Tears come to my eyes. "And so she does." I twirl her around and laugh with a joy I had almost forgotten. I put her down and she watches me fall into my brother's arms. At a loss for words we hug and cry, hanging onto each other. I had no idea how much I missed him.

Nathan backs away still holding my arms. "I cannot believe my eyes. I did not trust I would see you again."

"And I you, my dear brother. So much happened since I left."

"There is so much to tell it will take thirteen full moons to catch up." He takes my sack, puts his arm around my waist, and leads me into the hut. Rena is still watching.

"Nathan, I do not recognize this place. You added so many sections."

"What else could we do with six children? You will share a space with the older girls. Rachel will return soon."

"You did well, and now I can help. How wonderful." I examine his face. "But you did not mention Ima."

"She is here, somewhat worn, but still manages to get around the village to take care of others. She will be back any moment."

My hand goes to my heart. "I was so worried. I could not be here for Abba and need to spend time with her."

"And she with you. She said this morning how sorry she was we could not hear you sing in Shechem."

"You did know."

"Yes, but with Ima and the children it was not possible. And if you were that close, you were coming home."

"That was my plan all these years." Nathan and I hold each other for a long while. I break away. "I have something I wish to say. Please excuse me for the many times I got angry with you. I was not always nice to the sweetest person in my life. I love you. And one more thing. I do not remember you hurting me, but if you did, I pardon you."

"Foolish girl." And he hugs me again.

"You still think of me as a girl."

We separate and he goes outside to take care of the children. I sit on the mat. What is my mother like? Did she change or will it be like before? Someone once said, "Your family got rid of you." It was not the truth, but it did feel that way. A familiar voice makes me turn toward the entrance to the hut and run. "Ima, Ima, I am home."

"Elisha," she shouts, and folds herself into my open arms. I cry. She does not.

She moves away and I study her face. I do not like what is there. She is haggard and bones were almost all there was left to feel. "Are you well?"

"Yes, though I am in my advanced years."

The quick twisting of her tunic tells me she lied. "I am glad. You seem marvelous." My lie is defensible.

"Elisha, my child. It is wonderful to have you near, but I hope you are not here to make trouble." We gaze at each other.

She is the same. "Why would you think that?"

"Come into the hut. I walked too far and need to rest. We will talk after the meal."

Even with my arm around her she leans on her stick and her steps are unsure. We make our way inside. For the first time, I yearn to take care of her, love her back to the healthy woman I left long ago, though that is not possible.

Once inside she sits and I take her hands. The darkness removes all the wrinkles. "How have you been since Abba left us?"

"A great sadness took hold for a long while, but I am used to enduring it."

"I know you miss him as much as I do."

Tears come to her eyes. "Who do you think you are? He was my husband."

"Of course, I did not mean—you know—I was not here." Together for a moment and already I said the wrong thing. Ima lies down on her mat and falls asleep. I must cherish any moments we have left.

Another female voice yells, "Where is everyone?"

It must be Rachel. I go to greet her. She and Nathan are teasing each other. "I am so happy to meet you, Rachel." We enjoy a big hug.

Rachel's curls fall around her face and cascade down her back. She is pretty and her essence sets alight all around her.

She goes to the cook fire.

"May I help you?"

"No, you may not." Rachel laughs. "This is your first meal here and after your long journey I demand that you rest."

"I obey. I do not want to get into trouble the moment I arrive." We hug and laugh. I am glad. It gives me a chance to observe the family.

The children are well behaved. They stare at me and whisper to each other. Rachel is the perfect mate, Nathan's equal whether they tease or are serious. They are happy, and my heart is content.

The children are asleep and we gather around the fire to ward off the cool of the evening. Nathan was good to me, but there is a part of me that was jealous. He had friends and could go wherever he wished, climb trees, and shear sheep. All I could do was keep house.

"Tell us of your absent years," Rachel encourages. Her eyes invite me.

I will not hold anything back. The evening is spent in recitation of the vast length of time away. I speak of the journey and Resheph's abuse and watch their faces change and eyes grow dark. They light up with tales of Sandalphon, Abraham and Sarah, and again when I speak of Doron. The pain in their eyes at the separation from Doron reaches across the flames and into my heart.

When we finish it is well into the darkness. "Before we part, I must tell Nathan something." I turn to him. "The blade you made for me was stolen along with my harp. I am so sorry."

"Silly girl. Not to worry. I am sure we can borrow a harp from someone."

There is love in this home, but my recitation brings up questions. Was that the life I was meant to live? My girlish dreams were of marriage and children. My life was an adventure of difficulty, joy, and learning. What more could I ask for? It is time to settle down with my family and do what I can to make life easier for them. Many burdens are lifted. They accept my life for what it was, trying and glorious.

. . . .

I wake to Nathan calling my name. "Yes, Nathan, what is it?" Rena is watching.

"Someone saw you, and there is a request for you to attend a meeting in the hall."

"Now? You just woke me. A request or a command? Oh, Nathan, has nothing changed?"

"Things here are about the same. We like it that way."

I say the wrong things, but do the men still beat their wives? "I did not mean . . . will I have to go through the same thing again?"

"I do not know. Get dressed and have a quick meal. I will go with you."

Being with my family warms my heart, but I will not stay if I can be only what they want me to be.

. . . .

My mother insists on joining us. "Must you wear that fancy tunic?"

I will not fight with her. "Sarah gave it to me and it is all I have." My arm is around her. "We will walk at your pace. If it is not too much, I would like to see the changes in the village." We pass some new huts. They are no different from the old ones and we head for the new building.

"I hope the chief knows I do not wish to have trouble."

Ima is beside me. "After the number of years you were away and what you accomplished, they do not dare."

Her words are more precious than Abraham's wealth and make me feel better. We get close to the hall and an army of villagers has gathered to chant.

"Go back where you came from." "No evil people are wanted here." And every other mean sentiment.

My head is as high as Abba's at the council meeting long ago. Have these men learned nothing? I grab onto Nathan's arm, and he wards off those who try to hurt me. He yells, "This is my sister. You know me well. Leave us alone."

We make our way into the hall at last, and I can lean against the mudbricks and mortar of the wall and take a moment to calm myself. My mother takes my face in her hands. "You will be fine, Elisha. Do not speak out of turn and be polite."

I grit my teeth. "Thank you, Ima."

A man appears. "Come this way."

In front of us is a large meeting room. Many of the village men are still filing in, a small number the children I grew up with.

The guide points. "Wait here."

While we wait for the guide, I close my eyes. Under my breath I make amends. "I forgive and remove all guilt from those who hurt me, including the children even if they are no longer with us."

The guide comes back and points the way into the large room.

"Who is that person?" I whisper to Nathan.

"The son of the chief who banished you."

"Galina bat Shamgar, please come forward."

"Excuse me, my lord, but I still use the name Elisha."

Nathan pokes me in the back. "Do not make it difficult," he whispers. I move away from him. My mother gives me the eye.

The chief stares. "You were banished, why do you return? You are not wanted."

"My lord, my family wants me." Ima pulls on my garment. "I left countless moons ago, traveled, studied, and saw much. I wish to spend my final time helping my family."

"That is your reason? What can you offer this community?"

"A heartfelt apology for what happened as a child and my promise to be a productive member of my birthplace."

"I am aware of what you have done. This village needs assurance that you no longer speak to unseen voices."

"Does that include God and his angels?" Nathan pokes me harder. Someone snickers.

"Of course not." The chief is annoyed.

"The voice I speak to is an angel who helps musicians. His name is Sandalphon. According to your views, he is one I can speak to."

"He is the single one?"

"Well, there is God." I hear my mother cry out.

"Are you willing to swear to that?"

"If I must."

"Please approach." I leave my brother standing with Ima and walk up to the Chief.

"Put your hand on your heart and swear in your own words."

"Before I do, chief, may I ask a question?"

"Go ahead."

"In the many years I was away I traveled through most of this land, studied with Abraham and Sarah, and saw things the people of this village could not imagine. My adventures are part of who I am and not something I am able to discard. I would like to know if I may speak of them."

The crowd screams disapproval. Nathan gasps. Ima has her hands over her ears.

"Quiet. One more sound and this crowd will leave." The chief rings his bell until they quiet down. "That is not something that can be approved now." The crowd yells their assent. "Perhaps in the future, but you must prove yourself first."

"What does that mean, my lord?"

"You will prove that you can live in peace and have something to offer. That is my final decision. You may now pledge to the village or leave and not return."

"I swear to those present, that except for God and the angels, I do not speak to any voice not contained in a person's body."

The chief is smiling. "Welcome home, Elisha."

We turn to leave. "Nathan, what was that? He welcomed me and called me Elisha."

"I am not sure, but I think it might be a way to do his duty. Elisha, it is over. You are home and safe."

"But not free. I am bound by the rules of who they want me to be."

CHAPTER THIRTY-TWO

Nathan is content. "Now you can settle in with all of us and start a new life."

"Please do not be upset, but I want a place of my own."

"What for?"

"It has nothing to do with you or the family. I need quiet time. That will not happen in the hut."

"With my brood, I agree. What are you proposing?"

"Remember the tent you once offered?"

"A tent."

"Do not be surprised. I lived in Sarah's tent all that time. But this is just for sleeping. I could live there, close by, and come to take care of the children and the meals. After the evening meal, I would return. That would offer you and the children some privacy."

"And Ima?"

"Her needs will be cared for, but she is with one friend or another, like now."

"She is baking date cakes to welcome you," he whispers. "Are you sure?"

"In my travels, I learned about contemplation and reflection. They take quiet time. While I love you all, that will not happen with the goings on in the hut."

"I understand."

"Thank you. I must tell you of something I came across. This family had a large tree in the garden like ours. They covered it with flax cloths, small branches, and leaves. We ate under it and the air was delightfully cool."

"Wonderful idea. There is so much to do. I will try to get to that."

. . . .

The time flies. I make sure to walk with Ima to assure she does not fall. "Thank you so much for the delicious cakes you made. I enjoyed every one." I made her smile.

The rest of the time is filled with cleaning two places, gathering what to cook, preparing meals, entertaining the children with stories and games, or taking them on walks. I do not dare teach anything like reading or writing, but the children become like my own. Rachel and Nathan enjoy more time for each other and their chores. Ima is spirited but her decline is clear. The question is still—am I acceptable?

Four full moons later, I am in my tent reflecting on my new life. Something has been disturbing me but what is not clear. I lie on my mat and allow my thoughts to fly. It is not long before I am successful. This village does not fit me. Or do I not fit it? As much as I love my family, do I belong here? Being the peculiar one already raised its head. What happened to my courage and boldness? I am no longer the person who deserves the special name, Elisha.

. . . .

The morning chores complete, I go outside to find Rena sitting near my mat. Her lovely brown eyes are staring at me. Before I can greet her she asks, "Dodah Lishee, can you teach me your songs?" Her eyes are open wide, her fingers are in her mouth.

"Do you like to sing?"

"Yes." Her light brown ringlets nod with her head. A serious face confides, "Not songs," she whispers, "but beautiful music comes to me before I sleep."

That happened to me as a child. "I will think about that. Now it is time for Dodah to prepare the midday food. Go and play." She pouts with disappointment.

Nathan's brood listened to me hum one of my songs while doing the wash. "No Dodah, we must hear your words," they insisted. Then they went out to play, except for Rena. It seems she wants to be wherever I am and tells anyone who will listen she is five seasons of growth.

Replaced with household chores and chasing little ones. the music, the learning, the journey and the excitement all disappeared. There is no resentment, they have my heart. I want to take care of my family, but something is missing. Is housework what I will do for the rest of my life?

If I teach Rena, I can do the same with other children. There is wisdom that says things happen as they are supposed to. Where did my boldness go? Come on, Elisha. How can you be comfortable not sharing what you know? The relentless hunger for life beats against my heart. If I were young, it would do what was asked. The strength of youth would fill my imagination. Not squawking or rasping as I do now but singing out with passion. How can anything be the same? My body is tired, worn out too soon. The children are young and ready to learn.

· · · · · · · · · · · ·

Old fears and doubts plague me, but my insides say this is right. I knock on the doorpost. "Chief, may I speak with you?"

"Yes, Elisha, do come in." The chief's hut has not changed except for a few windows letting in the light. "You look well. What do you wish to talk about?"

"At the last meeting you asked what I can offer. Mine is an unusual request not granted to women. I learned much on my journey that I want to teach."

"What makes you think I would allow this?"

I take a breath to calm myself. "I was taught by Abraham and Sarah and wish to honor them."

"Who do you want to teach?"

"The children. When they learn, they will pass it on to the next generation and the wisdom will be saved."

"What do you intend to explain?"

"Living a good life, the importance of forgiving, the difference between a want and a need, finding out what kind of person you want to be, kindne—"

"That is enough. You will not use Canaanite ways?"

"Chief, I know little about them. Though I lived among them, my contact was with Abraham and Sarah."

"Only what you studied from them will be taught, and I will visit and listen whenever I choose. Are we clear?"

He is saying yes. "You are welcome at all times. Is there a shelter in case of rain?"

"There is room at the meeting hall."

"I promise I will not disappoint. It is too important."

We rise from the mats and he walks me to the path going back to Nathan's hut. "Thank you again, chief."

"Understand that I must consult with the council members, and they must approve. I will let you know their decision." He sounded as if it was done. "Thank you again." Waving goodbye, I turn for home. What if the council will not agree? Right now, the problem is my doing well enough for the children to understand the lessons.

• • • • • • • • • •

My mother is uncomfortable through the evening meal. All is cleaned and stored before she speaks. "Elisha."

My mother and her challenging tone. "Yes, Ima?"

"What is this rumor about tutoring children?"

I forgot what it is like in a small village. "I spoke to the chief, and he is seeking approval from the council. The amusing thing is, my nieces and nephews will be included."

"You are making trouble. It is starting all over. What is wrong with you? There is no concern for your family."

I keep my voice soft and warm. "There is nothing wrong with me. My concern is not just for my family, but for all the villagers. The teachings will reflect that."

"Must I speak to the chief? The moment I saw you, I knew nothing changed. You will cause this family more heartache. I wanted to send you away when you arrived. Nathan convinced me to let you stay—to my deep regret."

"Speak to the chief if you wish. I am sorry you have no faith in me." She stares as if the stick is in her hand and walks away. She will not change. I do nothing right.

My nephew and nieces are playing in the coolness of the downward sun and heard our discussion. "What will you do, Dodah?"

"Do not worry. I will make my teaching plan and wait for the decision."

"We want to learn, and so do our friends." They run off.

Two suns later, a group of youngsters show up at the hut after the mid-day repast. "Peace be with you, my friends. Welcome."

The tallest boy moves forward. Fingers grasping his chin, he acts like an elder in reflection, except there is no beard, not even a light fuzz. "My name is Boraz, and this is my brother, Nadav. We were told you would teach us."

My nieces and nephews told their friends. "Oh, yes, Boraz. That is true." He shows pride in his stance and tries to be in charge. "I cannot begin lessons until the council approves."

Their faces drop. "Do not worry, I know how to fix this." Boraz thinks he can change the villagers. He will learn. The children's faces light up again and they run away.

. . . .

The next morning my mother is awake and ready to leave. "Ima, it is dawn. Where are you going?"

"A meeting of the village women was called."

"I will go with you. I would like very much to help in some way."

"No, it is taken care of."

I am not one of the women. What is taken care of? I watch her drag the stick, then lean on it as she walks. "Do you need help?" She shakes her head but does not look at me.

. . . .

The next few suns are filled with the usual chores and attempting to form a plan for the teaching. I do not hear from the chief and console myself. The council takes its time.

More suns go by before the call comes. The chief's messenger lets me know that I am to be at the fire before the evening meal.

Approaching the old meeting place brings back the memories of the last time when the decision was banishment. They will not do that to me now. The setting is the same as it was then, the men in half circles, the chief at his bell.

Shivers run up and down. I inspect the ground and say a silent prayer. I look up and cannot grasp what happened in that short moment. All the women of the village descended on the meeting. And my ima is leading them.

"Well," the chief is shocked, "there is no doubt you were not expected. Did you forget that women are not sanctioned to be at these meetings?" His eyes are slits. I am fascinated.

Ima steps forward. "No, Chief. We did not forget. There is something we came to say."

"To say? You are not allowed to speak."

"We will not leave until the council hears us out."

"Is that so? You are aware we can make you leave."

"Yes, Chief, but we will return and interrupt each meeting until you do agree."

He turns to the men, his ears are red. "We might as well hear it now. Women are determined creatures, there is no stopping them, and if they become vindictive who knows what can happen." He raises his eyebrows and winks. His shrug says, *What can you do?* The men laugh.

My ima takes two steps forward. "The children told us of Elisha's desire to teach them." This is about me? "We demand that she does so."

"Demand?" The chief's nostrils flare.

"Who could be a better teacher? She learned from Abraham and Sarah. Think of what she must know."

"I am aware of her studies."

"Of course you are, my lord. We are trying to remind you of how she can help. No one in this village can do better."

"You do have a point, but how do we prevent her from teaching the things she was banished for?"

I cannot stay still. "Chief, may I speak?" There is distrust on his face. "I knew nothing of this and was as surprised as you. I want to remind you of the promises I made."

"I remember. All the women are to leave. The council will meet right now. We will let you know the decision."

I join the women and run to help Ima climb down the rise. "Thank you all for your concern."

"It was not ours as much as the children. They explained what they wanted, and it took on a different tone. As mothers, we could do no less. Let us all go home and wait."

Ima and I bake as many breads and fig cakes as we can and decorate them with dried fruits. We bring them to the women as a thank you gift.

· · · · · · · · · · · · ·

I leave the hut two suns later and find the children waiting. "Why are you here?"

Boraz steps forward. "For the teaching, of course."

The women must have their answer, but I am not prepared. "Dear God," I whisper, "I never said a real prayer before and need help. I do not know how to work with the children. Please be with me." I cannot chew my hair.

Every child, every age forms a half-circle and is waiting to hear something helpful from me.

I join them and Boraz stands. "Within this group are the story-tellers who ensure our history is carried forward." His voice is not yet that of a man. "The elders taught that we are tasked with burning important stories into our remembrance, so we must memorize every morsel of your lessons." His name means prominent, and his presence would stand out if only for his height.

"But I am of no importance. Not a prophet, not a king."

Nadav stands. "You are a great teacher." He is young. His locks are dark and strewn with sun soaked straw-colored locks.

"Abraham and Sarah are the wise ones. That is well known," I chide.

"But the teachings will help us heed their words and understand," Nadav insists.

The children's long hair gleams many shades of warm brown in the late afternoon light. Mine is gray and lifeless. "Then let us begin."

I sit on my mat. Something light and fluffy makes waves across my shoulders like gently flowing water. It helps me feel strong, ready, sure. "Thank you angels," I whisper. I take a deep breath and plunge in.

"A common thing in all people is wanting." Their heads nod. "For some it is sweets, others it is salt."

"Who would want salt?" That came from Nadav and brings laughter.

"My uncle loved salt." Their surprise shines through the sandy dirt on their faces. Nathan's brood runs from their play to join us and gather around the back of the circle. Rena waves, she wants to be sure I notice her. I wave and signal her to be quiet with a raised finger against my lips.

They are as eager for the learning to begin as I was when I first arrived in Urusalim, excited to hear the words of Abraham. The song I wrote about wants and needs is the first lesson.

"There are many things we fancy. Some we want, and still others we need. Which is more important?" They do not answer but do not take their eyes from me. "Of course, it is what we need."

"What does that mean?" Caleb is one of the youngest children.

"What if you have to decide between food or something to play with? We would all want more food but," I make my voice low and mysterious like a sorceress, "maybe we do not want anyone else to have it. Then, we must question what kind of person we want to be." Boraz stands. "Yes, young man."

"The others want me to ask something."

"Is that what you want or need?"

"A need," one yells.

"If any of you also wish to speak, you are free to do so. Go ahead, Boraz."

"What if we want many sweet cakes? Is that bad?"

This tickles me but is important to them and a perfect teaching moment. "There is never one answer. Will you have a sick belly from all you eat?" Some make faces. "Then your ima would take time away from work to care for you. Or do you eat so many the family will not have enough? That would be selfish. Do you understand? It is not only about us and what we want." I stand up and yell, "However, I hereby declare that sweets are definitely allowed."

They are happy and kick their feet high in the air. We get into a circle and practice my song about wants and needs, so they will not forget. We yell out needs we cannot live without, water, food, shelter, and air. It becomes a game I hope they remember. The children bounce off the ground and back onto their feet. I enjoy watching their lighthearted play.

"Wants are pleasing, but we cannot live without our needs." No goodbyes and they race home. I must plan better for the next one. The teachings need to be simple.

· · · · · · · · · · · · ·

Here I am, a grown woman, and there is still fear of my ima. I was unsettled when I spoke to the chief. Ima seems indifferent, but I must speak. We are outside enjoying the mid afternoon sun.

"Ima."

"Yes, Elisha." Her warmth makes me wonder if this is indeed my mother.

"It is time to talk."

"Time? We always talk. What do you wish to tell me now about what I did wrong?"

"One thing I learned is that the past is never gone and can haunt us all our lives. Abraham said we must know ourselves." Ima gets up and heads for the hut. "How can I know if you do not let me ask?" She keeps going. "Why did you never say I love you like other mothers?"

She turns back. "Do not be ridiculous. Of course, I loved you and said so. You are making me an evil person. Does that make you happy? You are never satisfied."

My tone is serene. "No. You did not say it. I asked Nathan and he agreed. You were the same with him."

"How dare you? Go back to Kiriath Arba, I will not discuss this any further."

She walks away. Rena was near enough to hear. "Rena, dear child. All is well." I pat her head. "I am sure that your mother and father have had many differences. People who love each other often do. That does not mean we stop loving. Understand?" She nods her little head.

It is hard to talk about my childhood. My mother is a woman like any other. That is not true, she birthed me.

· · · · · · · · · · · ·

Nathan and Rachel agree Rena will be my student, and she stops following me. We work every morning and to my amazement she is able to understand my teaching. She is learning to strum a harp Nathan borrowed from a musician friend in the village. The words to my songs are memorized faster than I could have at her age. She sings my songs to whoever will listen. Too young to grasp their significance, they will be concealed in her head until the time is right for them to appear. I hope this ensures she will be ready to carry on my work.

A few suns later, Ima stops me in the middle of putting away the utensils. Nathan and Rachel already left for the fields. The children are outside playing.

"Please sit." I do. "I have considered what you said." The long silence is agony. "I want you to know the truth. I did not say I love you to anyone. Not to Abba, nor he to me."

"Did you love each other?"

"Of course, but speaking the word is not how we were brought up. It was not done. I now realize how that hurt you." Tears drizzle down her cheeks. She never cried in front of me before. I hold her hand. "I did not think about it as right or wrong until you spoke."

She pulls her hand from mine, walks away, then stops and turns back. "I am sorry. It is still hard for me to say, but I," she stops to gather courage, "always loved you." I close my eyes and take in the words.

"I love you too, Ima."

CHAPTER THIRTY-THREE

*T*he following morning before the first meal, Nathan calls me. "The chief demanded your appearance."

"Demanded?"

"Now."

We run to chief's hut, and he is outside waiting.

"How dare you?" I am confused. "You met with the children. I told you the council had to approve first."

"But chief, I do not understand. The children came to me. They said we could begin. I assumed the women knew the decision and wanted me to. I saw them that one time."

"You did not have permission. The council decided you are not fit to teach."

"Not fit?" I spit out the words.

"There will be no teaching." He turns and walks into his hut. I turn to Nathan. He shrugs his shoulders.

· · · · · · · · · · · ·

The following morning, Ima goes to another one of her sick friends and the chores are all mine. She is on the way back when the sun is well over the horizon. Her steps seem slow. I run to put my arm around her the remainder of the way. "Are you feeling well?"

She nods. "We women went to the chief again." My mouth drops open. "We were angry. It took time, but the chief has agreed to your teaching."

"Thank you, Ima. I cannot believe you women did this for me."

"It was not for you. We did it for the children."

"Of course they are most important. The funny thing is, I thought you went to a sick friend again. When I was a child and too young to understand what it meant to help others, they seemed more important than me, and I was jealous."

"What are you talking about, and what else did I do? You tire me."

"It is not about you but about how I thought. There is something I never told you, not because I did not want to, but I remembered it during the time with Sarah. Do you recall when I asked you why I was afraid of my friends?"

Her eyes blaze. "I have not lost my wits. Yes, in the garden."

"Those children who surrounded me, they also beat me. With fists, heavy branches, and rocks." I look her in the eye. "No matter how hard I cried or yelled, they would not stop. I waited to die. Some child's ima saved me. I hid the marks from you."

"Why would the children do such a thing?"

"They heard the villagers say I was evil."

Ima holds back tears. "Why did you not tell me?"

"You would have said it was my fault."

"Nothing has changed. You are just as trying now." She goes into the hut and I cry.

A moment later she returns. "I am sorry, that was a terrible thing to say. The sight of you brings back embarrassment and shame. I am sorry for your suffering. I did not know. Do you think your sneaking off to listen to the men's conferences was a secret?"

I laugh. "You knew? That whole time?"

"I may not be well-traveled, but I am not stupid."

Striking back. She cannot help it. "Why did you not stop me?"

"You would not listen. You are stubborn like your abba. It did no harm and gave you a chance to learn how men think. I thought it might help after you married."

"I am sorry. It is not like I could change it."

"What does that mean?"

How to not hurt her? "You were brought up in a tribe that had certain beliefs. You learned from them. But hear me. Not one sun passed when I did not hear what a bad girl I was. You beat me."

"I tried to take care of you. Show you the right way."

"You were convinced you were doing the right thing. That is what I am trying to say. I spoke to an angel. No one else did. That meant something was wrong with me. I asked to change my name, and we got into a battle over that. I never told you," I laugh, "but I called that fight over my name 'my mountain of full moons' because it took so long for you to agree."

"I was trying to do the right thing." She hangs her head.

"I understand. We were both caught up in our own problems. I love you, Ima." She will never admit her wrong doings and saying I forgive you will get her more agitated. I say it under my breath five times.

· · · · · · · · · · · · ·

I spend the rest of the day catching up on chores. Tired after the evening meal, I pull Nathan aside. "Do you remember me telling you before I left that I wrote a song about you?

"I think so."

"May I sing it?" He nods. When I finish, tears are dripping from his cheeks.

"Thank you," and he races to the fields.

· · · · · · · · · · · · ·

I lie down on the outside mat to consider the next lesson. I must have fallen asleep. A loud voice wakens me. It is a messenger asking Rachel if he can speak to me. She points the way. I sit up, already uneasy.

The man recites the news from Abraham. "My dear daughter, Sarah passed on and I no longer wish to teach. My heart went with her and in the aftereffects, also my passion for guiding others. Know I am well and will go on, but it will be in a way not yet clear."

His heart was divided between Sarah and Hagar. But it is not in him to stop teaching. His energy and determination cannot be gone. He will heal and teach again.

"Thank you so much for your message." I point to Rachel. "She will give you food and drink so you can go on your way.

"Just a moment," I call. "Please let Abraham know that the children in my village are hearing his words and Sarah's wisdom." He agrees.

My second mother is gone, and I was not with her. Why did I not know and go to her? She left much to be grateful for. Her wisdom, her love, and her understanding heart.

It is easy to be sympathetic for her anguish over a husband who would not come home and releasing her torment to the one person available. It could not be Isaac. I was the only one left. They buried her in Machpelah, the land he bartered long ago. She will be missed by all whose lives she touched.

About to go to my mat, my mother walks toward me. "I know about Sarah, and I am sorry. You were close to her."

"Thank you, Ima. She was my second mother." Ima draws away, the veins in her neck stick out. "But she could never take your place." Her back straightens a bit and the tension falls away.

"Do you enjoy your teaching?" Her smile is crooked from the pain, her back bent farther over the stick. I wonder which of us is more ill. I never told anyone. My pain is not visible and there are no herbs to heal it.

"I did not do enough to be sure, but yes. It is not what I expected to do, and I am not sure it is done as well as someone else could."

"From what I hear around the village, they are pleased with the little you did so far. And the children are ready to come. That is a wonderful sign."

"Thank you, Ima. I love you." She is proud of me.

· · · · · · · · · · · · ·

After the morning meal, I ponder the coming lesson. "Dear sister, the children will be here in a few moments." Does Nathan suspect my sickness? He hovered over me the past few moons.

While they wait for me to make myself as comfortable as I can, the children laugh and play. "Is everyone ready?" They quiet down. "This time we will try something different." I sing a song about judgment. Their curiosity is obvious.

"There was another woman in Abraham's group. She was beautiful. I was not. To me, her perfection meant no one could find anything wrong. But they could find a lot wrong with me. Do you ever feel like that?" Many heads nod.

"Close your eyes and picture a person who tells you that you are bad and is important in your life. It could be a parent, family member, or best friend, or me." They snicker. "If they say bad things about us, we accept they are right. Their opinion says we are not good enough." Heads nod. "We do not question it. Those bad feelings gets stored inside us and everything we do is weakened. Have you experienced this?"

"Yes, yes," comes from all over the circle. There are a few no's. Is the teaching not clear?

"What do you mean by weakened?" asked Eitana, one of the young girls.

I smile. "Good question. Picture someone telling you that a chore you did was not done properly. How would you feel?"

"Terrible."

"Is that a definite feeling?"

"It is very strong."

"Strong is an appropriate word. That is what your name means." Eitana looks up. "If you have a bad feeling, the ache from it does not permit you to do any work well because there is fear of doing it wrong again." She nods. "That is your answer."

Some children laugh. "Do you want to be laughed at for learning something new? Do not laugh at others. We need to learn all our lives." I turn to Eitana. "Remember you are strong."

I take a moment to slow down. "Back to our exercise. Close your eyes and bring back the picture we had before of the judging person." I wait. "This person is trying to help, not do harm. They act as if they know what is best, yet no one knows what we learned from our mistakes, or our thoughts, or struggles." The children's discomfort makes them shift around. "Someone else's way does not leave room for your imagination and a new way you might find."

They are settled and I smile. "You have done well. Abraham and Sarah would be proud." They laugh and dance with delight on their faces.

When they use up some energy, I continue.

"What I am saying is that each of us is unique. Judging says we have to behave as someone else wants, and not be bold enough to do things our own way." The group is quiet, and I let them sit with their feelings.

"My parents will never let me do anything different." Anneke is soft spoken.

"You could try doing it your way and see if it turns out well."

"What if it fails?"

"As someone once said to me, 'Why think about failing before you begin? And do not give up after one try.'"

"I could never do that." Caleb's face is pale. His parents must be strict.

"Think about what I said to Anneke."

Zara raises her hand, and I nod for her to speak. In her whiny voice she asks, "Are we finished yet?"

"In a moment. One last thought. Change is frightening. It takes courage and boldness. I found that out and so will you." There is silence. We sing my song to remember the lesson.

"Does anyone have a question?" More silence. "That is more than enough to think about until next time." They gather their things. The slowness of their walk and the silence tells me this teaching was right for them. I hope my teachers would approve.

CHAPTER THIRTY-FOUR

What woke me this morning were the tangles of my life. There were so many mistakes, so many failures, because I did not listen to those who tried to help.

I was a child and they called me evil. Then I was betrayed by Resheph and lost Abba. Doron was the greatest hurt of all. What was it all about? Do I thank you, God, for the painful lessons of love? It is time to go to the wash stand. Nathan stops me. His face is pale, and he is agitated.

"What is wrong?"

His hand grasps my arms as if to steady himself. "Ima. She is gone."

"Gone?" I put my arms around him and we cry together. Rachel comes out of the hut and joins us. "She was kind to others and lived a good life," is all she can say. We cannot let go of each other. This will be the most difficult thing I will do in in my life. My feet drag toward her sleep space. I gaze at my mother's stillness and wait for her to get up and go to a sick friend. Rachel looks at me. "We must do our duty."

Wailing signals the rituals. It reminds me of a fox or a jackal's cry but is the sign for our neighbors to burn lavender, rosemary, and pieces of oak to disguise any odors. Rachel expects me to join in the washing of Ima's body. Is a daughter supposed to see her mother unclothed? Or clean what came out of her at the moment of death? Her skin is wrinkled and hangs loose. The smells makes my stomach retch and heave. We clean and wash her, then cut her hair and nails.

My hands shake as we rub all manner of perfumed oils onto what is left of my ima. Then we dress her in strips of white linen strewn with spices prepared earlier knowing her time was coming near. The spices try to disguise the scent and make it sweet, but not like the day she was born.

Sleep does not come that night. Visions of the body I came out of do not leave my head.

. . . .

At sunrise, I am unable to take in food. The others eat their meal. The village men began work moving the boulder away from the cave's opening. We carry her outside and the entire village gathers to be with us. They encircle our group, the scents of oils and spices wrap around us as we carry her to the burial place.

The men are gentle setting her on the shelf built into the rock. She lays not far from Abba and her parents. Rachel and I draw her knees up and place her hands across her chest in order to fit into the small space. Time stands still. The weeping starts. It is so final. I cannot cry.

The rite of bare feet and tearing our clothes is completed. The children enjoy the freedom from sandals. There is one more step before we leave.

The men of the village gather around the immense boulder again. They struggle to roll it back to the opening of the cave. Each step assaults my heart. The final push, which fills the hole, means she will be protected from invasion from man or animals, but makes me wish I could disappear. The one comfort I have is that my mother is not among the less fortunate who have no shelf, only the ground to lie on.

I do not know what the family is feeling, but as the rock is secured, my heart wants my arms to hug it, to climb inside and be near her for the last time. I stand there staring at it. My ima is in there. I cannot drag myself away. Nathan does not say a word. He waits. And waits. He puts his arm around my waist and moves me back to the hut.

We sit in mourning for the next seven suns, and villagers come to visit. They offer food and help, and if possible, they sit to discuss my ima's life. My mother's death softened them toward me. They are pleasant, and nothing of the old times shows on their faces or in their eyes. It is still hard to make conversation. They do not stay long, there is work to do. They do this for ima and will soon do the same for me.

. . . .

Before the next sun, I brood on how to teach the group the importance of words. I cannot fail. This may be my last chance. I reclined during the morning in the healing sun to relieve my discomfort, but it is now time for the children.

They come running and drop onto the ground. "Can you move closer?" I have not been this nervous since the first teaching and wait for their movements to stop. The next breath fills my nostrils with the fresh scent of their soaped bodies.

For the first time it feels strange to teach in one of the fancy tunics Sarah gave me in Kiriath Arba. The children's garments are the same as the ones we wore as youngsters. Either beige or brown, to the knees for boys, and the ankle for girls. They have never changed.

The group grew to more than thirty children, six to ten seasons of growth. They sit in three half-circles in front of me. I never did memorize their names.

"The teaching, please." Dodi has limited patience. She is small like me, with a shining face. Her eyes are like Nathan's, brown with yellow flecks.

"I am going to tell you how Abraham and Sarah taught me to know myself. To do that, I will tell you a little about me." They settle in ready for a story.

A little one stands and declares, "I want to grow vegetables."

"That is excellent work," I assure her. She sits again, happy.

"Many of you will not leave this village and will work with the soil or animals. All work is admirable. It is necessary and helps us and others. But do you learn about yourself? You can if you know how.

To do that you ask why. I was privileged to travel through most of our country, but that did not mean I learned about me. I had to be willing to do the work that would bring the change I wanted. Are you willing?" Many heads nod.

"Do you want to continue feeling angry, unhappy, confused, hurt, or defeated?" They shake their heads. "Do you want these feelings to change? To understand why you said that mean thing and hurt someone?" They nod.

"We learn and grow by asking why I did or said that. Was it jealousy? Was it meanness? Did I want something? Once you recognize the answer, the ability to change opens. It takes time but it can be done.

"You can tell by the way I use music to teach that I love it. My parents were against it." Some of them sit up. "They said it was a waste of time and did not help with work." The children are sad, and some with lined brows and half closed eyes seem to have the same sort of problem. "When you were little, what did you love to do, not work, do?

"Even if we love work it is important to pay attention to the part of us that wants something of our own." I look around the group. "It can be more than one thing. For me it was music and an altar where I collected special things. Here is a question to take home and ponder. Are you willing to dig deep and ask yourself why?"

The grass is rustling. It warns me the children are restless. I lean toward them. "It is time to end. We will be together again soon." I snuggle into the covering to rest. The youngsters are doing well, but am I missing something? Resheph would tease about needing to be perfect. The telling of my story was the right thing to do. The children accepted it without question.

CHAPTER THIRTY-FIVE

Another messenger arrived this morning to tell me Abraham brought Hagar back to Kiriath Arba as his wife. That man could hardly walk and was exhausted. He accepted food and water. How dare Abraham? That is Sarah's home not Hagar's. And, they are promising to produce many more children. It turns out that in the end, Hagar knew. Abraham wanted her.

. . . .

I do what I can these days, but the pain increases. I rest on my mat outside, but I am not complete. There are still things that must be done before I leave this realm. I hope they can hear me.

To Resheph:
*It is a long time since we were together, Resheph, and
I do not know where you are or what you are doing. I
hope you took Abraham's lessons to heart. Yes, that is his
name now. I choose to hold true that you did not know
the harm you caused me, for I could not love an evil
person. To believe you would not violate me if you knew
how horrific the consequences were.*

I no longer blame myself, I am sure of that now.
Sandalphon once asked me if you were a want or a need.
It took a long time for me to understand you were just a
want. I lost myself in you and gave you my power, sure
you would love me because I loved you so much. I wanted
to please you and in doing so, I forgot myself.

Until now, I could not pardon you. It was not in
my heart. Remember the lesson? Now I am ready, for
I too question things I did and am not proud of. The
difference is I now claim all I am. Good and bad. I no
longer blame you, but still cannot forgive what you did.
And for now, that is all I can do. I wish you well.

Now for one more.

To the chief and the villagers:
I want to make clear that I am not odd or peculiar.
When I studied with Abraham, I found out that there
are many others like me. But I am sorry for the problems
and exasperation I caused. I did not do it on purpose.
I was young and no one understood me. Now I wish
to clear away any misunderstandings. I forgive you for
everything that happened and if I hurt you, I hope you
can excuse me. And know that you are in my heart.

The last and hardest one.

Dearest Abba,
I did not do this earlier because I could not be sure of
what I wanted to say. The one thing I am sure of is
missing you so much. But that is not what I want to
talk about. I am sorry for the anger I caused. I did not
mean to. Life was frustrating for me. I did not belong

anywhere. I was different, stupid, not worthy. You gave
me a harp, and I could not play it. You did not want me
to sing. But I never stopped loving you. Never wanted
you to stop sending me the smiles that warmed my heart
and said you loved me.

   You left us before I could tell you of my wonderful
life with Abraham and Sarah and what they taught me.
And how I could teach the children. But what I must say
is that I forgive you for the times you hurt me or did not
let me do what I wanted. I now understand the reasons.
I explained that to Ima. About learning things as a child
from your parents and believing those things without
question. You are in my heart forever.
Your loving daughter, Elisha.

. . . .

"Elisha, the children will be here soon." That is Nathan, making
sure I do not forget. As if I could.

   "Nathan?" I call after him. "Thank you."

   At the first meeting, the children's greeting astonished me.
They marched toward me, in perfect step, and said, "Peace be with
you, Ancient One." I wanted to protest and say that it was two
moons since I was a girl. Their description now fits.

   They are about to sit, and I come alive and vibrant again. That
is what Sandalphon meant about feeding my soul.

   "Peace be with you." There is a tremor in my voice, and I gulp
down water. "I am glad to see all of you. Are you enjoying the teaching?" That gives me time to get comfortable. They are here, that is
all that matters.

   "If you were to feel wonderful all the time, what do you think
would happen?"

"I would be happy." Zara's name implies she feels like a visitor and has few friends. But her singing sounds the way I imagine the angels do.

"Would you like that?" They shake their heads. "I will show you how I did it."

They quiet to listen. "Please close your eyes. Say thank you for all the good things that happened since our last meeting. Be sure it comes from your heart.

"Was that easy?" They nod. "Who would like to tell what happened?"

Gianna raises her hand. "I was more than happy, but there is no name for it."

"It is joy and comes from being grateful. Anyone else go through a different experience?"

"I felt as if I could do anything," says Hana. "It gave me strength and confidence."

"Did any of you think that being grateful could make life better?" The faces they make say they understand. "Imagine if you do this each sunrise, how you will feel, what you will accomplish.

"Who else would like to share?"

"I felt light as if I could reach the clouds. My heart quivered and sang." This child has music in his heart.

"What we are learning is to feed your soul. Who likes to sing and dance?" They all get up and dance.

"Where is the singing?" They sing a folk song and end with a song I wrote. "Time to work. Who wants to tell us how that went?"

"It was fun, and I feel perfect." That is one of the older boys.

"Did you worry if you were doing it right?"

All their heads shake. "No," comes from around the gathering.

"Wrinkling your brow does not help to solve problems, it just makes you pace the floor or bite your lips. Feeding the soul brings soothing feelings of warmth in your whole body. Then you can focus on solving your problem with ease. Will you remember this the next time you have concerns?"

"Yes, yes, yes," they yell. They sing and dance, and I can rest.

The children tire and we continue. "I want to add one more thing. Music is healing. If we hear happy music, we are inspired. Sad music, we are gloomy. If you wish to change how you feel, make or listen to music. Now I want to tell you something that happened to me. I was walking through a forest and a bird was singing. I imitated its song and it answered me. Our conversation went on and on. I do not know what message it wanted to give me, but it was a delightful experience and made me happy for three suns."

"Is that true?"

"I promise it is. Here is another way to feed your soul. Remove your sandals." They look at me to be sure I am not fooling. "Yes, sandals off. I will join you. Now, into the grass. Stand here and feel the ground underneath the grass. Note what you feel. Walk a little. Feel. Walk again and then stand still. See if you can feel connected to the soil." I give them a moment. "You know how this works, who wants to speak?"

One of the younger children raises his hand. "It felt good."

"Can you use another word to explain?"

His forehead furrows. "Light, no troubles, big, held up, like my mother hugged me."

"Wonderful, thank you. Did anyone have another outcome? No? Try all the things you learned and pick your favorites. One last lesson. Lie down and put your hands on your middle. Breathe in and send the air to your stomach. It will go up as you fill it and down as you let the air out. Practice until you feel a big fat belly, then sit back up. How was that?"

They all get up and dance around. I wait, not wanting to restrain their fun. They settle in once more and I tell them, "Now you know many things you can do to be strong and feed your soul. Thank you all for being wonderful students."

CHAPTER THIRTY-SIX

When I woke up the first thought I had was that I did no teaching since I told my story to the children, thirteen full moons ago. Nathan brought my sleep mat to the fresh air and I settled into the smoothness. This was not the life I expected to live, fighting for women. In the end our village women stood up for the children and me, but what if it never goes any further, if it was a waste of time? If my songs are not heard? Never bear fruit. If the children pay no attention to the things I tried to teach? If Rena never has the awakening I was privileged to? I pray each child will find a driving passion.

I drift off to a beautiful dream. I am walking with Doron and the donkey is behind. Holding hands, our strides are as matched as our harmonies. Whether it is the love and caring we share, or the sustenance of food and drink, the abundance of our life together surrounds and bathes us in contentment.

A song joins the picture in my head, but I cannot make it out. Is it one of mine? Am I sleeping or are the children here? I open my eyes to angelic voices and children sitting in front of me. There are more rows of people I do not know, and more behind them. Some are older. Are they the ones who sang? I feel as if I am in a dream and wonder why the chief is here. One of the women comes forward and takes my hand. I cannot get up.

"We are the grandparents and parents of the children who came to hear your teachings. We are here to honor you for the work you did."

They value my efforts. Sandalphon would say they ate their leaves. "Thank you for being here."

I thought those women did not take my words to heart. That the best song I wrote was not acceptable and I did not accomplish what I wanted. It was my failure and disappointment that the village women did not change even a dew drop.

The woman holding my hand continues. "On behalf of all who are here, thank you for your instruction of our children and grandchildren. By teaching them, you taught us. We heard the words of Abraham and Sarah and took them to heart. We are grateful."

I smile. These women have changed. They came to let me know. Memories of the concerts I sang whirl through my head. The woman is crying and I wipe away her tears. It is difficult to speak. "Thank you," I whisper. Doron teased that my words were spoken at the top of my voice. I wonder if he would laugh now.

"It is our honor," she says.

"Sing another of my songs. Let me hear your beautiful voices." She moves away.

Someone else takes my hand. It is the chief. "Thank you, Elisha, for your contributions to our village."

I nod and take in the chief's words. My visitors are singing. Their sound is glorious. It speaks of not just understanding the words, but of the lyrics living within them. The music surrounds me and like a warm covering wraps me in its serenity. I float on air.

My work is realized. Childhood dreams were not to be, but I received so much more. In this moment, I know in my bones there will always be another woman who will stand up and speak for those who cannot. Maybe not with song, but in their own way. I listen with my eyes closed. The harmony is so pure I am taken to higher realms.

I look up and a color of the rainbow swirls between the blues and whites of the clouds. It is purple and grows closer. It is Sandalphon. He is waiting for me. His purple color flashes across the sky. I am lifted into the blue near it. The last sound I hear is Doron. My love came back. He calls for me. Elisha. Elisha. Too late.

ACKNOWLEDGMENTS

I could not have written this book without all of you. I send you my heartfelt thanks to:

My giving mentors Joyce Sweeney and Margetta Geerling who never stop giving.

My entire critique group for the valuable comments that made my story work.

Sonja Karlsen for the sharp eye that got me over the hard places.

Florence Ellman, my beta reader, who found the first flaws needing to be fixed.

Gail Ehrlich and Marcia lamel, who encouraged me to keep on going.

If I forgot anyone please forgive me.

ABOUT THE AUTHOR

Born in New York City, Irene Kessler is a Jill of many trades. As a single mother of three, she was the Polaroid Camera Girl, sold jewelry, and held makeup parties to supplement her alimony. She moved on to sing minor roles at New York City Opera, the Metropolitan Opera, and the Teatro Principal in Barcelona, Spain. Irene received her master's degree in psychology, moved to Florida, and became an eating disorder specialist at Glenbeigh Hospital. She completed her PhD in 1997 and went on to work at the Radar Institute and Renfrew Center. She was in private practice for over thirty years, during which time she also joined a local quartet that performed opera, operetta, and Broadway tunes at venues in Broward and Palm Beach counties. She was inspired to begin writing after attending a presentation by writer and teacher Joyce Sweeney.

SELECTED TITLES FROM SHE WRITES PRESS

She Writes Press is an independent publishing company founded to serve women writers everywhere. Visit us at www.shewritespress.com.

Elmina's Fire by Linda Carleton. $16.95, 978-1-63152-190-4. A story of conflict over such issues as reincarnation and the nature of good and evil that are as relevant today as they were eight centuries ago, *Elmina's Fire* offers a riveting window into a soul struggling for survival amid the conflict between the Cathars and the Catholic Church.

Dark Lady by Charlene Ball. $16.95, 978-1-63152-228-4. Emilia Bassano Lanyer—poor, beautiful, and intelligent, born to a family of Court musicians and secret Jews, lover to Shakespeare and mistress to an older nobleman—survives to become a published poet in an era when most women's lives are rigidly circumscribed.

Faint Promise of Rain by Anjali Mitter Duva. $16.95, 978-1-938314-97-1. Adhira, a young girl born to a family of Hindu temple dancers, is raised to be dutiful—but ultimately, as the world around her changes, it is her own bold choice that will determine the fate of her family and of their tradition.

The Sweetness by Sande Boritz Berger. $16.95, 978-1-63152-907-8. A compelling and powerful story of two girls—cousins living on separate continents—whose strikingly different lives are forever changed when the Nazis invade Vilna, Lithuania.

Lum by Libby Ware. $16.95, 978-1-63152-003-7. In Depression-era Appalachia, an intersex woman without a home of her own plays the role of maiden aunt to her relatives—until an unexpected series of events gives her the opportunity to change her fate.

Eliza Waite by Ashley Sweeney. $16.95, 978-1-63152-058-7. When Eliza Waite chooses to leave a stagnant life in rural Washington State and join the masses traveling north to Alaska in 1898 during the tumultuous Klondike Gold Rush, she encounters challenges and successes in both business and love.